Coti's

Iron Wolves MC
Book 9
By Elle Boon
elleboon@yahoo.com

Hiya April
Get ready for
a wild ride for this story
is one crazy adventure.
xoxo
Elle Boon

Coti's Unclaimed Mate, Iron Wolves MC Book 9
Copyright © 2018 Elle Boon
First E-book Publication: July 2018
Cover design by Valerie Tibbs of Tibbs Design
Edited by Tracy Roelle
Cover Image: Wander Aguiar
Cover Model: Jonny James

Dedication

I'd like to give a big huge thank you to all my family and friends. Y'all have been such an amazing group who have kept me grounded through all the ups and downs. Without you, I'd have probably gone crazy this past year. Well, crazier anyhow. I think...don't quote me, but I think this marks my 30th book. HOLY SHITE!

Thank you to all who've read my stories and wanted more. I hope you enjoy Coti and NeNe's story because y'all, this is gonna be one wild freaking ride. Plus, NeNe is named after my best friend since 3rd grade (Hey girl, Hey) I know that the road to a happily ever after isn't always smooth and hope I gave y'all one hell of a ride in their story. Stay tuned as the Iron Wolves series evolves.

Of course, to my wonderful hubby who makes my life. Yep, I am saying he makes my life, because he does. Love you to the moon and back, Mr. Boon, 22 plus years and counting.

Love y'all so hard,
Elle

Other Books by Elle Boon

Erotic Ménage

Ravens of War

Selena's Men
Two For Tamara
Jaklyn's Saviors
Kira's Warriors

Shifters Romance

Mystic Wolves

Accidentally Wolf & His Perfect Wolf (1 Volume)
Jett's Wild Wolf
Bronx's Wounded Wolf
A Fey's Wolf

Paranormal Romance

SmokeJumpers

FireStarter
Berserker's Rage
A SmokeJumpers Christmas
Mind Bender, Coming Soon

MC Shifters Erotic

Iron Wolves MC

Lyric's Accidental Mate
Xan's Feisty Mate
Kellen's Tempting Mate
Slater's Enchanted Mate
Dark Lovers
Bodhi's Synful Mate
Turo's Fated Mate
Arynn's Chosen Mate

Coti's Unclaimed Mate

Contemporary Romance
Miami Nights
Miami Inferno
Rescuing Miami

Standalone
Wild and Dirty

SEAL Team Phantom Series
Delta Salvation
Delta Recon
Delta Rogue
Mission Saving Shayna
Protecting Teagan
Delta Redemption

The Dark Legacy Series
Dark Embrace

Chapter One

NeNe took her helmet off and placed it over the handlebars. "Dammit, why do they both have to be home instead of at a bar?"

She stared at the doublewide trailer she shared with her dad and younger brother with disgust. The beat-up pickup her dad drove had more rust than not. The motorcycle her brother owned wasn't much better. Both men were mean as rattlesnakes when sober and even worse when drunk. She rubbed a finger over her bruised eye. "I won't sit back and take it this time," she promised herself.

It would only take her five minutes, tops, to get what she needed, then she'd be out. Hopefully, by the time she returned, they'd both be passed out drunk. "Where's my wishing rock when I need it?" When she'd left the Iron Wolves club for the last time, she'd stumbled upon a rock shaped like a heart. The small stone fit in her palm and had a small indent where her thumb fit, making the perfect worry, or wishing stone to her mind.

"Talking to yourself again, girl?" her dad asked, then belched. He wore a red wife beater tank top, a step up from the dirty white one. The jeans he had on were clean and appeared new. She wondered how he'd bought them when he hadn't gotten paid in weeks.

"Yep, you know me, always off in my own head." She pocketed her key as she strolled by him.

Her dad grabbed her by the arm. "You're just like your mama, thinking you're better than us."

She jerked out of his hold, watching as he spit over the railing. Mental note. Never date a guy who chews. Her file of mental notes was long and had more filing cabinets than the national library, but they all had good reasons behind them, most having little notations regarding her father and brother. Lord, he may look clean, but she could still smell the stench of whiskey on his breath.

Harold, her father, hitched his jeans up. "One day, your reckoning will come just like your mama's, and then, you'll find just how low you can fall. Standing on your pedestal like you do, it's bound to hurt."

NeNe ignored him and his blathering, like she did most days. He'd been telling her how worthless she was since she'd been knee-high to a grasshopper. Tonight was no different.

Thankfully, her brother Harry wasn't in his favorite spot when home, which was in one of the recliners in front of the television. She hurried into her bedroom and shut the door. She needed to change out of her day work clothes and into her night work clothes. Her dad and brother may be happy to live in their piece of shit trailer, but she had plans. Now that her friends were happily involved with men who didn't want her around, she wanted out of this town. Since graduating high school, she'd been saving her money, squirreling it away in a savings account for a rainy day. The five-figure sum would get her across the country and allow her to start new. Start where people didn't call her trash, where her friends' men didn't look down on her.

She shoved her tennis shoes off followed by her slacks and top. Working at the bank, she had to dress in proper attire, but at night, she had a totally different persona. There, she was NeNe the flag girl and waitress. If they'd only let her race, she could make more money in one night than in an entire week, but her bike wasn't fast enough to go up against some of the faster ones. She could've used her savings and had the Iron Wolves fix it up, but then they'd be privy to her private life. No, better to allow them to fade away. Her real passion was interior design. She'd been so close to finishing her schooling. However, her dreams of becoming an interior designer were just that, dreams.

Her chest ached at everything she'd lost in such a short span of time. Last year, she had friends, dreams, and a promising future. Now, she had money in a savings account, but nobody to lean on. One by one, her friends found boyfriends, pulling away from her so quickly NeNe didn't quite understand why. Hell, she wasn't clingy, didn't expect to be invited over for movies and shit every night. In all honesty, if they would've called once a week she'd have been fine. Yet, they'd cut her out of their lives like she was some pariah, like the trash she'd come from. The trailer trash girl from the other side of the tracks. Yep, that's exactly what she was called growing up.

Looking around the tiny room which had been her bedroom for the last ten years, she cringed at the apt description of trailer trash. Oh, she tried to keep the place clean, but with two grown men who were slobs living with her, the only room she truly had a chance with was her own. Even that could be a chore if one of them decided to ransack it while she was gone.

NeNe swiped at a tear. The loss of her friends hurt, but she'd found a way to cope or a replacement of sorts. The bikers who'd moved in gave her a job that paid good money for her to show up, wave the flag at the beginning of a race, and pass out drinks. Not a glamorous life, but she was past the point of giving any fucks. After giving her notice last week at the bank, the manager had almost seemed relieved, the jackhole. She'd been there for four years, never missing a day, always on time. The least he could've been was upset to lose a loyal employee. "Fuck him," she muttered.

"Who you fucking now, sis?"

NeNe spun around, holding a shirt in front of her. "Get the hell out of my room, Harry."

He shrugged his shoulder. "I was just checking on you, thought I heard your bike roll in. So, where you off to?"

She gave him her back, pulling the tank top over her head. Whatever gods were watching, she sent up a silent thank you that her brother hadn't come in when she was wearing only a thong. Damn pervert.

"I'm going out with some friends," she lied easily.

Her brother pulled his can of chew out of his back pocket. "Is that so? Well, you have fun now, you hear?" He shoved a huge mouthful of snuff into his lower lip, then smiled.

NeNe wanted to tell him how nasty he looked with bits of tobacco stuck in his teeth but kept her mouth shut, letting him leave without another word. A quick glance at the clock had her shoving a change of clothes into her backpack along with her ID and some cash. Everything else of value, she kept in a locker at the gym she worked out at. Her dad and brother had taught her long ago nothing was sacred in their house. She also had a go bag stashed outside of town with another ID and some cash. Her *just in case you need to get out of town bag*, she called it.

After digging the key to her bike out of her pocket, she straightened her spine. Opening the door, she took a deep breath, looked out in the hall, exhaling in relief to find it empty. Shoulders back, head high, she marched outside and to her bike. Both her dad and brother stood on the porch, their hands resting on the railing. She wished the damn thing would collapse beneath them, but luck wasn't on her side.

With a backward wave, she tossed her leg over her bike and started it. The deep rumble always made her giddy. She grabbed her helmet and strapped it on. One last look at the trailer, which used to be blue and white, but looked more grey and grey, she turned the wheel and headed out. One more week and she was out of here.

Coti listened as Arynn told Lyric about her friend NeNe having a black eye. For the other man to have seen it from across the street, the bruise had to have been pretty bad. His fists clenched. The urge to fly into a rage and beat whoever touched the female had him on edge. Whoa, she's not yours to protect, he reminded his wolf.

His little reminder didn't stop him from heading toward the door and his bike. He'd just drive around town and do some looking, see if one little female crossed his path.

A short time later, he was about to head back when a Harley Roadster driven by a crazy female sped past him. He'd recognize the bike anywhere as he'd seen Lyric and Syn out with their human friends several times. Truth be told, Kellen and Xan had ordered him and several others to shadow them to make sure they were safe. Now, he was shadowing a human and couldn't for the life of him figure out why.

He turned around, heading in the same direction she went. His wolf went crazy the farther outside of town they got. Finally, he saw lights and dozens of vehicles parked along the highway. There looked to be a small town set up outside the city, a thriving area he'd never noticed before right on the outskirts of Iron Wolves' territory. He made a mental note to speak with Kellen about it. Waiting a half hour before driving forward went against all his instincts, which were screaming at him, but he was more than just an animal.

With his enhanced vision, he could make out several tents and could hear music blaring hard rock. When he was within ten feet of the area, a truck filled with men rolled in front of him. He'd seen their vehicle off to the side, had noticed they'd been drinking and smoking something other than cigarettes, but he wasn't there to judge.

Coti placed his feet on the pavement alongside his bike. "Evening, boys."

"You wanting in on the race or fights?" a man with a potbelly asked. He had a shotgun resting on his shoulder, giving him that lead courage men got when they had a weapon. Coti could have taken the gun away without breaking a sweat. Nothing would save him if he so chose to take him out, but humans didn't take well to being told their guns didn't mean dick to him.

"Fights for starters," Coti answered. Hell, he didn't know what kind of fighting they had going on, but he was pretty confident he could take whoever he came up against.

"It's been a while since we've had fresh meat. Let him through. What's your name, boyo?" The leader asked, slapping the gun against his palm.

He lifted his lip in a snarl. "Wolf, you can call me Wolf."

"Well, Wolfman, you picked a hell of a night to show up. Hope you got a strong stomach."

Coti heard one of the other men mutter how it didn't matter since the Wolfman wouldn't be leaving except in a body bag. Shit just got interesting.

"Who do I need to see about these fights?" Coti asked.

"Drake, but don't worry none, he'll find you. You might want to have a few shots and see if you can get laid before then." The man snickered.

Coti scratched the side of his nose with his middle finger, then revved his engine, going around the truck. "What the hell you got yourself into, little NeNe?"

The thought of leaving his bike unattended didn't sit well with him, within this makeshift town, but he knew he had other means of transportation. Four legs to be exact. After making sure it was as secure as he could, he eyed his surroundings. His bike was nice but didn't look any better than the ones around him. The matte black paint looking incongruous. However, he was sure his ride was worth more than all the others parked in the area.

He had to duck his head to enter the first tent, the pop-up bar had a real wooden countertop with stools and tables set up. Each chair was filled with mean looking men and the women who looked eager to please. Fuck, this wasn't a place for a nice girl like Lyric's friend.

NeNe swatted the hand of another man away. "I swear by all that is holy I'll rip your hand off and shove it so far up your ass, even the good lord ain't gonna find it."

"I do love a bitch with a mouth on her. How 'bout you, Tank?"

Tank glared at her. "I can think of other things she could do with her mouth."

She turned away from Tank and Bales. Both men gave off creeper vibes the likes of which made her wish she could shoot them and forget about it. If she'd still been in the pop-up bar, she'd have a little more protection, but out on the line, she had to fend for herself, or so Mac had informed her. If she wanted to continue working, he wanted to see her.

"Rose, get your fine ass up here," Mac yelled.

NeNe hated when he called her Rose. It made her want to stab him with a really big thorn...In his fucking dick eye. "Whatcha need, boss?" She never called him Mac, didn't want him to think she thought they were friends. Him boss. She employee.

"One day, you're going to scream my name. Get me a beer, and it best be cold when it gets here."

She hurried back down the rickety ladder to fetch the asshat's beer without commenting, heading for the cooler that was stocked and guarded like it was Grade A liquor. One more week. That's all she had to put in. Actually, only two more days, and then she'd be done with the Hell Makers.

Reaching into the stock Mac kept for himself, she pulled two out. The two men sitting behind the mini fridge grunted but didn't say a word. She'd learned to never just take a single drink; he never wanted just one.

Before she could climb back up, she stopped and adjusted her ponytail. With quick flicks, she wrapped it around and around, making it a messy bun. Much harder for anyone to grab a hold of. Revulsion shook her at the memory of the last time she'd had it down, and how close she'd come to being pulled into a position she never wanted to be again. "Fucking hate all these asshats," she muttered.

She took a fortifying breath and made her way back up, passing one of the other girls who served alcohol to Mac and his buddies. The look of hate and something else flashed across the redhead's face. Gracie, who had a lady boner for Mac, hated NeNe since day one. Why was anyone's guess, but she didn't have the time or inclination to give a single fuck about Gracie or her group of bitches. "Watch yourself, NayNay," Gracie snarled.

NeNe didn't correct Gracie on the pronunciation of her name. Hell, NayNay or NeeNee, at least she wasn't calling her a cunt, or one of the other lovely names she and her merry bunch of hoes had come up with.

How nobody had caught on to them, their little city outside of the city, still flabbergasted her. "None of your business, NeNe. You're out in one week," she muttered to herself.

Coti heard her whispered words and fought the urge to make her tell him what her plans were. The closer he got to where she was, he smelled shifters. His wolf snarled. The men at the gate had been human as were the ones at the pop-up bars he'd entered, but these men, they were not. He'd walked right into an unauthorized pack territory that wasn't his and was about to find out just who he was fighting that night. Coti had a feeling it wasn't going to be nearly as easy as he'd thought.

He rotated his neck back and forth, shaking out his arms and grinned. Yeah, he definitely came to the right place. Everyone at the Iron Wolves were pairing off and while he was as happy as a freaking puppy getting picked at the pound for them, he wasn't in the mood to sit around and sing kumbayfreakingya and shit. Give him a good fight, let him bleed someone, and he'd be happy to sing a few lines at the end of the night, preferably between the thighs of a female.

With the ease of one of his kind even though he hadn't had to do it in years, he masked his scent before walking up to the big man by the makeshift octagon.

The huge shifter, bear if Coti were correct, looked him up and down, his lip lifting in a half grin. "You're a big one, son. You think you got what it takes to take on Champ?"

Coti looked around, getting his first view of Champ. His snort almost escaped, but he managed a nod without rolling his eyes. "Guess we'll see," he said.

"What's your name?" The man eyed Coti up and down, his nose flaring.

"My friends call me Wolf." He dropped the name and waited.

The bear shifter laughed. The booming sound had those around them turning to stare. "That's fucking rich, man. Hey, we got fresh meat named Wolf going up against Champ."

The crowd grew, spectators anticipating a good fight. Coti was glad he'd taken off his jacket with the Iron Wolves logo on it before entering. Now, dressed in a pair of jeans, T-shirt, and his leather Harley boots, he glanced at the barefoot man across from him. "What're the rules?" Since there were humans present, he assumed there was a no shifting rule, especially since they thought he was human.

"Fighters fight until one of ya are unconscious or one of ya tap out like a pussy. Champ there ain't never tapped out, just so ya know." He spat a brown stream of spit, the shit landing too close to Coti's boots.

Narrowing his eyes, he got up into the man's face. "Watch where you spit your shit," he growled. Although the man thought he was human, and by all appearances Coti was, the alpha power rolling off of him would be hard to ignore.

"Fuck off. Either get ready to fight or get out of here." The snarled words were said, but he didn't crowd Coti. Smart man.

Coti gave a nod, knowing he'd made his point. Keeping his eyes where he could see the bear shifter and his opponent, he took off one boot followed by the other. His wallet was in his pocket, hooked to one of his belt loops by a chain. If something went south, there was nothing in it that'd lead back to the club, nor could they find anything he didn't want them to. He opened his billfold, took out a fifty before closing it and stuffed his wallet into his boots. Looking around, he spotted a young kid who appeared as if he might have a decent bone hidden in his gangly body, Coti motioned him over. "Watch my stuff?" He held the fifty out in front of him.

The kid nodded, reaching for the cash. "Yes, sir," he agreed eagerly.

Coti reached behind his head, pulling his shirt off and handed it off to the boy. "You sit right here and holler out if someone tries to take it. I'll hear you," Coti promised, pointing to the area next to his boots. When the kid sat down, pulling his boots into his lap, he shook his head, then entered the chained octagon arena. Although he'd fought many times in the cage at the Iron Wolves Club, he'd never felt the same energy surrounding him as he did now.

The people watching began making bets as they took his measure. He walked to the center, making eye contact with several men who were shifters. Fuck, since when did wolves, bears, and cats start hanging out in a free-for-all pack community?

"Alright, folks, get your bets in. We got Champ. He's undefeated six weeks in a row, against a newcomer. Look at the fresh meat, men. We've got Wolf, who stands a couple inches taller than our champ, but don't let that make you think he can defeat our boy."

Cheers erupted as the 'Champ' stood. Coti sized up his opponent. At six four, he was a couple inches taller than the other man, but the champ was every bit as muscular. His eyes though, they looked dead. Black as pitch and filled with nothing. Coti met the other man's steady gaze and tried to gauge what was going through his mind but saw a void. It was as if the man had no thoughts. While he'd given his name and had been announced as such, his opponent was called Champ. Surely, he had a name.

"Once the bell rings, you fight until you can't fight no more. You want to tap out, you tap the ground three times. Or if you pass out, then we'll get him off ya," the bear shifter laughed.

"What's his name?" Coti asked.

A bell sounded as he asked, and then Champ was moving toward him, his gait steady and sure like a cat stalking its prey. The big bastard slapped his left bicep with his right palm, then repeated the action with his left hand, a grunt accompanied each hit.

They circled the cage, each of them eyeing the other up, looking for a weakness. Coti subtly inhaled, watching as the lion shifter did the same. His long, matted mane of hair needed washed, his nails needed clipped, but he was clearly in excellent shape. He'd been so focused on the man's looks he wasn't paying proper attention and almost got his head knocked off as Champ shifted his feet in the dirt as only a shifter can do, and leapt the distance separating them. A big fist aiming for the side of his head would've been a killing blow, which shocked the fuck out of Coti as there were human spectators, but he ducked, taking only a glancing blow that knocked him against the chain link fencing.

Coti shook his head a couple times. The rattle of the fencing had the crowd going wild, chants of Champ echoing around them. Champ spun, facing him with dead eyes.

"Come on, fucker, is that all you got?" he taunted. He walked forward, done with the circling shit. As Champ came at him like a crazed animal, Coti met him in the middle, his arms up, fists ready to do some damage. The lion shifter swung on him, but he blocked it with his left arm, punching out with his right, following with his left and right again. Blood flew from Champ's nose, but Coti didn't let up and neither did Champ. Shit, the bastard smiled as he wiped across his face, looking at the red smear, and then licked his own blood.

"Is that all you got?" Champ mocked.

Those were the last words that were uttered as they both fought; each hitting and kicking the other. Coti fell to one knee as Champ landed a vicious blow to his kidney with a kick that sent him staggering backward. He could hear the crowd yelling 'finish him'.

He kept his head down, looking at the blood splattered dirt, listening to the beating of Champ's heart as he got closer. His other half, the one that allowed him to mask his scent pushed forward, focusing on the other fighter. Coti could see the other man was hurt a lot worse than he was. His right lung was punctured, along with a bruised kidney, not to mention broken ribs and a possible broken leg which the man was dragging. Coti couldn't tell for sure as the injury looked older.

When Champ got within striking distance, he jerked up, punching Champ in the solar plexus, before hitting him with what his brothers called a haymaker. Champ looked dazed, then he fell backward, landing on the hardpacked dirt littered with their blood. Coti wondered how many others had bled there before them, and just how many had lost their lives there as well.

The chants continued with 'finish him', only they were aimed at him. Coti walked over to where Champ lay, his eyes closed, his breathing deep and even. "I say that's a definite tap out, folks," he growled.

"You gonna finish him?" a deep voice growled from behind.

Coti looked over his shoulder, eyeing the man who spoke. "Nah, the rules stated the fight ends when your opponent is knocked out, or when one of us taps out. He," Coti pointed at Champ, then met the other man in the eye, his stare steady. "I'd say is the former."

"Interesting. Come, let's have a drink."

Without looking back at Champ, or whatever the hell his real name was, Coti made his way

toward the exit and his shit, glad to see the kid still
had his boots. "Thanks, kid."

He shoved his feet into his shitkickers after
pulling his shirt on and tucking his wallet back into
his pocket and connecting his chain to his belt loop.
His fob was still there as well, which meant the kid
did a good job of watching his shit, or whoever
went through it was quick.

"Sounds good," he agreed. Looking back, he
watched as the kid ran into the cage, helping Champ
get to his feet. Those black eyes locked on him,
blinked once then gave a nod before getting to his
feet. Coti followed the obvious alpha up a set of
rickety steps, fearing he was going to bust through
the damn things at any moment. "Shit, these things
gonna hold up?" he asked once he reached the top
and looked back down.

The man slapped him on the shoulder, his hand
staying and gave a squeeze. Had Coti been human,
it probably would've hurt. As it were, it pissed him
the fuck off. Not because it hurt, but because he had
to either act as though it did, or he'd give himself

away. With a slight flinch, because he could only act like a pussy for like two point five seconds, he shrugged the man's hand off.

Chapter Two

"You're done for the night, bitch. We got this," Kris said.

NeNe looked at the black-haired girl who was Grace's little bitch. God, how she wished they'd just go fuck off and maybe even, fuck off again. "I'm not done until Mac says so, Kris, and you know it. Last time I checked, he's the one who pays me." And she hadn't received her money for the night, except for the tips she'd made.

"Do you not have a brain in that head of yours?"

She turned to see Paula enter the tent that acted as a place for them to relax. Of course, it was the one place they could come and reapply makeup, deodorant, and use the bathroom without fear of getting felt up. Not that Grace, Kris, or Paula cared about the latter. To hear Paula ask if she had a brain was so funny, she snort laughed. "Oh, good one, Pauly." The nickname came out before she could censor herself.

"My name is Paula, you little twat," Paula said, shoving NeNe into one of the tables.

"Hey, what's going on in here?" Grace walked in, her red hair pulled into a ponytail.

NeNe noticed for the first time that all three girls had their hair pulled back. Usually, they wore their hair down and had more hairspray holding their curls in place. Between the three of them, they were probably the cause of some of the ozone issues. The next thing she took in was their lack of earrings. She started doing some calculations and didn't like the answers she came up with. Nope, three on one was only sexy in a book, and that was if it were three guys and one girl, and it was sex.

"So, what's your plan?" she asked Grace since she was their leader.

Grace flipped her ponytail around. "Why, I think it's pretty simple. Since Mac seems to find you attractive, we're gonna do something about that."

NeNe rolled her eyes. Their logic was fucking flawed. Hello, she would heal, then what? They going to kick her ass every night at closing time? Newsflash, she was out of here in a couple days. "Listen, I don't want to fight with any of you. I don't want Mac or any guy here for that matter. I just want to do my job and go home." Gah, she hated the whine at the end. She was pleading for them not to beat her ass. Heck, one-on-one she was pretty confident she could take them, but three on one was a no brainer. She was going to get her ass whooped.

"We could just let her go," Kris offered.

The sound of flesh hitting flesh had NeNe looking over her shoulder. Paula glared at Kris who was now holding her palm against her cheek, anger radiating off of both of them. Well, fuck her running. "Alright, I guess that's a no, then?"

Before Grace could decide to make the first move, NeNe tried to rush toward the door, her flight instead of fight kicking in.

"Oh no you don't, little girl."

NeNe was shoved back inside by a man she'd met several times as she delivered drinks to Mac.

"You in on this?" She blinked up at him, watching him shrug and look over her shoulder.

"Pussy's good, sweetheart. You shoulda put out."

She looked behind her, a sick feeling entering the pit of her stomach as Grace stood there with her two little bitches. The three of them didn't think anything was wrong with spreading their legs for the men wearing cuts. Never mind the fact none of them in this club would respect them in the morning, or make them theirs in any way, except for the moments of pleasure if they gave as good as they got, which she doubted.

NeNe wasn't a virgin, but she sure as shit chose her partners wisely. Of course, it had been a long dry spell for her. Ever since she'd seen one tall, tatted biker who looked right through her. Nope, she wasn't going to think of him.

"So, you're saying if I'd put out I'd have been safe? Yet, the reason the three of you are going to give me a beat down is because Mac wants to fuck me? Do you even hear yourselves? That's fucked up

on so many levels. Look, I'll go and not come back.
Problem solved." She dusted her hands off in front
of herself, showing how easy it would be, hoping
they agreed.

Grace tossed her head back, laughing. "Ah,
sweetie, you're so funny. No, now we just really
want to hurt you. You've walked around here,
strutting like a bitch in heat who was too good for
any of us. Now, it's time for us to teach you a
lesson." As one, they moved forward, cracking their
knuckles.

Lord, did they watch movies and take notes on
what to do when in situations such as the one they
were in? Cracking their knuckles for fucking crying
out loud. Next, they'll be pulling out a set of brass
knuckles and a ball bat. Holy shit, she prayed on her
Great Aunt Stella's grave that didn't happen.

NeNe felt a big hand on her back give her a
shove toward the trio, her cowgirl boots kicking up
dust as she tried to keep on her feet. From years of
avoiding her father and brother's abuse, she ducked
between Grace and Kris, elbowing Kris in the back

of the head, then latched onto Paula's ponytail and jerked hard. The woman landed on her back at the unexpected attack.

Grace spun around, smirking. "Ah, look at her, she's got claws."

She had more than claws in her right boot if she needed it, but NeNe wouldn't pull the blade out unless things got real messy. Facing the three of them again, she held her palms out in front, her legs bending slightly as she balanced on the balls of her feet. Grace attacked first, her fist flying out, but NeNe blocked, hitting the other woman in the jaw, moving away quickly.

"You're gonna pay for that," Paula shrieked.

NeNe hit, kicked, blocked, and rolled from more punches, yet in the end with three on one, she knew she didn't stand a chance. Blood dripped from her nose, and she couldn't see out of one eye thanks to Paula's foot that had come down on her head.

Now, she rolled into a tight ball, trying to protect her face and stomach as best she could.

Another kick hit her in the side and she swore she heard something break.

"Enough," a man roared.

Coti had only drank half his beer with the man named Mac, self-proclaimed alpha of the Hell Makers, when he felt a tug on his mind. The man was jawing about his business savvy and how great he was. All Coti wanted to tell him was that a man who had to proclaim how much a king he was, clearly had to be a fucking pussy. However, he kept his thoughts to himself and sipped the beer, a fucking Corona. What self-respecting alpha male drinks a damn Corona?

"Gentlemen, I need to take a piss," he announced standing in the middle of Mac's blathering about something Coti couldn't recall.

"Just go hang your junk off the side, ain't nobody gonna say shit, unless you're one of those who need a little privacy?" Mac made the word privacy sound like an offence.

He shrugged, chugged the rest of the drink being played off as beer. "Need to make sure my dick and balls are still in the same condition as before. You wanna look for me?" He raised his brows, a slight challenge in his tone.

Mac tossed his head back laughing. "Champ's a tough sonofabitch, huh? You must've got him when he was weak. Next time, watch your shit." Mac pointed his bottle at Coti.

The implied threat didn't bother Coti, not when the tug on his mind was screaming at him to get somewhere fast. Fuck, he wanted to squeeze his temples. Instead, he made his way back down the damn stairs, which surely were going to collapse under him at any second, allowing his senses to lead him. Instinct was a fine thing, and what had kept him alive as long as he's been. It was what had led him to the Iron Wolves all those years ago. He sure as shit wasn't going to ignore it now.

Making his way back toward the entrance, he nodded at humans who called out to him, never breaking stride. One of the men he'd seen with Mac stood outside a tent, his arms folded across his chest. Coti stopped, his nostrils flaring at the familiar scent and the coppery smell of blood behind the man.

"Keep walking, boy," the man snarled.

Coti shook his head. "No can do, boy." He moved to go around the wolf shifter.

He put his hands up, trying to shove Coti back. Coti looked down at the hands on his chest, then up into amber eyes. "You don't want to do that," he told the shifter. "Take your hands off me and walk away."

The other man shook his head. "Fuck you." He tried to grip Coti's T-shirt, his face twisting in a snarl.

Had Coti truly been human, the fact that the other man half-shifted would've freaked him out. As it were, he allowed his own wolf to rise just under the surface, lending him strength. He grabbed hold of the shifter's wrists, squeezing until he released Coti's shirt. Much harder and he'd have crushed bones. They'd have healed in time, but Coti didn't care. The man was blocking him from NeNe and she was hurt. "I said move, fucker. Either get the hell outta my way, or I'll make sure you can't walk." The real threat was clear. This man had seen him beat the shit out of Champ. Coti could see him thinking of shifting, then the decision to walk away was made. His grip relaxed, Coti's shirt fell from his fingers. For good measure, Coti gave one final tight squeeze before letting him go. The man stepped around Coti, muttering about pussy not being worth it. He wasn't sure what he'd expected, but the vision of three women surrounding a tiny lump on the ground wasn't it. His wolf howled in his head. His other side wanted blood. The females' blood.

"What the hell are you doing?" he roared. Shit, his wolf was up and so was the other half of himself. They were uniting, and neither were happy.

All three women turned to him, blood on their fists and clothes. Their own, and his NeNe's...Ah shit. They were claiming her, yet he couldn't seem to stop the growl as they stared at him.

A redhaired woman placed a hand on her hip, looking him up and down before she spoke. "Go on about your business, this doesn't concern you."

He moved toward them, silently cheering when they scattered away from the prone form of NeNe. "Hey, you." He bent and brushed back a hank of hair that had fallen over her face. Her heart raced, the whoosh whoosh sound reassuring to him.

"You can't just come in here. This is our space."

Coti glared at the red head. "You speaking again? Really, you should probably shut the fuck up and run. All three of you, get the hell outta my sight, but make no mistake, I've catalogued every single thing about each of you." Oh, he knew he could find them in a crowd at anytime from that moment on. Once he told Lyric and the girls what happened, these three bitches were going to wish they were never born. He watched the redhead's eyes flicker to amber, her wolf wanting to come out and fight him. The fact he was still masking his scent was the only thing keeping her in check. Of course, if he allowed his wolf out, she'd become a bitch in heat begging him to forgive her or some shit. There was no forgiveness for what was done to his female. She may be his unclaimed mate as of now, but that was going to change, soon.

The three females quietly rushed from the tented space, the flap closing quietly behind them. He opened his senses, allowing himself to flow into NeNe while he kept a presence in his own body. "Fuck," he swore as he imagined the internal damage she suffered from their beating. Being human meant she didn't heal like shifters, nor was she as strong. If he attempted to lift her and carry her out, there was a chance he could kill her. Yet, he also knew if he didn't do something she was going to die. "Those fucking bitches." Looking around the space, he nicked his finger with his incisor, watching as the tip filled with ruby red blood. The rich lifeblood of his kind would help heal her enough that he'd be able to carry her out and get her to a human hospital, he hoped. With his other hand, he tilted her head back to make sure her breathing was steady and stuck his finger into her mouth. At first, she didn't do anything, her stillness making him think she wasn't going to accept his gift.

After a few seconds, he felt the soft rasp of her tongue flick against his finger. He ran his hand over the back of her head, feeling a huge bump. "Motherfuckers," he whispered, his palm moving away from the injury. Her mouth closed around his finger, cheeks hollowing out as they sucked. Goddess, his dick became fully erect, which made him feel like a complete pervert since she was near death. Slowly, he eased his finger out, knowing she had enough to start healing, yet not so much humans would wonder at the miracle.

One big green eye blinked open. "I've died and gone to heaven," she whispered.

Coti chuckled. "Pretty sure that's the first time I've been accused of being in heaven."

NeNe moved to sit up, then groaned. "Oh god, I've been run over, then backed up on for good measure. Where's the sisterhood of the traveling bitches?"

At the reference of the trio in question, he growled, then the scents hit him. Shifters were coming, and they were coming quickly. "Can you stand?" His blood was powerful, but he didn't know if she'd had enough to work that quickly. Her right eye was still swollen almost completely shut since he'd concentrated on her inner injuries.

"Well, I can breathe without feeling like I'm going to pass out, and I can feel, everything. I say that's a good thing. Help me up?" she asked, holding her hands out.

Coti stood, grabbing her under the arms and lifting, not wanting to jar her too much. What he really wanted was to carry her out, but if he was going to fight, he'd need both arms free. "Can you shoot a gun?"

She pointed at her face. "I'm a good shot, but not sure if I would be with only one eye?"

He nodded. "I'd rather you be honest than accidentally shoot me in the ass."

The flap was jerked open, allowing several men inside followed by the sisterhood of the traveling bitches as NeNe called them. "He threatened us because she got what she deserved for disrespecting us." Grace pointed, her voice grating.

A huge man, clearly a bear shifter, placed Grace behind him. "Boy, you don't come in here disrespecting our bitches. You may've beaten Champ, but that was in the cage. Out here, there ain't no rules."

The sound of fabric ripping let him know some of the shifters were partially shifting, agitation making them lose control. Fuck, what the hell was wrong with this pack that they not only allowed humans to lead them around by their dicks, but they'd shift in front of them and have fights between shifters and seemingly full humans for fun? "Listen, I don't want to fight any of you. I'm taking my girl here, and we're leaving."

"Looks like your girl ran into some trouble. Why don't you let us take care of her?" The bear shifter offered.

Coti's wolf wanted to break free and rip the assholes throat out, but years of tempering both sides of his being kept the animal reigned in. "Nah, I got this."

"Yo, you got a problem, Coti?" Joaquin asked.

Seeing a familiar face in the crowd along with several of the man's MC brothers, Coti gave a lift of his chin. Joaquin not only was a shifter, but he was Coti's alpha's cousin. If he opened his mind, he'd be able to connect with the other man, but Coti didn't trust easily, nor did he want to give Joaquin an opening to his own thoughts. Instead, he met the alpha's stare, a thousand words conveyed between them.

None of the shifters could miss the scent of NeNe's blood or the fact she was one hundred percent human, while the three bitches hiding behind the wall of shifters weren't. The fact the little firecracker was alive was a testament to her strength.

"What the hell, man? Who fucked up your old lady?"

"Real fucking subtle, Blade. I think that's a question we're all wondering." Joaquin looked around the space, his eyes going to the three women with blood on their white tank tops. "Haven't you heard it's better to stick with black? It don't show blood as easily." Joaquin moved closer to Coti and NeNe, putting himself between the crowd.

Without a word, several other men came to stand in front of Coti and NeNe, creating a wall of tattooed muscle. "Looks like we got a standoff. What's it gonna be, boys? We gonna have a brawl inside this here tent, or you gonna let our boy and his lady walk out of here?" Joaquin asked, his tone sounding bored.

"You can't let her leave." a female voice growled angrily.

"What the fuck is going on in here?" Mac called out, making the entire space go quiet.

Coti allowed his other being to close itself off so only his wolf was apparent, then opened a link to Joaquin. *"I'm leaving here with NeNe if I have to kill every motherfucker in this place, including that bastard pretending to be an alpha."*

"I feel you, but let's try to keep the bloodshed to a minimum. There's more going on here than what you see on the surface." Joaquin shifted closer to Coti.

"Rose, girl is that you? What the hell happened? Come, I'll take you to our physician." Mac held out his hand.

NeNe whimpered, pressing herself closer to Coti. "Sorry, man, but she's mine."

Mac's brows rose. "Is that right? You've been here all of five fucking minutes. How'd that happen?"

Coti could see the man was fighting to keep his wolf in check. "I actually came here looking for her. We sort of had a fight. Took me a minute to track her down. Luckily, I did." He put his arm around NeNe, feeling her shiver at his touch.

The crowd parted as three more men filed in, their scent let him know they were cat shifters as well, but these men he knew. Of course, they were usually on his side, but Coti wasn't willing to risk

NeNe's life on the off chance they were playing for the other side.

Damn, he really wished he'd called his pack before he'd walked into this shithole. Before everything could go completely to shit, he opened his link to Kellen, hoping like hell he wasn't intruding on 'sexy time'. *"Hey, man, sorry to pop in unannounced, but there's some shit going down."* He gave a quick rundown while keeping his eyes on the gathering crowd, waiting for Kellen's response.

"Well fuck, son. You sure know how to ruin a guy's boner. The Fey Queen's out of commish for the time being, but I can send a fiery little dragon. She's kinda made herself available in Jenna's place."

Coti pictured the pink haired crazy female popping into the already full tent. *"Not just yet. Let's see how this shakes out. I got Joaquin and a few of his guys. Hell, Ace and the cats just strolled in like they were out for an evening walk."*

"Cats make me sneeze," Kellen snarled.

"You should see the fucking menagerie we got here. Lions, tigers, and bears, alongside wolves." He joked, not mentioning what all he was. *"Oh, and let's not forget the dragons."* Yeah, their world was getting crazier every damn day.

"You forgot to say 'Oh my' you know. Don't get killed, and just so we're clear, there's gonna be a mandatory meeting when you get out of the situation you've found yourself in. Check in with me as soon as you get your ass out of there. Me and the boys will be paying Mac and his crew a visit real soon." Coti heard the threat in the growled voice inside his head. The Iron Wolf was not to be fucked with, which made him wonder why Mac and his merry bunch of shifters had settled so closely to them.

"Alright, I need to focus on the circus in front of me. I'll try not to get dead." Although Kellen had said it like a threat, Coti and the rest of the pack were an intricate part of the Iron Wolves. When one was severely injured, or Goddess help them, killed, Kellen felt the loss deep within him. An image of

Kellen's middle finger with the Wolf head ring on it flashed in front of Coti's eyes.

"You ready to roll outta here, Coti?"

He turned, meeting Ace's eyes. The huge shifter moved subtly, showing Coti he was packing a couple guns. "Ready when you are." Which meant he was up for just about anything.

"I think I'm going to be sick," NeNe whispered.

His gut clenched at the image of the fiery little female tossing her cookies in front of the crowd. "Come on, let's get you out of here." He swooped down, lifting her into his arms, trusting his pseudo pack to have his and his unclaimed mate's back. Of course, if shit went south, his other half would come out, then none of them would be safe.

Chapter Three

NeNe tried to control the rolling of her stomach. Lord knew she didn't want to appear any weaker in front of the bitches who'd literally beat the living shit out of her, let alone the rest of the asshats who'd gathered, but damn if her body wasn't having other ideas.

As Coti lifted her into his arms, she was sure the motion would be the final straw, yet her body relaxed, the nausea dissipating, thank you, lawd. Forget decorum, or women's lib, she wanted to snuggle up to the big tattooed biker. She wanted to let him fight her battles, well at least until she healed, then she was going to find each of those bitches one-on-one and beat the fuck out of them. Of course, she'd have a goddamn bat with her because those bitches knew how to hit, hard.

"Easy, we're gonna walk out of here," he murmured near her ear.

She blinked at his whispered words. Her body trying to curl into a ball in his arms. Looking into his eyes, she thought she saw a flash of red. However, with only one eye, she was sure it was a trick of the lighting, or the bitches had fucked up her sight. "Am I going blind?" she whispered back.

Coti tilted her chin up. "You're going to be fine. Just hold still."

It was then she realized her arms were wrapped so tightly around his neck he had to be uncomfortable. She took a deep breath, pain in her wounded ribs made her wince, but she forced her arms to relax slightly. Up close, she could smell his masculine scent. Damn, she wished she wasn't missing the vision in one eye. At such close proximity, she'd have been able to study his tattoos, then she'd be able to ask him if they had meaning. God, she hoped he had a story behind each one, instead of just getting them because he was bored. For her, getting ink was special. Each of her tattoos had meaning. She didn't judge those who went out and got one because they wanted to, but for her, they were cathartic.

"Hey, stay with me," Coti said.

She jerked upright, not realizing she'd almost drifted off to sleep. Crap, they were almost to the entrance of the little makeshift town Mac had created. "My bike," she croaked. God, it felt as if she'd swallowed sand, then proceeded to gargle it for shits and giggles.

"Where'd you park it?" he asked, not breaking stride.

NeNe wondered how far they'd make it before gunfire would erupt. Knowing the men who manned the gates, she wouldn't put it past them, or Mac, to have them shot as they drove off.

"NeNe, I need you to tell us where your bike is," Coti said with a little force behind his words.

Running her tongue over her lips, she tried to sit a little straighter, trying to orient herself in Coti's arms. "I can walk," she offered.

Coti grunted. "Bike?"

She gave him the general location, praying like a good little church girl that it was still there, only breathing easier when they reached it.

"Ace and his boys are going to trailer it back to the Iron Wolves Club, along with my bike. Now, before you open those lips that are too damn bruised for me to kiss shut, don't. Just don't," he growled.

"Hey," she said. He wants to kiss her lips? "What was I going to say?" she asked.

"Damn wolves always making the females lose their minds." The one she thought she'd heard called Ace muttered as he walked by. "We got this. We'll also follow you out just to make sure you ain't picked up no shadows."

"Thanks, man, I owe you a solid."

"Don't fuck up my car, she's special," Ace said.

NeNe placed her head back on Coti's chest, her mind whirling. These men were taking over, talking as if she weren't there. She should be putting up a fight. Heck, her bike, her baby, was going to be trailered away by men she didn't know, yet all she wanted was to lay down and rest for a week or three. "I think I have a concussion." That was the only reasoning she could think of.

Her words had Coti stopping, his face screwing up as if he was in pain. "No, you're just exhausted. Once we get out of here, you can rest."

"Gee, thanks for that great triage, Dr. Coti," she snarked.

Coti winked at her. "Want to see my stethoscope?" He wiggled his brows.

The absurdity of his words and the fact she actually did want to see his "stethoscope" made her laugh, then regret doing so when the pain struck her. "Oh god, don't make me laugh; it hurts my face," she moaned.

One of the men from the tent came up next to them. He reminded her of Kellen Styles in looks and demeanor. He kept pace with Coti while the other men could be heard talking behind them.

"Your face hurts me too, little girl. Why did they beat you like that, may I ask?"

"Joaquin, don't." Coti stopped walking.

"There's more at play here than you know, Coti. I need to find out if she knows anything." Joaquin didn't raise his voice, but the command was there like she'd noticed with Kellen.

Coti adjusted his grip on NeNe. "Don't try me with your alpha bullshit. I let Kellen do it out of respect 'cause he's my alpha. I don't owe you shit except gratitude for helping me get my…NeNe out of that place alive. You want to have a sit down with her and I, you give me twenty-four hours to see to her needs. Fucking rattle my cage, you won't like what I become."

Ace, Dalton, and Norris moved up beside him, flanking him and NeNe. "I don't want to war with you, but on this, I'm immovable." Damn cats were becoming things he was beginning to like.

"Coti, what's going on?" NeNe whispered. "They want to know why I got my ass handed to me? That's easy to answer. Mac wanted me, but I didn't want him. Grace is a jealous bitch, and her sidekicks are twatwaffle's who'll follow that cuntamungous anywhere she goes, do anything she tells them, like the trained bitches they are, without question. There ya go, there's your damn story. I didn't do anything nefarious to deserve this." She pointed at her face. "I didn't fuck my boss or any of the other porchdickasshats that hangout there. I show up to work, do my job, and remember what they like to drink. I make sure to have their next one to them before they ask for it and make great tips because I do all of that with a smile, not because I don't wear panties under my skirt. That's it."

He barely restrained the growl as he listened to her explain what she did and didn't do. "You wear a damn skirt around those fuckers?"

NeNe huffed. "Really, is that all you got out of what I just said?"

"How long have you worked there?" Joaquin asked.

Coti glared at Kellen's cousin. "I said twenty-four hours. You got your explanation, now you get the fuck outta my space." He hadn't been joking about rattling the cage he kept his beast locked behind. Hearing her speak as if she'd been fucked with on a daily basis had him wanting to go back and rip the heads off of men who touched her, uncaring if they were human or shifters.

"Can I make a suggestion?"

He turned and met Dalton's gaze who was Ace's second in command. "What is it?" he asked.

Dalton tipped his head toward the way they'd come from. "I suggest we all stop our fucking yammering like a bunch of bitches, no offense, ma'am, and get the hell outta Dodge."

"None taken, since I'm not a bitch," NeNe said.

Dammit, he was doing a piss poor job of taking care of his mate. "Where's your vehicle, Ace?"

"You can't miss it." The cat pointed toward the only car that was parked between the trucks.

"You gotta be joking?" Coti looked at the low-slung sports car, then at the huge shifter. "How the hell do you fold yourself into that thing?"

Ace shrugged. "With care. Now, off you go. I'll make sure your toys are delivered safely and I'll trust you to do the same."

Coti barely kept from rolling his eyes as he strode toward the vehicle Ace had pointed out. How the damn thing hadn't gotten jacked while it sat in the lot he had no clue. The closer he got to the vehicle, he allowed his wolf to surface when a sensation of being watched washed over him, making him halt and look around.

"You didn't think I'd leave Lucile out here all alone, did you?" Ace scoffed, then whistled. Several shadows moved, sleek in their silhouettes, blending in with the night.

"Please tell me those weren't real panthers, or whatever kind of large cat they looked like," Coti muttered.

"Okay," Ace agreed.

"What're you talking about?" NeNe asked, looking around as he bent and placed her on her feet.

"Nothing, I was commenting about the fact Ace owns a damn Jag and actually left the cat out here. You know, a sleek jungle cat waiting to devour its prey or be devoured if caught by a bigger predator." The sound of the other man's laughter made him want to chase his ass down and feed him some damn catnip.

"You say some weird stuff, Coti."

He opened the door, helping her buckle the seatbelt before going around the hood. "You've no clue, NeNe love. No clue at all," he muttered.

The little human's world had just gotten turned on its head, but he'd do all he could to even it out and help her acclimate to her new normal.

"Love you too, boo. Love you, too." Ace laughed.

Coti met Ace's glowing eyes across the hood of the Jaguar F-Type convertible. Coti may be more of a jacked up truck or Harley guy, but he knew cars. The sleek black cat on the steering wheel was one Coti wouldn't mind having in his garage. "Is this car even out yet?"

Ace shrugged, a grin split his face. "If you know the right people. Clearly, I do. Take care of Lucile for me. She's only a babe, fresh out of the factory." Ace looked down at NeNe and winced. "Sorry about your face."

NeNe lifted her hand, her fingers ran across her right cheek bone. Coti wanted to punch Ace for reminding her about the damage. She surprised him though as she gave a wry chuckle. "I'll survive. I guess it could've been worse." She yawned, groaning in pain.

His blood was working through her system, repairing the worst of the internal damage. In all truth, he'd been surprised she hadn't zonked out within minutes. "Let's get out of here. See you," he said to Ace. The other man tossed him a fob for the car through the open roof, making Coti shake his head. Damn vehicles and their lack of keys. With a push of a button, the vehicle roared to life.

"She's an eight speed quick shift."

He looked out the side window, not in the least surprised to find Ace next to him. "I'm gonna have to ask you to no," he growled.

"Gonna need you to be more specific." Ace stood with his hands on his hips, looking confused.

Coti pointed at him. "You just appearing there like a fucking ghost. Not okay."

"Ah, so you're asking me not to explain?" Ace kicked a rock, biting his lip.

"You don't do the innocent look well," NeNe said, her one eye staring through the darkness.

Coti bit his tongue, hoping NeNe didn't question how Ace got from one side of the vehicle to the next so quickly. "As for needing you to explain? I think I can figure out how to drive this puppy." He revved the engine, the fine hairs on his arms rising.

"I'm the one who's gonna have to tell you, to no," Ace growled.

"Hey, what's she top out at?" Coti asked as he shifted into drive but didn't wait around to hear what Ace said. More than likely, the other man was cursing him and his future children.

"That was kinda mean." NeNe's soft voice had him glancing over at her.

He loved the tone of her voice, just the sound of it soothed all of him. "Nah, he knows I'm just fucking with him. Besides, if I messed up his baby, I'd take care of it."

"This looks really expensive." Her hand ran across the console.

At the bruised and swollen knuckles, rage threatened to consume him again. His little warrior had put up a hell of battle against three female shifters. The fact she was alive to tell the tale was a testament to her strength and endurance. "Yeah, it's not cheap." He didn't want to tell her the thing was probably worth more than a hundred and twenty grand, depending on the extras Ace had installed.

"Can you turn the dashboard lights down?" She placed her palm over her one good eye as she spoke.

"Shit, are you hurting?" He looked in the rearview mirror, making sure they weren't being followed before signaling to pull over. Ace had custom lights that made the dash and door handles glow a bright blue, which could irritate if one was having eye or head pain. He allowed his mind to open, flowing into NeNe's, searching for the source of her injury. He sent a flood of healing energy from the crown of her head, much like one would do if they were meditating, only his was on the corporeal level. His wolf whimpered, feeling it's mate's pain as if it were his own. It took all his concentration to soothe the beast, his other being rising, becoming more dominate as he too wanted to take control.

Once he felt he'd done the best he could without a full-on healing that would alert her, he pulled back, his hands moving on her temples in a soothing motion. "Oh, that feels amazing," she whispered, her breath fanning across his forearm.

Dick. Hard. That was his state, which was completely and totally inappropriate given the woman was beaten within an inch of her life, looking like she'd gone a couple rounds with Mike Tyson, and lost. "Feel better?" he asked, already knowing the answer.

"Mmhmm," she mumbled.

He settled back in his seat, pushed the turn signal on, and began the trip back to his place. Not once had he contemplated how he'd explain to NeNe why he'd brought her to his home, instead of hers. In his mind, she was his, and that meant what was his, was hers.

Turo had come out, telling the pack he was hundreds of years old. The revelation had shocked the pack since most were still young pups. They knew shifters lived a longer lifespan than humans, but the oldest of their kind, they knew was only a hundred and fifty or there about. However, Coti and his kind were different. No, scratch that, Coti was different.

"Fuck," he grunted. The thought of explaining to NeNe what he was, what the Iron Wolves were, was daunting to say the least. A human didn't feel the same pull as his kind, or shifters, did. Some humans fell in love and said they had a "soulmate", but there were still instances of divorce. Hell, divorce rates among humans were almost fifty percent. Those numbers were staggering. He didn't understand why they even went through the travesty of agreeing to be with one person for the rest of their lives if they didn't mean it. For him, his people, and other supernatural beings, when they found the other half of their souls that was it. There was no one else for them. Of course, he'd heard the Goddess had made exceptions in cases where a mate was killed, but those cases were rare, such as with Niall, the alpha who'd lost his first mate to a hunter. Now, he was happily mated to Alaina and raising a cub with another on the way.

He glanced over at NeNe, hating to see her so pale, her beautiful face black and blue. His wolf snarled with the need to exact vengeance for the damage done to it's mate, but the man pushed the urge back. She was human, and he was far from what anyone thought he was.

The Jag ate up the distance to his place tucked away just inside pack lands. He took a deep breath, finally feeling at ease as he pulled into his driveway. While most of the other members of the club had built or bought homes that were more cabin-like, he'd opted for a modern home. One that was all sleek lines and more defensible in his opinion. To the outside eye, it looked as if it were glass and concrete. However, it had bullet proof glass and the concrete exterior was thicker than it appeared. Not to mention, the windows were smoked and could go dark as night, keeping the sun and any onlookers from being able to see in, or out, depending on the need. His brothers in the MC hadn't asked how he'd afforded his home, mostly because they hadn't seen all his gadgets. Living a long life gave a man the opportunity to shore up funds and resources.

Hell, if Turo the gun loving son-of-a-bitch, ever got a peek at his gun room, Coti was sure the bastard would be walking out with one or two. Not that he'd steal them, more like procure a few for keeping the peace, but Turo was Coti's best friend so he'd allow it. He was also one of the best shots Coti had ever had the pleasure of training with, but still, he hated the thought of losing one of his babies.

He dug into his pocket and pulled out his cell. With a couple swipes, one of the bay doors opened. The empty space was quickly filled with his friend's car. Coti made sure the door was closed before he got out, opening his senses even though he was sure his home was secure. With NeNe's safety, he wasn't taking any chances. The smooth drive combined with the luxury interior made it remarkably easy for NeNe to relax, so when he opened her door, it didn't surprise him to find her half asleep. "Come on, Armina, let's get you inside."

NeNe groaned but swung her right leg out. "Do I gotta? How 'bout I just stay right here?"

He chuckled. "You'll hate this car in a couple hours. Let's go, I'll carry you," he offered. The need to feel her in his embrace was one he wouldn't think too much about at the moment.

As he strode toward the door leading into his home, her head rested on his shoulder, her arms wrapped around his neck as if they'd done it a thousand times. Neither spoke as he placed his palm on the security pad, waiting for it to register his imprint. The red light turned green, then the door was sliding into the wall. Once he was on the inside, he made sure the door closed and locked before going farther. He hadn't lived as long as he had without being cautious, and he sure as shit wasn't going to start fucking up now that NeNe was in residence.

The lights came on in each room as he entered. The dim setting kept them from blinding him as he made his way to the other side of the house. Once he got to the hallway where he could either take NeNe to the guest suite, or his, the decision came quickly. His. She was his. Again, lights came on, but they were set to low, creating a nice glow so they wouldn't hurt NeNe should she open her one good eye. His hope was to get her cleaned up and give her another healing session before she got a good look at herself. If she didn't see the damage to its full extent, he wouldn't have to explain how she healed so quickly. He could almost hear his mother's lyrical laugh in his head.

With a nod, the door to his ensuite opened, the shower already on and warming. He was glad little NeNe seemed to be dozing again. "Come on, let's get you cleaned up, then you can sleep."

"I think I'll just stay right here," she mumbled, nuzzling her face against him.

Coti felt her breath on his neck, the sensation more erotic than any other experience in his life. Using a little more of his powers, he undressed NeNe, pushing into her mind the memory of her undressing. If there was a medal for most chivalrous act, he was sure he'd win as he stepped into the shower stall, large enough for six grown men, still clothed with a naked NeNe in his arms. His fucking cock was going to be scarred with the imprint from the zipper, however knowing his little human was comfortable was all that mattered to him. Motherfuck, he was joining the growing list of pussywhipped.

Chapter Four

NeNe wasn't sure how her clothes had come off, or that she even cared right then. However, having Coti, the one man who made all her girlie parts wake up and sing, pressed up against her ass, she couldn't work up one single fuck. Nope, not a one. What kind of woman did that make her?

Coti chuckled, his peppermint breath making her lean back to look up at him. "Why are you laughing?"

"You say the craziest things," he answered.

She froze. Dammit, had she said that out loud? Gah, her brain had clearly been rung too hard by Grace. She bit her tongue, hoping she hadn't said anything about her girlie parts with her outside voice. She noticed for the first time the rough feel of denim against her ass. "You do realize you're getting your clothes soaked, right?"

His grunt was her answer, but she smiled. Her Coti wasn't a man who wasted a lot of words. She stared at his hands. They were large with tattoos on them. The designs each probably having meaning. Her fingers trailed over the rings he wore, one on the pinky of his left hand the other on his middle finger. Anytime she'd seen him flip off one of the guys, she'd always wondered what the crest on the ring was for. Now, her fingers traced it, but she couldn't get the words out of her mouth.

"This was passed down through my family." Coti ran his thumb over his opposite hand. The action made it feel as if he were hugging her.

The feel of his hard body wasn't easy to ignore, yet he didn't press his erection into her like most guys would. Instead, he leaned forward and grabbed some body wash from a shelf. With deft hands, he squirted a generous amount into his hands. She stared as he made a lather of the fragrant gel, then all coherent thought left her brain when he brought his soaped-up hands to her chest. God, she'd fantasized about having his hands on her so many times she could literally fill diaries with them. Nowhere in any of those imaginings did they come close to how the reality of having his rough, callused fingers tracing over her flesh truly felt.

Her breath whooshed out the moment his thumbs scraped over her nipples. At some point, both her eyes opened, the swelling having gone down enough she could see out of both eyes, and good god almighty, she was so freaking happy since she wanted to catalogue what it looked like to have Coti Sharp's hands on her. He stood behind her, washing her front, then moved onto her hair, making sure to rinse the shampoo and conditioner out completely without getting any in her eyes. "A girl would think you've done this before," she joked, although the thought of him doing this to other women made her feel stabby.

"This is a first, I'll have to admit."

"Oh," she gasped.

"Does this hurt?" he asked, his hands tracing over her ribs.

NeNe didn't understand why he was asking her such a silly question until she looked down, seeing the purple and red bruising on her hip bone. Damn Kris and Paula and their boots. "No, not too bad." In fact, she didn't seem to be feeling any pain at the moment. She could've died tonight, of that she had no doubt. Grace and the other two bitches would've continued their torture without stopping, had it not been for Coti.

Coti's hands moved lower, tracing over her upper thighs, skipping over where she most wanted him to touch. Knowing he was too honorable, she turned in his arms, the warm spray hitting her back. Coti's hands immediately landed on her ass, pulling her into him.

"I want you," she said.

She watched him close his bright green eyes, his breathing deep and even. "You're hurt," he gritted.

"I'm not that hurt. Sure, I got some pretty colorful reminders over my skin, but they'll fade and be gone, much like I plan to be one day. For tonight, I plan to take what I want, and that's you

Coti." For once she was laying it out there. Yes, she was the girl from the wrong side of the tracks. Looking at his shower, she could tell he had money. Heck, his bike was worth about ten of hers, easily.

When Coti growled, she stepped back. "It's fine, you don't want me, no big deal." Which was such a lie. His rejections always hurt, the pain like a knife that cut deep, but the wound would heal, like it always did.

"Are you kidding me? I want you so damn bad my dick is going to be permanently scarred." He pulled her palm to the front of his jeans.

Whether he thought she'd run screaming at the feel of his hardness or what his reasonings were, she had no clue. The only thing she could think was 'Holy shit, the man was huge' and 'Dang that has to hurt,' both of which she didn't say out loud. Instead, she let her fingers trace his length up and down, then feeling bolder, she unsnapped the front of his jeans. The soaking wet fabric made it hard to get them undone, but NeNe was nothing if not determined. Once the button was open, she looked up, shocked to find his eyes closed, yet she was sure she could feel him staring at her. "Are you okay?"

"Yes, your hands are softer than silk against me. Let me," he said, easing the zipper open.

NeNe laughed at the pained sound he made. "Were you worried I'd hurt him?"

"If you did, would you kiss him all better?" Coti asked.

She looked down at the monster escaping the tight confines of the wet denim and thought of taking him into her mouth, or her vajayjay. God yes, she'd kiss him all better. "Absolutely," she answered, her hand wrapped around his dick, her fingers not quite meeting.

"We shouldn't be doing this." Coti's hand covered hers.

"Why not?" She tried to move her hand up and down, but he wouldn't let her. NeNe stuck her bottom lip out. "Please tell me you're not a virgin. But, if you are, I promise to be good to you this first time, Coti." She gave a gentle but firm squeeze.

"What?" he choked. "Baby girl, I ain't been a virgin for a long damn time, trust and believe that." His eyes rolled closed as she brushed her chest against his. "Damn, you're a tease."

"So, if you're not a virgin, and I'm not a virgin, then what's stopping us?"

NeNe was lifted off her feet, her back landing against the shower wall as Coti got into her face, holding her up with his hips, yet he was gentle. "I don't want to hear about other men and you. Ever!"

Yep, he was growling, but instead of getting irritated, her body was saying *do me*. She lifted her legs, wrapping them around his waist. For a heartbeat or five, he held her there, breathing hard. "Goddess, you drive me crazy."

She opened her mouth to reply, but then his mouth was crashing down on hers, silencing her with a kiss. His tongue demanded entrance, licking, dueling with her own. Peppermint filled her mouth as if he'd been chewing sweet gum. He brought his hand to the back of her head, the other going down the front of her, shivers wracking her frame from the contact. Everywhere he touched she felt electrified, the need for more making her twist against him. His thumb trailed down, stopping on her unbruised ribcage.

He broke away from the kiss. "When'd you get this?"

Looking down at her side, she looked at the phoenix covering her from breast to thigh. The hours it had taken, not to mention the pain was worth it. "A year ago." She didn't know what he wanted her to say, why he was still standing still, and not touching her. Hell, he was sleeved on both arms and had most of his chest covered. From his neck all the way over his shoulders and down his back, told the story of his life. She'd had fantasies of her tongue and hands, tracing over them for hours.

"Female, you're trekking on dangerous grounds." Coti pinched her nipple between his fingers, making her cry out.

"Hey, what did I do?" she asked. The sharp pain sent a tingle straight to her clit. She wondered if she thought dirty thoughts if he'd do it again? Heck, was the man a mind reader? Closing her eyes, she wiggled in his hold and reached between them, flicking his nipples.

"Who did it?" he bit out.

NeNe groaned. "Are you kidding me? I'm naked, nearly impaled on your ginormous dick, and you want to know who inked me? Why, you in need of some new ink yourself?"

Coti blinked at the little female in his arms and fought not to laugh. Shit, he was harder than he'd ever been in his entire life, and that was saying a lot for a man who was close to two hundred years old. "I'm always thinking of my next piece, but no, that's not why I asked. I need to know who I need to kill for seeing all of you." There was no way in hell whoever inked her hadn't seen her perfect pussy, or her gorgeous tits as they were laying the needle to her. The details of the phoenix with the subtle shades of purples and reds made it even more gorgeous than if it had been done in all black. He wanted to lay her out on his bed and examine it under the light, yet he needed to find out the name of the male first. He was all about lists and order. Get name, decide best way to kill, then get rid of him. Of course, if he had a family, Coti would make sure they were taken care of for the rest of their human lives, he wasn't a Neanderthal, after all.

Her musical laughter had his cock jerking, the action making him grunt as the poor abused appendage wasn't in the place it wanted, which was inside NeNe. "Coti Sharp, you can't go around threatening to harm innocent people. Besides, Morgan is a sweet woman who has mad skills with the tattoo gun."

His need for killing an unknown man went out the window at the image of a female doing the seeing and touching, until the diabolical woman bent forward, her teeth nibbling at his ear. "Of course, she does like women. I think she offered to help me do aftercare at my house."

Coti reached out and shut the water off, knowing his little warrior was messing with him, but decided he'd had enough. NeNe wanted to see him out of control, well she'd done rattled his cage one too many times and he'd yet to cage his beast completely. "How about I show you how I do aftercare?"

He spun her away from the wall, taking them out of the shower and into his bedroom, uncaring they were dripping water everywhere. With only a thought he could've dried them, but was too engrossed in stamping his possession on the woman in his arms. He didn't stop to question the unreasonable need, only knew she was theirs. Theirs to love. Theirs to protect. Theirs to fuck and fuck hard. Goddess, he wanted to claim her in the way of his people, but she wasn't ready. Hell, he wasn't sure he was either. "It's not too late, you can say no," he offered.

NeNe tightened her legs around him, her arms held his head as she brought her lips to his. "Not. Gonna. Happen. Fuck me like you mean it," she said, then bit his lower lip, the sharp pain making him growl.

He placed her on the bed, hunger beat at him.

"God, you taste divine. Like seriously, what the hell do you do, swish your mouth with peppermint or what?"

Coti was sure he should've focused on her words, but seeing her laid out on his red sheets, her once flawless skin now mottled with bruises, he did the only thing an alpha male could do. Kiss her hurts away, each scrape, bruise, and lump he found, he lavished with attention, seeking to wash away the pain she'd felt with pleasure. If he could, he'd go back in time and erase the three women who'd touched her, wiping them from the fabric of time.

"Oh, that's nice," she whispered.

Never had a woman said he was 'nice', in bed. He didn't like it. Coti wasn't nice, not in bed and he sure as fuck wasn't nice out of it. He was dirty, filthy, and by damned, he'd show NeNe just how much. His mouth latched onto one pert nipple, letting his hand wander south, trailing over her belly continuing down between her thighs, sliding through her slickness. "You're wet. Let's see if I can make you wetter." Her gasp was music to his ears as he alternated between breasts, sucking and biting, not hard enough to break skin, but enough to give her a bit of pain. He'd already figured out his mate enjoyed an edge of pain to her pleasure, which suited him perfectly. Urging her thighs farther apart, he moved down her abdomen, tracing her belly button with his tongue, leaving a trail of wetness behind. Her sweet arousal called to him. He wanted to have her cream coating his face when he entered her for the first time.

"Oh, fuck," she gasped.

Coti chuckled against her pussy, circling her clit with his thumb before pressing two fingers into her smooth pussy. The slick opening tightened as he pushed inside. "I need to hear what you like, don't hold back," he said as he watched her biting her lip.

Curving his fingers inside her wet, welcoming channel, he pressed against her inner wall, working them in and out in slow measured strokes. NeNe tried to lay perfectly still, but her legs quivered slightly as if she worried the wrong move would make him stop. His warrior woman would learn he loved her taste, could spend hours right where he was and still want more. She bucked against him as he found her G-spot, a rush of moisture coating his fingers. Not wanting to miss a bit, he trailed his tongue down, lapping around her opening as he increased his thrusts. Over and over again, he worked that special spot that was right inside and up, the one that had her crying out, her body lifting into his mouth, gasping and rewarding him with her cream.

"Please, oh fuck, I want you in me, Coti. So long I've fantasized. Please don't make me wait," she admitted.

With an inarticulate groan, he gave one last swipe of his tongue from bottom to top of her pussy. "Nothing could stop me from claiming this tonight, NeNe," he said, placing a kiss on her clit.

NeNe squirmed beneath him, her legs moving restlessly. Coti ran the head of his cock through her slickness, coating him with her cream before lining himself up to her opening. "Look at me, armina. I want you to watch me as I take you." He braced one hand next to her head, the other he used to lift her leg up higher on his hip, opening her up more for him while he pushed inside, slowly, smoothly. Finally, when he was balls deep, filling her completely until he felt as if they were one, his breathing was fast, his heart was thundering in his chest like he'd been running for hours. "Fuck, you're so tight. Am I hurting you?" He opened his senses, needing to make sure she wasn't going to lie to him. Not in this. Not in anything, but especially in this.

"No, I mean, you're huge, but just give me a moment," she said on a sigh.

He was glad her breathing was choppy like his, and then remarkably, their hearts began beating in the same rhythm. Coti thought he was losing his mind since only bound mates claimed to have that bond, but he could hear her blood as it rushed through her veins, could feel the echo of each beat of her heart as it matched his. "Are you ready?" he asked, his wolf and the other part of himself needing to claim their mate to make them whole, but he couldn't, wouldn't do that to her until she knew what he was. For now, he'd sate them with her body.

She nodded, lifted her arms, welcoming him. He rested his forehead against hers, giving thanks to the Goddess for the gift she'd given him, then started to move. In, out, he thrust inside her. With each move, she lifted with him, her breath escaping in sighs that urged him on.

NeNe scraped her nails down Coti's back, lifting her legs as he began pounding into her harder and faster. She felt his muscles tensing, could feel he was racing toward his pleasure. She arched up to meet him, his pelvis hitting her in just the right place sending tingles of ecstasy that had her crying out, her legs gripping him tighter. The movements of his body became one of beauty, something she wanted to catalogue forever. Her fingers ran along his shoulders, feeling the flexing muscles, loving the sweat dampened skin even as tension coiled inside her, winding tighter and tighter with every in and out stroke of his cock. "Shit, I'm right there. Harder please," she begged, lifting her legs higher along his back, urging him further inside her.

Coti drove into her harder, faster, his breath fanning her neck as he worked relentlessly to bring them both over. "Come for me, armina, need to feel you surrounding my dick with your tightness."

She thought she felt him bite down on her neck, the sensation driving her closer as he pumped his hips faster. The edge of ecstasy appeared out of nowhere like a blinding light, shattering her and putting her back together with a strangled cry. She wasn't sure, but in her mind, she thought she'd yelled out she loved Coti. Her muscles locked down, waves of pleasure rocked her to the core, locking her entire body in a vice-like grip unlike anything she'd ever experienced. She bit down on his shoulder, stifling another cry of completion. Coti was there with her, his body jerking inside her, growling against her neck as he came for what seemed like forever to NeNe.

For minutes or hours, they lay there, neither moving or saying anything. Coti finally rolled, taking his weight off of her, but she'd liked having his body blanketing her. Now, she felt cold until he pulled her on top of him, his arms enclosing her. The fading tension of her orgasm still pulsed through her, but Coti didn't say anything, just lay there, holding her. His calm, easy breathing as he ran his hand through her hair, calmed NeNe. If she'd shouted she'd loved him, he'd have already tossed her to the side and offered her a ride home, right?

"Are you okay?" he finally asked in the silent room.

NeNe ran a finger around one of his flat male nipples, light from the bathroom gave her just enough illumination to see. "I'm fine. Um, I'm sorry I bit you." Gah, she'd never been a biter. Ever. Heck, she'd never even allowed a guy to give her a hickey, but if her memory served her correctly, Coti had bitten her too. Yikes, they were a bitey couple.

Coti wrapped his finger around a hunk of her hair. "I loved it. Your teeth sinking into me was almost as fucking amazing as your pussy kissing my cock."

She snorted. "You're such a dirty talker."

He gave a tug on the hair he held. "I'm a lot of things, and dirty is only one of them. Is that going to be a problem?"

NeNe bit her lip. "Are you trying to scare me off?"

"Hell no, I'm trying to keep you. If I need to temper myself, I need to know what it is you don't like. I'm not saying I'll be able to change a lifetime of habits, but for you, I'll try." His green eyes seemed brighter.

"I don't want you to change for me, just as I'd hope you'd never ask me to change for you. I'm not even sure why we're discussing this." NeNe didn't get to finish as he pulled her down for another deep heated kiss. Her body ached, but not from the beating she'd taken earlier, which had her pulling back.

"I forgot to thank you properly for saving me tonight."

Coti sifted both hands through her hair. "You don't owe me any thanks, armina."

She propped herself up on his chest. "What does that mean?"

He laughed. "Warrior woman. It's an old German word my grandfather used to call my grandmother."

She could tell he had great affection for his grandparents. "I'm sorry," she said.

"For what?" he asked, puzzled.

"I didn't mean to bring up a sad subject." Propped up on his chest, she should've been uncomfortable lying naked with him, but she wasn't. It was as if they'd done it hundreds of times. Heck, he was so damn big, he made the perfect bed except for the large pole currently nudging her.

Coti shifted her down and then up, teasing her with his dick. "I'm not sad. My family are the Iron Wolves."

Before she could comment, he lifted her higher, then pushed her back, impaling her on his length. "Fuckkk," she gasped. In that position, he felt larger, taking up even more space. "Oh god, I think I feel you in my tonsils."

He barked out a laugh, then eased her up a bit. "You set the pace and depth. I could come with you just squeezing my cockhead." He groaned as she worked her inner muscles doing just that.

The last time he was fast and furious, and she was every bit as impatient. This time, she thought she'd work them both up to a fever pitch. However, she couldn't wait. She bent, seeking his mouth, sucking on his tongue, tasting peppermint again. She wiggled on the cock inside her, adjusting left and right, searching for the right angle. Coti growled, his eyes locked onto her face. His eyes glowed as he pushed up, twisting until he was over her, his body pushing into hers, his pelvis circling, working deeper until they were both groaning.

Pleasure slammed into NeNe. She tried to hold it off, but the sensation was too overwhelming as if she was feeling Coti's and her own body at the same time. His strong body gripped hers tightly, held her firmly while he pistoned inside her. The sound of their bodies, the wet slap of skin on skin, reverberated throughout the room, ramping up her excitement, making her want to get closer, to feel him everywhere. God, she didn't know where these feelings were coming from, this out of control need that erased every other thought but this, what they were doing. She tightened her pussy, raising her hips up off the bed to meet his thrusts. "Yes," she yelled when the angle was perfect. Coti growled, the sound seemed to vibrate through her body. She felt his cock jerk, making her climax rip through her, shocking in its intensity and speed.

With each clench and release of her inner walls, she could feel his dick jerk even as Coti continued to move. Her own body spasmed again, her nails raked down his back. He buried his face against her neck, creating a sense of intimacy she wanted to lock away inside herself forever. God, the thought of another bite there made her clench down on him.

Coti sucked on the muscle where her shoulder and neck met but didn't bite. She could feel him kissing, licking, his hips still flexing. When he lifted his head, his eyes locked onto hers. "Best fucking night of my life," he swore. "In all my time, I never thought one tiny little warrior woman would be the best, most amazing ruin of me. I'm a lucky bastard." He pressed a kiss to her mouth, then whispered words in a language she didn't understand. NeNe thought whatever he said sounded beautiful, but then darkness washed over her.

Chapter Five

Coti looked down at his mate, the one female he should've stayed away from, yet he couldn't. Fate had other plans for him and now it was time for him to face the Reaper. He slowly climbed from his bed, making sure NeNe slept soundly. He'd given her his ancient blood twice. Once in order to heal her, and once when she'd bitten him. He'd felt her little teeth sink into him and damn near exploded right then and there. His own teeth had broken through her delicate flesh, but he'd had the sense to pull back before giving her a full claiming bite. However, he knew that the seal would be broken on his crest. He'd felt it as soon as she'd bitten him. Damn, he'd never thought a human could actually do such a thing. Running his thumb over the ring she'd admired, the one with his family crest, he shook his head.

The Iron Wolves were the family he'd chosen, a pack that had called to him. For over a hundred years he'd roamed. He'd sensed Turo was an older wolf, but he'd not realized just how old until he'd mated with Joz. Everyone seemed to take the news he wasn't like the rest of them fine, but Coti knew it would be different for him. He wasn't hiding just his age, he was hiding a beast within himself, one he'd wished with all his heart wasn't as dominate as the wolf. Of course, if wishes were granted he'd be fine, but that wasn't the case. He was a trio-dominate, something his family believed was a danger to them all. Like he wanted to hurt any of the fuckers. If he'd wanted them dead, he'd have killed them instead of allowing himself to be shoved out at the ripe age of twelve.

His mind went back to when he was being shunned from his clan. The look of sadness on his grandmother's face while she held his hand, still had the power to make him rage. He'd been a boy of twelve winters, yet he was taller than his father and already stronger. Still, he was a child.

"It's time you made your way in the world and found your mate. She's not here, and until you and your others are settled, none of us are safe, Ulric Chlodwig." His father had said, his tone leaving no room for argument.

Coti had looked at his mother, her eyes red rimmed and sad. He'd known how much it hurt her seeing what was happening. He could feel her suffering. If he fought his father, he'd win, but it would destroy his mother, and their entire house. Straightening, he gave a nod and picked up his small bag. *"I shall do you proud, maman."* His father thought he'd become a raper and pillager of the young and innocent, or at least that was what he'd accused his son of on many occasions. Coti thought his father was a bastard, but he'd kept his thoughts to himself. He knelt in front of his little sister and younger brother. Seeing his siblings were normal, deep within himself, the knowledge that he was doing the right thing by leaving, resonated. *"You be good for maman and do as she says. I'll be back before you know it."*

His grandmother handed him his grandfather's ring with the family crest. *"When you find your mate, this will unlock the crest, and all will know. You'll then rule the house of Chlodwig."*

Coti didn't want to rule anything, least of all a house that hated him. His father was the ruler. Ulric, the name his father was given, meant Wolf Ruler. The first born was always named Ulric, yet Coti wasn't just a wolf. His mother, a distant cousin of the Vampire Kings, had met him when she'd been young and fallen in love, hiding her true self from her mate until it was too late and he'd bonded with her. His mother had assured his family their offspring would all be shifters. Coti came first, followed by his sister, and a brother the following year. All seemed normal until his family was attacked. A five year old boy should've been easy pickings, yet he'd shifted into a huge white wolf and taken out three grown men who'd thought to kidnap him and his siblings. Blood had dripped from his fangs and covered almost every inch of his furred body, while he stood guard. From that day on, his father eyed him with distrust, challenging his abilities, and later, seeing how far he could stretch his punishments without killing him. He would snarl the Cordells' name and laugh when Coti would ask to go to them for training.

Coti wanted to snort at the thought of being related to the Cordell twins, but they were so far down the line their blood would be diluted to the point of non-relation status. His mother's family had been Gypsies. To hear his father talk, they were lower-class relations that none of the Cordells would spit on if they were on fire. However, it didn't take away the fact he'd been gifted with the ability to do all the things a vampire could, plus all the things as a shifter, yet had none of their weaknesses. Silver, daylight, none of them hurt him like others of his kind. His father tried and failed, until his only recourse was to send him away. Of course, he'd not been decapitated and didn't want to try that either. "Son of a bitch,' he snapped, running a finger over the crest.

Throughout the first ten years, he'd been so
damn lonely, missing his family to the point he'd
tried everything he could think of to find a mate.
Yet, he was a boy on his own. He may have looked
like a young man, but he'd been twelve and cast out
to fend for himself. The first harsh winter would've
killed a normal being. Hell, most shifters would've
perished as well. He'd hunkered down and
survived. Year after year, he'd soldiered on, making
his way across the world, searching for that elusive
someone who would make it okay for him to go
home. After fifty years, he'd given up. Goddess,
he'd pretty much given up on everything and
realized he was virtually indestructible. That was
when he'd realized his father was scared of him for
a reason. Nothing the bastard could've done
would've killed the son who would soon take his
place. Yes, Ulric, his son, or Coti as he was now
called, would've snapped one day and killed his
father for the way he treated his mother. So, instead
of heading back to his family, he'd looked to the

Goddess his grandmother had worshipped and asked her for guidance.

It had taken another hundred years, but the Goddess had finally led him to the Iron Wolves. "Why couldn't you have let me have more time with her?" he asked the darkness.

Without waking NeNe, he padded naked out of the room. He needed to think. What had been done to her needed to be addressed. Plus, the fact there was a bunch of shifters congregating just outside the Iron Wolves territory, yet they hadn't announced themselves to Kellen, the alpha didn't bode well. "Fuck, Kellen's not gonna be happy," he whispered.

Knowing he couldn't put it off any longer, he opened the link to his alpha, giving the equivalent of a mental knock in case the other man was getting busy with his mate. It didn't take long before he felt the answering connection. Unlike the other wolves, Coti was able to control the link instead of being controlled. Of course, he didn't let on to the others that he could. An alpha wouldn't want another in his pack who he couldn't control.

"What's up, Coti?"

He didn't waste time, sharing what had occurred, skipping over the mind blowing sex and keeping his past hidden, for now. Hell, he didn't know how long he was going to be able to keep his secrets. Forever seemed like the perfect length of time, but he had a sinking feeling that wasn't what the Goddess had in store for him.

"Shit, why didn't you reach out to me sooner?" Kellen growled.

Coti looked back toward his suite, then stared out toward the front lawn of his home. He felt time ticking away like the switch on a bomb. *"My duty was seeing to the comfort and safety of my mate first,"* he said without heat and waited for his words to sink in.

"Shit, son. NeNe's yours? How the hell did you not know that all the times she'd been here with the girls?" Accusation laced his voice.

He turned from the view, heading toward the opposite end of his home. *"Really? You want to explain how you turned your mate away for how long and almost lost her to two men? Don't fucking lecture me, alpha.*" He wasn't going to show his damn throat, not over why he hadn't wanted to claim what he knew was his. His life wasn't cut and dried like Kellen's and the others.

A snarl echoed through his head followed by an image of Kellen snapping huge jaws at him. Coti flashed an image of him batting the wolf down with a huge paw, startling the other man.

"*You got big balls, Coti, always have. So, tell me more about this pack. Did they appear to be the friendly sort? Are they just passing through, or what?*"

He placed his hand over the sensor and waited for the light to turn green. Once the panel accepted his imprint the door slid open soundlessly. His computer blinked, showing he had messages. "*I think we need to have a meeting with them. They're most definitely not a friendly bunch, Kellen.*" Coti couldn't get the feeling he needed to do something quickly to ensure NeNe's safety out of his head. His hand went to his chest, rubbing over his heart. The thought of leaving her undefended made his wolf half crazy while the other part of him thirsted for blood. Neither was a good thing for anyone.

"Be here by noon tomorrow morning." Kellen didn't ask if that was a good time before severing the link.

Coti laughed at the arrogance the Iron Wolf alpha exuded. Sure, the man was a fucking beast who could turn into a wolf that would scare the shit out of just about anyone, yet Coti didn't fear him. Maybe that made him crazy. No, scratch that, he was most assuredly crazy. However, none of them had seen what he could do. "Goddess save them all if they ever did." He understood why his father had sent him away. Until he could get all three parts of himself on the same level, he was a danger to all if he was ever truly rattled. It was why he was always joking, staying light, and never caring kept his beasts at bay. His mind sought NeNe, checking to make sure she still slept peacefully. His carefree life was no longer a possibility. If he were honest, it hadn't been since he'd recognized the little human as his, but he'd been able to deny the truth until tonight. Now, there was no stopping what was to come. "Fuck a goddamn sonofabitch," he growled. "Why'd you give me a human for a mate?" he asked the empty room. The fates had a way of fucking with everyone, but to give him such a fucked-up fate was on a level he didn't think was possible.

NeNe rolled to the side, her body aching in spots that hadn't seen action in forever. Memories flooded her from the previous evening, making her freeze in the act of turning back over. She remembered vividly getting her ass handed to her by the three crazy bitches, then Coti saving her. Things got hazy for a bit. Her memories foggy of people and faces, but she distinctly remembered arriving at his house, which holyshitballs, the man had to be rich as fuck. She blinked, shocked to find the ability to see out of both eyes. "Huh, guess they didn't hit quite as hard as they claimed, bitches," she whispered. The red silk sheets felt divine under and around her. She wanted to roll around in them but worried he'd come in and catch her. Nope, she was so not going to act like the trash she was accused of being. Just because she'd never slept on anything as soft didn't mean she had to act like a hillbilly.

She shoved herself into a sitting position, pushed her hair back from her face and wished she had a hair tie. "Note to self. Do not go to bed with wet hair. Ever."

His room was huge and very masculine. The longer she sat there, orienting herself, she realized she was waiting for him to come back. When he didn't, she began to feel stupid. "Get up and get going, girl. It was a one-night stand." Not that she'd ever had any, but last night was a first of many, she hoped. She swung her legs over the side, wondering where her clothes were.

The door opened behind her, making her gasp and grab for the sheet on the bed. "Fuck me, you scared the shit out of me," she yelled.

Coti raised a brow. "What're you doing out of bed?"

He strolled into the room wearing a pair of sweats that hung precariously low on his hips, carrying a tray. The heavenly scent of coffee and eggs made her mouth water. "Um, I was just going to get dressed and head out."

"Hm, and how were you going to do that?" He asked, setting the tray down before coming around the end of the bed.

NeNe tried not to drool at the vision he made, but seriously, the man had too much on display. "What did you ask?"

Coti's chuckle sent a delicious shiver down her spine, making her nipples bead. "I asked how you were going to accomplish those tasks. Your clothes were ruined, so I tossed them. Not to mention, you don't have a vehicle here. How were you going to get a ride when you're nekkid?" He stood in front of her, his warmth urging her to lean into him.

She knew she should demand he get her clothes back, but his nearness was frying her braincells. "I can borrow a shirt and pair of your sweats."

His deep chuckle made her angry. "Armina, my sweats are three times too big for you. However, one of my T-shirts would be like a dress on you. Yeah, you'd look good in one of them," he agreed.

She held the sheet over her breasts. It's silky fabric kept slipping when she moved. "This is not a joking matter, Coti. I need something to wear."

He reached out, placing two fingers between her breasts and gave a tug. NeNe tried to hold the fabric in place, but in a tug of war, he would always win, damn him. The sheet fell between them, leaving her completely exposed before him. "Damn, you're even more beautiful than I remember," he murmured, bending to kiss her.

NeNe expected him to try and seduce her or take what he wanted. Hell, she wanted him just as much, but he only kissed her before stepping away.

"I brought you some coffee and eggs. I actually do have something more for you to wear, even though it's a shame to cover up perfection." His fingers traced her collarbone to her breasts. "I'm sorry you were hurt last night," he said, anger making his features hard.

She licked her lips. "It wasn't your fault."

He pulled her against him, one arm going around her back, the other tilting her chin up so she had to stare into his eyes. "I'm not so sure about that, armina." He kissed her one more time before releasing her. "Eat and have some coffee, we need to head to the club. Kellen's called a meeting. We can't be late or he'll not be in the best of moods." He winked, not wanting to scare her. "I let you sleep in because you needed it. Hardest fucking thing I've ever done."

The huge bulge in the front of his sweats was a testament to that fact. Her body remembered what it felt like to have him inside. She wanted to experience that again, wanted to know what it was like to have Coti possess her during the day, night, in every way imaginable.

Coti inhaled. "Female, don't. I left you some clothes in the bathroom. You best get your ass dressed, and then eat before I piss Kellen off and say screw his meeting."

Truth was stamped on his face. If she made one move toward him, she knew he'd take her back to bed, but Coti was nothing if not a man of his word. If he'd told Kellen they'd be there, then he wanted to be there. She didn't want to be the reason he wasn't. She thought of wrapping the sheet back around herself, but he'd seen all of her, kissed all of her. With her head held high, she skirted him and the bed, and went into the bathroom. Once inside, she let out the breath she'd been holding. "Wow, the man is potent," she whispered. The outfit he'd laid out for her had her narrowing her eyes. The tank top looked new and appeared to be her size with the Iron Wolves logo emblazoned on the front. The jeans also looked new and her size. She wondered who they belonged to, and who she needed to cut. Like Coti, she felt the urge to hurt every woman who'd been with him. Of course, his numbers had to be a lot more than hers, but she wasn't going to tell him that. "Coti, there's no panties," she yelled.

"I know," he answered.

She rolled her eyes, then picked up the jeans. "I'm not putting on some other woman's pants without panties."

Coti came to stand in the doorway. "They're yours. I had them delivered for you this morning while you slept."

She stifled the yelp when he appeared almost soundlessly but was unable to suppress the sigh. How the man could look sexy leaning against the doorframe with his arms crossed over abs that were more than a six pack…did they come in eight packs? Damn, he seriously had her mind running in circles. "Do I want to know how you got me clothes so fast?"

He shrugged his massive shoulders. "Ace brought them when he came to get his car. I asked him if he could procure you some jeans. I told him your size and that they had to be new since I figured you wouldn't want to wear some other female's."

The way he spoke, the way all the men referred to women was strange. She remembered the few times she'd been at the club and how they didn't say man or woman, but male and female. When she'd mentioned it to Lyric, her friend had made a joke about the reference. It was as if they were referring to each other as different species, which made her snort. "I must've really been out of it," she said instead of asking more. She didn't mind having her hooha up close and personal in a pair of jeans without panties, if no other ladies hoohas had been in them. She had rules and standards. No other lady juice, even if it had been washed out, was going to be next to her punani. "Give me ten, and I'll be right out."

She waited for him to leave so she could jump into the shower, but the too sexy for his shirt man didn't turn to go. Instead, he seemed to relax against the doorframe like he was getting comfortable.

"Coti, are you going to just stand there?"

He sighed. "I'd like to do a lot more, but that would make us late. I thought I could at least get a little pleasure."

The way he growled the last word made her shiver. He'd given her more pleasure the night before than she'd ever experienced in her entire life. She had a feeling if given the chance, he'd show her even more. "Well, I can't just shower while you watch. Go," she said, waving her hands toward the door.

"You'll do a lot more before I'm through with you, but I'll give you a reprieve. Besides, I hear someone coming up the drive."

She tilted her head to the side, wondering what the hell he was talking about. She was trying to remember the layout of his house. If her mind served her correctly, they'd parked in a garage, then it seemed as if he'd walked a bit before they'd made it to his bedroom. She distinctly remembered several turns and a hallway.

He pointed at her. "Get dressed. I'll be back in seven minutes."

Her mouth opened to tell him to kiss her ass, but he was gone. "Damn, how can a man as large as him move so fast?" Shaking her head, she jumped into the shower making quick work of washing. When she was dressed, wet hair wrapped in a towel, drinking the last bit of coffee, Coti returned, wearing a pair of jeans and a black T-shirt. His shitkickers didn't thud the way her dad's and brother's boots did when he walked. It was as if he walked on air. Heck, she was getting fanciful, and she was so not a fanciful girl.

"You 'bout ready?" he asked, looking her up and down.

She sat the mug back onto the tray. The eggs she couldn't eat since they'd gotten cold by the time she'd finished showering and dressing. Her stomach growled, a stark indicator she needed food. Once Coti dropped her off, she'd swing by a fast food place and grab something. At the thought of buying anything, she bit her lip. "Damn," she swore quietly.

"What is it?" Coti was at her side, his hands going to her waist.

NeNe shook her head, not wanting to explain to him how important it had been to her to get paid last night. How putting up with the drunks, and even Mac's bullshit, just to get tips, meant she could get out from under her dad's and the town's bullshit. Gah, the man was rich, he wouldn't understand how a couple hundred dollars would mean so much to her. "I don't know where my purse is." Which wasn't a lie.

Chapter Six

Coti didn't scent a lie, but he was aware she wasn't telling him the entire truth. Her scent went from one to another, never hiding anything from him. If she'd been a female shifter, she'd have known how to conceal her feelings, how to hide her scent from him. He was glad she didn't, glad she was human, and he could read every nuance in her facial expressions as well as her smells. Goddess, her smells could bring him to his knees.

"Let's go, we'll stop and grab you something to eat on the way." He didn't give her a chance to agree or not, knowing she had an independent streak a mile wide, and she'd argue just to argue. Damn, he was actually looking forward to disagreeing with her. Nekkid.

"What're you thinking about, right this minute?" she asked, halting directly in front of him.

He inhaled before answering. "I was thinking how sexy you are, especially when your back is up like a…well, I was going to say hissing cat. You get this glint in your eye like you're daring someone to test you. It's sexy as fuck. Makes my dick hard if you want to know the truth."

NeNe looked down, then back up, her eyes comically wide. "Seriously, your dick should be outlawed."

He brought her body flush with his. "I've been telling people that forever. Hence the names I call it." Coti steered them out of his bedroom before he got any other ideas, and decided to say screw the pack meeting, and screwed his sexy mate instead.

She laughed. "I can't wait to hear them. Go on, let's hear some."

"Heat seeking moisture missile," he said without pausing.

"Oh, that's a good one. I got one for the lady business. You ready?"

When she waggled her brows like she was ready to out do him, Coti was sure his mate was going to be his match in more ways than one. "Let's hear it."

"Wet tunnel." She brushed by him as the door to his garage slid open.

"That's not even sexy sounding." Coti looked toward the other side of his garage where he'd had their bikes stored but didn't want to chance having NeNe out in the open. The matte black truck with it's blacked out windows would give him a sense of security, plus he could reach across the seat and hold NeNe's hand. He led her toward the passenger side, laughing at her scoff. "Alright, my turn. You ready, baby?" He paused while opening the door and helping her inside the jacked-up truck. Once she was settled inside, he stood there, amazed how she could look sexy as sin, yet innocent and too perfect for the likes of him. At her nod, he grinned. "Mayo shooting hotdog gun," he said, winking before he shut the door on her chuckle.

"That was a good one. Mount of teetle." She waved her hand.

He waited for the bay to open, then backed out of the garage before talking. "One eyed yogurt slinger. And, before you say, *'oh that's nasty'*, he said in a high-pitched tone, before continuing, "you should try it first."

NeNe held up a finger. "Okay, first, never ever try to sound like a girl, because you just sound silly. Second, I wasn't going to say that. I was going to say, ewww. Now, my turn. Pie corner of succulence."

Coti licked his lips, thinking of eating some of her sweet succulence. "Purple helmet warrior of love."

"Oh my god, you did not. I can't get that picture out of my head." She scrunched up her eyes.

Her laugh was deep, rolling over him like a lover's caress. Damn, everything she did felt like she was touching him on some level. "What image would that be?"

She turned to the side, placing her back against the door. To look at her, one would've thought she'd been in an accident or brawl a couple weeks ago, not just hours. He winced at the bruising under her eyes he had to leave, so he didn't draw too much attention to what he'd done.

Seconds ticked by and she still hadn't answered him, he thought she wasn't, but then she laughed out loud. "I keep picturing you naked with your ginormous dick standing straight out in front of you wearing a purple helmet on the tip. There, you happy?"

The smell of her arousal mixed with a hint of embarrassment filled the cab of his truck. "No, my little warrior. I'm not happy that it embarrasses you to admit you picture me naked. I'm also not happy I can't create that scene for you, because I'd fucking love to do just that."

NeNe leaned her left arm on the back of his seat, resting her head in the palm of her hand. "But then we'd have another issue. Where would we find a little purple helmet?"

He reached over and ran his finger along her cheek. "I'd search the web for it. Hell, I'd find someone to make the damn thing if I had to."

His words made her laugh. "I can just see you explaining what it was for. Alright, my turn again.

Hm, let's see if I can beat the purple guy." She batted her lashes at him. "French withered pear."

"Ack, that doesn't even sound appetizing. Nope, redo," he said and grabbed her hand, not questioning the need to touch her.

"What? You don't like pears?"

Never in his long life had he joked with another female the way he was with NeNe and felt so calm. Sure, he talked to women, got along with them quite well, but with the woman sitting next to him, he felt, for the first time in forever, peaceful. He didn't think he'd ever get to that place. "I love pears. Sweet succulent pears. Not ones that have the word withered attached to them." They were getting closer to town, making a sense of anticipation begin to set in.

"How about a two-fer." She held up two fingers, a grin split her lips. "Huck hole and penis garage." She laughed but didn't let go of his hand.

He pointed out their choice of restaurants, making her turn in the seat to face forward.

"Hey, what's the matter?" Her relaxed pose had disappeared, which he hated to see.

"I don't have my purse or any cash on me. Shit, I just now realized I'm going to need you to drop me off at the bank." Delicate little teeth bit down on her lower lip, making him want to pull over and replace them with his.

"Ace found your stuff and returned them along with the clothes. Sorry, I thought I told you, but I think seeing you wrapped in my sheet must've short circuited my brain." Hell, he was sure he was a few cells short at the vision she made wearing nothing but her skin.

"Oh my god, he did? Where are they?" She looked over the back of the seat then around the front of the cab.

Coti turned the blinker on, then pulled into the parking lot of a shopping center. "Calm down, it's right here." He reached behind him, pulling the small bag out and handed it to her. He'd made sure there was extra cash added to what she already had inside. If he was to guess, the females would've taken any money she'd had inside.

"Oh, thank you lord Jeezus," she whispered, looking up at him with shining eyes. "I don't know how much I had in here since I just shoved it all inside. I usually wait to count it until I get to my bike, but—"

He tucked a strand of hair behind her ear. "That's good. Now we get you something to eat so your stomach quits yelling at me. Steaming seaman pump dong," he laughed.

"What the ever-loving hell? That is so not sexy, Mr. Sharp."

It may not be sexy, but it worked to take her mind off of the hows and whys of her money. After pulling through, ordering a couple breakfast sandwiches and a drink for both of them, they got back on the road toward the Iron Wolves Club. "I declare I'm the winner."

NeNe coughed around a bite of her food, grabbing her drink and sucking down some to clear her throat before she answered. "That would be a hard no, sir. How about we call it a tie?"

At the sight of the Iron Wolves' huge gate, he sighed. Tension filled him for what was to come. His mate was human and had no clue about other species. Shoot, the very fact there was more than humans walking the Earth was probably going to knock her on her sexy little ass. Throw in the fact he was a mix of more than one, and that his own pack had no clue? Yeah, he was most definitely not looking forward to the meeting.

"Sounds good. I mean, it's not like you can truly beat me, so I might as well let you tie with me," he joked, then caught her hand in his when she tried to smack him. Bringing her palm to his lips, he kissed the center. "Whatever happens, know I will protect you above all others."

NeNe searched his green eyes, knowing there was more to his words than what he was saying. "I trust you, Coti." The truth of that announcement amazed her. She did trust him for whatever reason. If he said he was going to do something, she knew he'd move mountains to see it done.

"Good, remember what I said."

She opened her mouth to ask him what he meant, but they'd pulled into the club's lot. She was stunned to see it filled with vehicles. "What the hell's going on?"

He gave her hand another squeeze. "Mandatory meeting by the big guy. Come on, let's get inside." Coti backed into a spot, shutting the truck off with a sense of finality, leaving a quietness that was almost deafening in the cab. He didn't say another word until he got out and came around to her side. "Want me to carry you?"

NeNe stared down at him from the seat. The huge truck gave her the advantage of being a little higher up than his six and half feet. Even so, she had no doubt he didn't feel inadequate staring up at her. Ace had brought a pair of flip flops along with the jeans and tank top. Now, looking at the number of cars, trucks, SUVs, and motorcycles, she didn't

think she was prepared to go inside half dressed.
"Why don't you go in and have your little thing
with your peeps? I'll sit out here and listen to the
radio." Surely his radio worked.

Coti shook his head. "No can do, my little huck
hole provider."

She laughed, slapping at his arm. "You can't use
my words. Besides, why do I need to go in there?"

"Because this meeting is about the place you've
been working at and the people who run it. We need
to find out as much information as we can, and
Kellen thinks you can give us that," he bit out.

Her hand came up and touched his cheek,
feeling the scruff of his beard. "And that makes you
angry?"

He nodded. "I wish I could shield you from all
of this, but I understand why he—we need to know
more. If at anytime you want to leave, you tell me,
and we're out. You need a break, you say the word.
Feel me?"

She traced her thumb across his cheekbone, down to his lips. "Do I have anything to worry about? Grace and the others?"

Coti sucked her thumb into his mouth before answering. "Those three won't be bothering you again if they know what's good for them."

The fact he hadn't answered her question completely didn't settle her nerves in the least. "Let's get this done then."

Instead of allowing her to get down on her own, he gripped her around the waist and lifted her out. "Wrap your legs around me, armina."

"I can walk. I believe we've gone over this before." She rested her arms over his shoulders, relaxing into his hold instead of fighting it.

"Yeah, we went over it," he agreed.

The sound of locks engaging, followed by a beep let her know he secured his truck. "Fine, carry me away my luscious, lickable, lollipop dong."

Her words had Coti stumbling in the gravel before righting himself as they reached the entryway. "Well, damn."

"That's what I was gonna say. How'd you get a female who says crazy shit like you?" Turo held the door open.

Coti gave her ass a squeeze then allowed her to slide down his body. "Lucky I guess."

"Um, hello, Turo. Is Joz here, too?" She looked around the big man guarding the door for her old friend, unable to hide the sneer.

Turo nodded toward the bar. "She's over there."

As soon as the door shut behind them, NeNe could've sworn everyone stopped talking. She backed into Coti. "Why's everyone looking at us?" she asked without moving her lips.

Coti rested his hands on her shoulders, giving her a little squeeze. "Because they're idiots. Come on, let's go see Kellen."

When her friends Joz and Lyric gave her a wave, but didn't rush over and say anything, she felt like they'd slapped her. Taking a deep breath, she wiped her palms on the sides of her new jeans and turned away from the women. Screw them and their too good for her attitudes.

"They know Kellen wants to chat with you. Everyone knows if they started talking we'd never get away," Coti whispered near her ear.

NeNe nodded. Let him think what he wanted. The women she'd thought were her friends clearly weren't. She wanted to throw up her middle finger and jack it up and down. "Let's get this over with, shall we?"

Two sharp knocks heralded their entrance before Coti shoved the thick door open. If she could back pedal, she totally would've right then and there. Kellen Styles looked big and bad from a distance. Up close, like a few feet away, he was even bigger and badder. His blue eyes bore into her, daring her. NeNe had no clue what he was daring her to do, but she damn sure wasn't going to do it. She took a step back and bumped into Coti. "How about I write you an email and explain to you what I know. I think better when I have a moment to, you know, process things. Besides, I'm not feeling too good." She placed her hand over her stomach. The truth of her words had her stomach rolling.

"Dammit, Kellen, simmer the fuck down or we're gonna have problems," Coti growled.

NeNe had no clue what Kellen could do to simmer down. The man was just standing there looking mean. Her stomach rolled again. She put her other hand over her mouth. "Oh lord, please don't let me get sick, and if I do, please don't let me get sick on Kellen," she whispered.

Her words had barely escaped her mouth, and then there were a few chuckles.

"I apologize, NeNe, please come in and have a seat. Would you like a drink?" He walked over to the corner, raising up a square decanter.

She shook her head. "I'm sure it's five o'clock somewhere, but my body says no."

The door opening had her turning to see who entered. She tried to remember the tall man's name as he sauntered in, thinking he always seemed so calm and collected.

"Hey, Arynn, how're the girls?" Coti asked Arynn before they hugged, pounding each other's back like guys do.

Arynn stopped in front of NeNe, his hand going to her head. "At ease, girl. My Rebel's raising hell, and my other girl Romie's walking around soothing ruffled fur after her. I'm a blessed father, that's for sure."

She didn't know what the man did, but her stomach instantly stopped tossing and turning as soon as he touched her. His gruff words nearly had her telling him to fuck off, however her food decided it liked where it was, which was in her instead of on the floor. She called that a major win and wanted Arynn with the magic hands to stay near. Heck, the next time she decided to try tequila, which was going to be the second Tuesday of next week, he needed to be there just in case.

"Your female has very strange, shoes," Arynn said.

NeNe looked down at her flip flops. "Okay, that's an odd thing to say."

"Can we forget about what the female's wearing and get to why we're here?" Kellen slammed the decanter down.

"Oh, is the alpha throwing a hissy?"

She sighed at the newcomer's voice. Was she going to be faced with every man she'd ever seen at the Iron Wolves, and have to explain to all just how badly she'd gotten her ass whooped? "Alright, can I ask who else is coming to this shindig? Because to be real honest, I don't like having to explain just how stupid I was more than once."

Coti spun her to face him. "Armina, you're never to speak of yourself like that ever again. Everyone who's here is only here because they have a vested interest in what you have to say. Not a single male here will say a damn thing in a negative manner about you, or they'll face me. Trust me, they don't want that."

Xan coughed, the words sounding like pussy, but NeNe didn't take her eyes off of Coti. She could see he meant every word he said. "Let's get 'r done then."

"She even speaks our language," Xan announced. He pointed at Kellen and held up his finger.

Kellen lifted his drink to his lips and drank. "It's too early to be drinking," he said after he finished the glass.

NeNe moved out of Coti's arms, turning to face the room full of men. Each one was gorgeous with muscles and tattoos, yet none held a candle to the one standing at her back. He gave her the strength and courage to speak without fear.

Taking a deep breath, she told them what she knew. "I've worked every weekend there for the past two months. Since I didn't really have much else to do, it seemed natural to find a second job, so I could save money up. The pay was good, and the tips were great."

"How did you find out about the position?" Kellen asked. He'd come to sit in one of the large leather recliners, his arms resting on the sides.

"They came into the bank where I work and asked if they could put up a flyer. When the manager told them no, I told them which businesses in town allowed that sort of thing. The guy asked me if I was looking to make extra money, and the rest as they say, is history." She shrugged, feeling as if they were all staring at her like she'd done something wrong.

Coti tensed beside her, a low growl coming from him.

"Let me ask you a question, and Coti leash your beast. Did you have any sort of relationship with the man who runs the place?" Xan asked. He too had taken as seat in a large leather recliner, yet he wasn't as relaxed as Kellen appeared.

She shook her head. "Fuck no, Mac was a dick from the get go. I knew if I ever let him near my punani he'd never respect me. Hell, he'd probably have fired me within the first day or made me his personal bitch. Either option wasn't good for me."

"Just for clarity, punani is your lady bits, yes?" Xan asked, then caught a can before it hit him in the head. "Hey, I have no interest in anyone else's punani other than my Breezy's."

"Back to the subject at hand. Can you tell us how many men Mac had with him?" Kellen steepled his fingers together.

"At the end of the night, there were at least thirty guys with Mac. They all gave off the same vibe as you guys. You know, don't eff with me or else," she explained.

Turo grunted. "I think we need to go pay this boy a visit."

Coti walked around to stand in front of her. "Can you go wait for me out in the bar? I need to speak with these guys for a minute."

She looked behind Coti at Kellen and Xan, both looking like they were ready to spit nails. "Mac's not a good man. I know what they were doing was probably illegal, but I also know I saw some of the city council members out at that place. Do you know what that means? It means he's got backing that you don't want to mess with. This place," she waved her hand toward the door. "You've built up a nice business and have a great clientele, but they've got dirty money. When push comes to shove, if Mac has something on them, they'll side with him. You all have families now. Sometimes it's better to just turn the other cheek."

Kellen got to his feet, getting right in front of her before he spoke. "Did turning the other cheek work so well for you, little girl?" His finger came up to touch her cheek, but Coti's hand snapped out, stopping him from making contact. Shivers danced down her spine as the temperature in the room seemed to drop.

The door opened, allowing Laikyn holding a little boy to enter. "Hey there, papa. This big guy wasn't having it out there with us females." She handed the boy to Kellen. Instantly, his face softened as he took his son.

"I'll just go on out and wait for you, Coti."

Coti grabbed her hand, halting her exit. "What did I tell you before we got here?"

His words ran through her head, making her look around the room at his friends. He nodded as if he could read her mind. "I meant what I said, armina. Go on and get a drink. No tequila for you though."

Chapter Seven

NeNe was sure she should be freaked out at how easily Coti read her and how much she wanted to let him take all her troubles away. That alone made her straighten her spine and head toward the exit instead of the bar where her old friends sat. She'd rather sit out in the sun and get a tan than have idle chit chat with the girls who no longer wanted to hang out with her.

"Where you going, little girl?"

She closed her eyes, hating how all the men seemed to walk on a damn cloud or some shit. "I'm going outside to get some fresh air. Is that okay with you?" Instantly, she felt bad for getting snarky with Wyck, when the man had never been anything but nice to her.

Wyck held the door open. "I'll just go with you then, if you don't mind." It wasn't a question, more like an announcement.

Knowing, even if she'd told him she did mind, he'd still meander out with her, which was why NeNe didn't agree or disagree. Once she was outside, she could breathe without feeling as though she needed to check in with Coti. Lord, what the hell was happening to her? She wasn't one of *those* women who had to be with her guy of the moment constantly. Actually, she'd never had relationships, which was kind of sad, but she'd accepted it and moved on. She called them her twelve-step programs, only she would admit her issues like a good stepper, then move the fuck on. NeNe excelled at step one and twelve, it was the stupid steps in-between she skipped. Her first boyfriend had said she was a first-class bitch, which was echoed by her next. Just because she couldn't give two shits if they didn't call or want to hang out all the time didn't make her a bitch, in her opinion. She'd seen what happened when one person in a relationship clung, while the other didn't. Nope, she wasn't ever going there.

"You look pensive. Something on your mind?" Wyck asked.

NeNe looked over her shoulder to see the man leaning against the wall, one booted foot resting on the building, the other on the ground. How men could look casual, yet dangerous at the same time she had no clue. "Wow, that's quite the observation. You've known me for like—a minute," she snarked.

Wyck looked toward the road, then back at her. "Yep."

She rolled her eyes. Men were frustrating in general, but the men of the club took it to a whole other level. It was like they didn't listen, unless it was what they wanted to hear. NeNe looked back toward the closed door, promising herself if Coti didn't come out in the next fifteen minutes, she was out of there. Before she could start the mental countdown clock, the door opened, letting out a gust of cool air and loud music. The petite form of Joz was followed by Lyric and Syn. The very last thing she envisioned herself doing was having a come to Jesus moment with these three women who looked gorgeous, while she had two black eyes and more bruises than she could count. Although, for all the colorful skin she was sporting, it was shocking she wasn't hurting more.

Not waiting to hear what they had to say, she took off toward the road. The distinct sound of an irritated male growl, which sounded deeper than she'd have thought, made her grin.

"We got this Wyck, go on inside."

Ah, if the man believed Joz, he was a fool, but she wasn't sticking around to hear more of their bullshit. Nope, her mama didn't raise no fool.

"NeNe, get your scrawny ass back here this instant," Lyric yelled.

She lifted her right hand in the air, extended her middle finger. "Go fuck yourselves," she called out.

"Goddammit, let me go. I promise I won't bite her, hard."

Syn's tacked on last word made her want to laugh. She shimmied through the gate, silently cursing that it wasn't still open like it had been

when they'd driven through. A hiss of pain escaped
her closed lips, looking down she grimaced at the
piece of metal that had sliced into her side. "Son of
a biscuit fucker."

Hearing her friends argue made her move down
the road quickly. For months they'd forgotten about
her while they got on with their lives. She wasn't
mad, exactly. More hurt that they'd thought she
wasn't good enough for whatever they had going
with their men. Okay, yeah, she was pissed. Just
because she didn't have super smarts like Joz or
grow up in their backyards, didn't mean she was
trash.

Her heart sped up at the sound of a vehicle
coming behind her. The deep rumble didn't sound
like that of Coti's so she didn't look up or slow
down her pace. The vehicle's engine sounded
closer, the driver clearly shifting down as he got
closer to her. She looked around the deserted street,
kicking herself for not thinking first before acting.
"Damn, too late to turn back now," she muttered.
Keeping her head down, she worked out her options

for running. To the right was the road, to the left closed up shops. Sundays before noon, most businesses weren't open yet. If she ran straight, whoever was meandering in the car would likely follow. However, if she turned around, they could easily jump out and grab her. "Think girl," she mumbled.

"You gonna keep talking to yourself, or you gonna acknowledge you know we're here?"

Fuck! *Acknowledge we* meant there was more than one. She chanced a glance over her shoulder, squinting as the sun kept her from getting a good view. "I'm sorry, do I know you?"

A deep sigh floated out of the driver's window. "Why do all the women forget me, Ace?"

The mention of Ace had her pausing at the corner. "Um, you're Coti's friends?"

"My name's Dalton. I know, you've blanked me out of your mind because I'm gorgeous, and you didn't want thoughts of me to mess up your thing with Coti. I understand." He tapped the side of the door, nodding.

Ace groaned. "Ignore him. We met briefly. So, why you walking all alone?"

She didn't know why he was asking her stupid questions. "Thank you for bringing me these clothes, Ace. I can pay you once I get my purse."

"Don't worry about it, girl. Come and get in, we'll take you back to Coti."

She heard Ace's voice as he spoke, yet she didn't want to go anywhere with the men. "Nah, I'm good. Thanks, though. You guys have a good day."

She began walking again, hoping they'd take the hint. The sound of another vehicle coming from the opposite direction had her groaning. Of course, it couldn't be Coti since it was coming from town. "You better move out of the middle of the road," she cautioned.

The truck heading straight toward the muscle car idling in the road didn't seem to be slowing. NeNe moved back, worried if one or the other didn't get out of the way there was going to be an accident. Shit! The crazy fools in the muscle car revved their engine, laughing as the passenger tapped the hood, a yell of yeehaw floated out as they jerked forward. "This is not going to end well," she whispered.

Two arms banded around her from behind. "Sure it is. How you doing, babe? You look like you had a rough night last night."

NeNe gasped and tried to twist out of Mac's arms. "What the hell's going on?"

Mac nodded at the road. "My boys are just having some fun. Wanna stick around and watch?"

She shuddered at the feel of his warm breath on her neck. The man was a grade A asshole, who didn't seem to understand the word no. "I don't think so, thanks. I was just on my way back to my boyfriend's." The lie slipped out easily.

"Don't fucking lie to me, bitch. I know when someone lies, and you stink to high heaven right now. Let me explain a few things to you, just to give you a fighting chance. One, don't ever fucking lie to me. Two, do as I say when I say it, and you'll live a little longer. Three, remember the first two things." He jerked her to him. "Let's go." He looked up and down the road.

"Listen, Mac, I'm not sure what game you're playing, but I'm not going anywhere with you. Last night was my last. I'm done working for you. I'm sure you'll have no trouble finding someone to replace me." Her words rushed out while she tried to get free. Damn, what did the man eat, steel Wheaties?

Mac laughed, the sound anything but pleasant. "I always did like the ones who fought."

While she was trying to work out his meaning, she was lifted and tossed over his shoulder, her ribs, which were still slightly sore, protested the treatment.

The two racing vehicles barely missed colliding into one another. Her only chance at being saved spun in a circle, Dalton and Ace whooping loudly, only to be side-swiped by one of Mac's other trucks. The huge vehicle had the image of devil horns and the HM written in the middle, his crew of

Hell Makers loved to make sure everyone knew
who they were.

Coti glared at Wyck. "What do you mean you
left her outside with the girls?"

Wyck shrugged. "They looked like they had
some shit to handle. You know as well as I do them
women can take care of themselves. Besides,
they're right outside."

His phone rang, the caller ID showing him it
was Ace. Shit, he'd already told the man thanks for
the use of his car. What the hell else did he want,
his first born? He let the call go to voicemail,
focusing on Wyck. "What do you make of her bomb
about the council members being in Mac's pocket?"

Kellen sat in his chair, rubbing at his jaw.
"Rowan's doing some checking. I'll have more info
on all of them within a couple hours."

He glared at his alpha. "By all of them, do you
mean NeNe, too?"

With a nod, Kellen leaned back and took a sip of Makers. "This is my pack, Coti. Like she said, we all have families now. I ain't risking any of them because some prick thinks to move into my territory."

He rocked back on his heels. "She's mine," he growled. He may not have claimed her completely, but she was his. With his fucked up heritage, he didn't want to bring her into his world not knowing which side she'd land on, but with the threat looming, he'd do it and damn the consequences.

"I'm aware she's yours, but you ain't claimed her. I knew she was yours months ago, yet you didn't claim her. Why is that, Ulric?"

Coti stared at Kellen, shocked to hear his given name come out of his mouth. "Because she needs to know what she's getting into beforehand. I'm not going to force a mating on her without her full consent." Every shifter in the room would be able to tell he was speaking the truth. Although it wasn't the complete truth, it was the truth.

"Are you ever going to trust me?" Kellen asked.

He tilted his head to the side. "I do trust you."
And he did. He wouldn't have given his loyalty and
oath to Kellen and the Iron Wolves if he hadn't.

Kellen sat the glass back down, then stood.
"There's more to you than what you've told me, but
I haven't pushed. One day, you're gonna have to
come clean. I hope that day won't be too late for
you or your unclaimed mate."

His phone rang again, the irritating ringtone had
him jerking it out of his pocket. "What the fuck?"
Seeing Ace's number again, he pressed the talk
button. "What's up?" he growled.

"You need to get your ass to moving. Your
girl's been taken by that fucker, Mac." Coti
registered pain in the other man's voice and the
sound of metal creaking in the background.

"Where are you?" He was moving toward the
door as he spoke, knowing the men in the room
could hear what was being said. Turo stood by the
door with Kellen's son in his arms, the little boy a
miniature version of his father but with an
intelligence that no toddler should have, held his

hand out. Coti gave the boy a high-five, thinking the cute kid wanted one. Coti jolted as his hand jerked back as if shocked.

"You not bad," Kellen's son said. At almost eighteen months old, the quadruplets were already speaking in full sentences and acted more like three or four year olds. They all assumed it had something to do with the fact they were conceived in the Fey Realm.

Which twin boy said it he wasn't sure since Jagger and Jaxon looked identical, but the alpha blue eyes held him in his enthrall. He wanted to ruffle the little one's hair and pretend the kid didn't freak him out a little. The phone in his hand beeped, reminding him he had places to go and a mate to see to. "Thanks, kid."

An image of a couple blocks away with what appeared to be a crashed muscle car alerted him to where Ace was. He typed in a quick question, wondering why NeNe was with them and not at the club.

Lyric came in, frowning. "What the hell is wrong with NeNe?"

Coti pulled up short. The last thing he should do is yell at the petite female who just so happened to be the second to the alpha's baby sister, but damn if he didn't want to shake the little thing. None of the females had thought what their desertion would do to NeNe. The tough as nails act was just that, an act. His mate was hurting long before last night. He'd sensed her pain and didn't step in. That was on him. "How about the fact her best friends turned their backs on her without so much as a fuckoff party, making her think she wasn't good enough."

Laikyn, Joz, and Syn gasped behind Lyric, but his give a fuck meter was empty.

"Brother, don't piss me off by insulting our women."

Coti looked to see that Turo had handed the boy back to his mama. "I'm stating facts, brother. I'm out." He brushed by the other man, ignoring the people he'd called pack for the past twenty years. His priority lay with NeNe.

"His mate's in trouble. Let's go," Kellen said.

The need to shift and chase her scent nearly had him allowing his wolf to take over, but Ace's image had shown him a vehicle, which meant his female was being driven. "Fuck, I should've chipped her ass."

Xan strode out the door, keeping stride with him. "I tried that with Breezy, but Laikyn said they'd just fall out the first time they shifted."

His steps faltered at the matter-of-fact tone. "I'm not even gonna ask if you're serious." He pressed the unlock button on his truck, climbed inside, and shut the door. The passenger side opened, allowing Xan to haul himself inside.

"You'd think they could come up with something that wouldn't fall out, especially with all these babies," Xan said, sitting back.

Coti shook his head, knowing the other man was being completely serious. "You going to buckle up?"

Xan looked at him with a raised brow. "Just drive, dickhead."

Chapter Eight

Coti bit his tongue to keep from telling Xan to
go fuck himself. Both his other beings were clawing
to be let out. Their mate was in danger. He felt it
clear down to the pit of his soul. Throwing the truck
into drive, he skidded out of the lot, kicking up
loose gravel as he went. Luckily, none of the
women were standing around. Even as pissed as he
was, he would never want to hurt any of the
females.

"So, where you think they're taking her?" Xan
asked.

"The territory they've claimed would be my
guess." He tapped his hand on his thigh, wondering
why they'd wanted her. Hell, why would Mac set
up an elaborate event for one human female,
especially knowing she had ties to the Iron Wolves.

Ace and Dalton stood off to the side of the road
talking to one of the local cops. He rolled to a stop
at the sign, expecting the other men to ignore them

altogether. When the crazy alpha cat walked away from the officer, holding his hand up in a stop sign signal, Coti's lips lifted in a half smile.

"Norris is on their trail, but that fucker is cagey, man. He had three other trucks parked all around this square. They know we're shifters, my friend. Each truck was either leaking gas, or some other shit, trying to screw with our sense of smell, dumbasses. We may be Pride, but we ain't lazy like our cousins. He also didn't go toward that set up he's got outside of town." Ace put his hands on his hips, looking down before he met Coti's gaze. "Norris said he took her into a trailer park on the other side of town, but a train kept him from being able to follow."

His stomach dropped. NeNe lived in one of the trailer parks with her dad and brother. Could this Mac be an ex? Fuck, he didn't know enough about her, but he did know she hadn't been lying to him. Whatever reason the other man had for taking her there, she couldn't be with him willingly. "Thanks, man. You need anything?" He lifted his chin toward the pile of metal that was still smoking.

Ace chuckled. "That was Dalton's baby. He'll be happy to have a new project." He jogged backward. "There's more to Mac than meets the eye, brother. Don't go in with a big head."

Coti shifted his truck into gear, easing around the wreck and the gathering crowd. "You still in for going across town?"

Xan looked at him then out the side window, indicating backward. "I'd say we got plenty willing to go across town, bro."

His pack were lined up behind him in trucks, SUVs, and even a couple motorcycles, all to help him rescue his mate. Goddess, he hoped she wasn't hurt. The Iron Wolves would see the worst of him if his mate, unclaimed or not, was harmed.

NeNe looked out of the window as Mac's driver drove them through town. He'd dumped her unceremoniously into the backseat, following her inside before she could scoot out the other door. She recognized where they were heading. "Why are you taking me home?"

For that matter, how did he know where her home was?

"Your shit should be packed and ready. I don't like loose ends, and this is a loose one," Mac answered.

She scooted as close to the opposite side as she could, putting whatever space she was allowed between her and the crazy man. "You're making no sense whatsoever. Listen, I'm not sure what the hell is going on, but you need to have your guy pull this car over and let me out." Her voice came out a little shaky, but she was proud of herself.

Mac reached across the space, eliminating her sense of security. "You really think you have the right to order me around, girl?" His hand fisted in the back of her hair, twisting until he brought her face close to his. "You'll speak when I tell you to. Do as I tell you to. Are we clear?" He gave a hard jerk, making her head bob back and forth.

Her hands went to where his were, trying to pry them off of her. "You're hurting me."

Even before he laughed, she knew he was going to do something vile, yet she still hoped she could get away. *God, what the hell did I do?* Mac chuckled, then his tongue licked up the side of her face before he covered her mouth with his. Sharp teeth bit into her lower lip, making her cry out, giving him access to stick his nasty tongue inside. She closed her mouth, teeth clamping down until she tasted blood. She wanted to bite the damn thing off, but the hard grip on her hair jerked her back, followed by a slap to the side of the face.

"I really do like it when my females put up a fight, to an extent. You try that move again, you better pray for a quick death, little bitch."

She wiped her hand across her lips, seeing a smear of red. "If you think I'll let you...you touch me without a fight, you got more than a few screws loose. I'd rather die fighting, than lay docile like one of your bitches," she sneered. The taste of his blood ran down her throat, making her stomach roll.

Mac tossed his head back and laughed, the booming sound shaking the windows of the car. Shit, she didn't know what the hell was going on, but the black eyes he turned on her looked nothing like they had a few moments before. Nor did his teeth. Oh, god, did he appear to have hair sprouting all over his face, not just where he had a beard?

"Listen, I think you need to calm down." She pressed against the door, the handle biting into her back. She felt around looking for the lever as his body rippled before her eyes, his jaw elongating and his teeth became huge. The sound of his clothing ripping made the decision to jump from the moving vehicle easy. Whether she was hallucinating, having a bad dream, or if she was in a waking nightmare, she had no clue, but the man in front of her was ripping out of his skin into a monster that appeared to be a cross between a bear and a man. She didn't wait around to see if he completed the change, so he could rip her into pieces, or to see if she woke up. Falling out of the car, backward, while it drove a steady twenty miles an hour hurt like nobody's business. She landed on her side, then rolled half a dozen times, rocks and dirt flew while she raised her arms to try and protect her head, with the wind knocked out of her, NeNe lay panting. A roar split the air. "I'm going to die," she groaned.

In movies, people jumped out of cars and got up, but her limbs didn't cooperate. Oh, she could feel them, each appendage hurt like a son-of-a-bitch. Yet, getting them to do what she wanted was like moving a freight train. It wasn't happening. Tears rolled down her cheeks unchecked. She was a fighter, always had been. "I can't," she whispered brokenly. The thought of being back in the car and letting that man touch her, do as he pleased, was worse than having the beast eat her.

She heard him before she saw *it*. His hot breath hit her first, followed by a drop of drool that made her shudder. NeNe wanted to close her eyes and think of something good as her last thoughts. An image of Coti kissing her hurts away, his gentle care of her the night before made her smile. She wished she'd not been such a rash brat and stayed at the club. Of course, if wishes were hand grenades, she could blow this fetid breath fucker into tomorrow. The reminder had her shivering in spite of the heat. "Fucking kill me and get it over with, you bastard," she said through gritted teeth.

An angry growl made her look up, then she wished she hadn't. The huge grizzly stood next to her, his dark brown fur was tipped in black, and his black claws were massive as he stepped closer. Fuck, they were going to hurt.

Another step closer, and he was straddling her with his front paws. Angry sounding growls and spittle dropped on her. His massive head lowered, showing off teeth that were stained yellow. NeNe imagined he could swallow her entire head in one gulp. His deep rumble shook her entire frame, even the gravel around her moved.

In a move that was swift and violent, he lunged, teeth snapping, the huge bear latched onto her shoulder. NeNe screamed, pain shot through her entire body, burning her from the inside out and in again. The light faded, turning everything dark.

Every fiber of her being burned, her bones broke, the snapping making her cry out again as agony washed over her in never ending waves. When total blackness took her, she welcomed it.

Coti looked at the amount of blood in the middle of the road, NeNe's blood overlaid with a shifter. His wolf howled. His demon rose. Both beings fought for supremacy. The ability to push them back took effort, more than he thought he had, but NeNe needed him.

"Whoa, brother, your eyes are red," Xan said, stepping back.

He knew in that moment there was no keeping what he was from them any longer. His arms fell to the sides as he turned to face the rest of the Iron Wolves. Kellen, Turo, Bodhi, Slater and Wyck came to a stop behind Xan, their wolves ready to come out and play, only they didn't know what they'd be messing with. "Stop right there, boys. My mate, or in the words of some of my ancestors,

Hearts Love, has been taken. You may feel you're owed an explanation, and yeah, maybe you are. Right now, though, I ain't giving you one. NeNe's hurt. That," he pointed at the ground. "That's her blood. Once I get her back and exact revenge, I'll deal with you. You want to bail, do it." He shed his skin, becoming mist and floated on the air, following the scent of his one.

"Well, fuck me running. Did he just do what the wolpires can?" Xan asked.

"I think he also used their term as well, but I don't smell the same thing on him as I do them," Kellen growled.

Coti didn't look back at his pack, blocking them from his mind when he realized no one was following him. He'd fought bigger battles alone in his life and won. This time, the stakes were a lot higher, and he had no doubts he'd win this one too, after he made sure the shifter who thought to take what was his paid.

It was easy to find where they'd taken NeNe. Her scent was like a beacon, shining brightly for him. At first, he'd thought they were going to her old trailer, and from the looks of the destroyed home she'd shared with her father and brother, they'd been there. He kept to the air, looking for where they were keeping her, the smell of her blood everywhere, like they'd painted the walls with it. Mac, the alpha's blood was everywhere too. In the form of mist, it was hard to truly take in the myriad of scents, yet he got an overwhelming sense that his mate had put up one hell of a fight. One the bastard hadn't expected. He wanted to cheer at the thought of NeNe giving him hell. Of course, that meant she was more than likely hurt even worse. A prospect that made him angry.

He left the room with the cloying scents that was literally painted red with a mixture of shifter blood.

"Did you see her? Goddess save us all if she's the alpha bitch. She'll kill every single one of us." A tall female shifter whispered.

He paused after hearing her words, waiting to see what else they said.

"I can take her. Just because she's a bear doesn't mean she's the strongest bitch in the pack."

Recognition hit Coti when the last woman spoke. Grace, the woman who'd tried to kill NeNe was speaking with the other woman. His mind replayed her words, freezing at the description of what she'd called NeNe. His mate couldn't be a bear. Fuck, the goddess had to be playing a trick. No way would she fuck his world up in such a way. He'd yet to meld all that he was, hoping that when he finally mated with his one true mate she'd seal his ragged soul and complete him. His mate would have to be one of the three that he was, not a completely different species.

The women were still speaking, yet he tuned them out until he heard them plotting how they'd kill NeNe. The crazed female bear had been shackled since she was out of control and nearly killed the three strongest men of their pack. Coti wanted to cheer hearing his girl was totally bad ass, but she wasn't his. She couldn't be. Now that she was a different shifter, the goddess would have changed things. His heart ached, his soul cried out for the loss, yet the tentative bond still vibrated. He'd been inside her mind, had forged a path when he'd helped heal her. They'd exchanged blood, although she didn't realize it, they'd already begun the process of becoming mates. Coti opened the link, hoping it still worked, praying she was still his.

Madness swamped him. He tried to sooth NeNe, pain, anger, and uncertainty beat at him. *"Sssh, armina, it's me, Coti. Calm down, everything's going to be okay. I'm coming for you."*

The sound of her huffing, jaw clacking, followed by a roar so loud, he was sure windows would shatter if there were any, let him know she wasn't listening. Shit, he needed to go in on two legs and face down a female grizzly. A pissed as fuck grizzly.

"Oh, my goddess, I'm out of here. You want to get eaten by her, it's your death warrant, Grace, but I'm out."

"Kris, you run and so help me, I'll track you down and beat you for being a little bitch," Grace warned.

The female named Kris laughed. "Yeah, good luck. If you survive that one, then I welcome you to try."

"She's chained to the damn wall, what can she do?"

Coti opened his senses, searching for others. The men had clearly left NeNe alone with the two women to watch over her. Pussies. He floated to the ground, materializing as he landed, making sure he was clothed in a pair of leather pants and vest. Two of his favorite katanas were strapped to his back, although he hadn't used them in over fifty years.

"Female, don't even think to open your pie hole. The only thing it's good for is sucking cock, and, you ain't going anywhere near mine." He held up his hand, silencing her with a thought. Years of non-use had his other being rising, power flaring to life. He popped his neck from side-to-side. "I know, you like freedom, but don't get used to it," he muttered, talking to himself. The railroad cars they had set up as living quarters were lined up front to back with doors at the back that clearly allowed them to move from one to the other. The thick iron-coated metal made it hard for shifters to get a bead on what was inside, which was obviously how Mac and his band of merry fucking fuckups had stayed under Kellen's radar. He shrugged, zero fucks given about his old pack.

Three cars later, her scent became stronger, making his wolf claw at him to take over. Pressing his shifter back, he stayed focused, searching for anyone hiding. The last car shook, the clacking and roars from an enraged bear weren't as loud, clearly signaling she was tiring. He took a deep breath, hands itched to pull the swords free. She was his mate or would be if the goddess saw fit to make it so. He wouldn't harm her, no matter what.

The huge brown grizzly that was three times the size of a normal one, was chained down by all four legs, the smell of burning fur and skin had him seeing red. They'd put cuffs on her they knew would damage her. He'd never known of a made shifter turning so quickly and wondered if it had anything to do with him and his mixed bloodline.

NeNe's head turned toward him; a growl rumbled up as she tried to stand.

Coti waved his hand, quieting her. "Hush now, little one." Although touching the cuffs wouldn't hurt him, he knew if she broke from his thrall, she could bite his head off. That whole decapitation thing would probably be a killer for him. He tried to think of a way to keep her head from moving around and snapping at him. Deep inside the bear, his mate was in there, yet she wasn't cognizant of him or herself anymore. For all he knew, she never would be.

Doing something he'd not done since his eighteenth winter, he called upon the Cordells. Sure, he'd seen them at the club, knew they were mated to the Fey Queen Jenna, but he hadn't asked for their help since their grandfather had turned him away. The old bastard had sneered when Coti had shown up, wanting to find out how to combine his beings. His harsh words, telling Coti he should meet his death and do them all a favor made him turn from the grand castle, vowing never to seek their help again.

"What's this, and who are you?"

He rolled his eyes, then turned to face his distant cousins. "For fuckssake, you've seen me at the Iron Wolves, pretty sure we've been introduced even." Coti kept his arms at his side loosely.

Lucas tilted his head to the side. "He's a Cordell alright. Look at that cocky bastard. Why did we never recognize it before?"

"I was busy."

Coti waved his hand. "Listen, we'll catch up on family drama later. Right now, can you help me with my mate." He pointed over his shoulder, not taking his eyes off of either man.

Lucas raised his hand. "Son, I don't care what you've heard, but we aren't in the business of bear trainers."

Damien raised his hand and high-fived his brother. Coti moved faster than either man could track and close lined both Cordells, taking them to the ground, his katanas out and at their throats. "Seriously, this is no joking matter. See that bear? She's my mate, who was human only an hour ago. We're in the middle of some fucked up shifterville train car, so I'm gonna need you two to act like your three thousand years old, instead of three days. Feel me?" He misted across the room.

"He's so our family. Ps. That's your one freebie. Now, what do you need us to do? I'm not gonna lie and say this is in my wheelhouse, 'cause in all my years, which by the way was rude of you to call out, I don't think I've ever wrestled a bear. You?" Damien asked Lucas.

Lucas held up his hands. "Can't say that I have."

"I need you to ensure she doesn't bite my head off when I remove these cuffs. They're hurting her." He winced when she made a chuffing sound.

"We can hold her enthralled while you take care of them. Now, my next question is this. What are you going to do with her once you have her free?" Lucas asked.

Coti looked at the black eyes of his female, sorrow seeping into his bones. "I don't know. I can't reach her when she's in so much pain."

"We can see if Lula can take her to Fey. It might be the only way to reach her. When something like this happens to a human, a forced shift, it can fracture their minds unless they're strong enough to survive. When was she bitten?" Damien asked, he and Lucas moving closer to NeNe.

"About an hour ago," he answered.

The two Cordell men looked at one another, then at him, their expressions saying they couldn't believe what they were hearing. "My mind is open. You can see for yourself."

He allowed them to search through the front of his memories, keeping a wall up between his past.

"That's…that's unheard of. Let's do this. I've called out to our Hearts Love. She said Lula will be here in a jiffy."

They signaled for him to proceed, which he quickly did while they both worked to keep NeNe still. Sweat poured down all of their faces by the time he got the last of the locks off of her huge paws. He stared down at the black claws that could rip and render a being, thinking about their differences.

"Yoohoo, your fairy dragon is here. Oh, now, who do I need to kill for hurting such a gorgeous girl?" Lula asked, going up to NeNe and rubbing her face over the bears head. "Ah, your fur is so soft, sweet one. Come, you and I will go and run through the fields and get right with the Goddess."

Coti coughed, drawing the pink-haired female's attention. "Um, Lula, a word please."

Lula rolled her eyes, then whispered loudly into NeNe's ear. "These alpha men are so bossy. Coming, sir."

"Thank you for getting here so quickly. Ah, yeah, so she's my mate. Can you tell me what's going to happen?" Coti put his hands on his hips, the sense he was talking to a being who could wipe the ground with his hide had him deferring to her.

The tiny female leaned in. "Psst. Just so you know, I'd never use your carcass to wipe anything. And, she's unclaimed as of right now. I sense two claims in her, which is confusing the dear bear. You and the beast who put the beast in her. She's confused, so me and my dragon are gonna get her unconfused. We'll be in touch. Toodles," she waved, and then they disappeared.

Coti jerked backward, nearly falling on his ass. "Shit, she just took her. I didn't get to say bye."

Damien clapped him on the back. "Simmer down, she's fine. Lula will take good care of her as will our Hearts Love. Jenna will make sure she's well enough to come home, or—"

He glared at the man who spoke. "There is no *or*. NeNe is coming home to me." His heart ached. His soul screamed worse than when he'd fought an entire pack of rogue wolves who tried to kill a farmer and his family in order to claim their land. The pack of seven grown shifter men, in their prime, had fought dirty, but he'd killed each and every one of them, sustaining injuries that nearly killed him. Yet, the pain from that battle combined with every other one, didn't come close to what was coursing through him at the thought of never feeling NeNe's skin under his hands. Never learning all the things that made her who and what she was.

Coti sheathed his swords with a thought, then dropped to his knees, unable to stand. "I thought nothing could kill me. I've tried, throughout the years you know? I've tested what could and couldn't kill me. This, losing her, will kill me." He would claw his own heart out. A man couldn't live without his other half, the woman who was made just for him. He didn't care if she was a bear, a sprite, or even a damn dragon. She was his.

Coti felt his two beings expand inside himself, the wolf and vampire, merging. He wasn't like Damien and Lucas, born with the abilities of a shifter, but essentially a vampire. He was, or had been, three beings in one body, each one co-existing. Now, they merged, strengthening. His vampire half and his wolf rolled around inside his head, then forged to become the man.

"Damn, I think Grasshopper has become the teacher. Should we call dad and Ezra?" Damien asked, backing away from Coti.

Coti rolled his neck, his skin feeling too tight. "We're on the same side, right now."

"What the hell is going on?" Kellen growled, his claws out.

"Well, you see, this one here, is like a superhero being. Kind of like Deadpool of the vampire shifter world, I think. Only, he doesn't look like an ugly avocado that nobody wants to have sex with. Ouch, fuck! Damien, I will beat your ass if you do that again." Lucas pulled a knife out of his leg.

Kellen pointed the iron claws at Coti. "Alright, so you've got some shit to explain. However, we're about to be converged on inside this mothereffen train car. The last thing I want is to rumble in a tin can with that," he pointed at Coti. "I say we get the hell out of here and into an open field."

Xan held his hand up. "I'd just like to point out, that you shouldn't be pointing your freaky ass Freddy Krueger like knives for claws at someone and saying shit. Just saying."

"Don't kill him, yet. We might need him," Turo implored.

"I can call Creed," Lucas said.

"Who's going to open this tin can up?" Bodhi asked, bouncing on his feet.

Coti raised his hands, but the top of the train car groaned, a hole forming within seconds as the upper half was ripped off.

"Yo, anybody home?" Creed asked, looking in through the top. "Ps. I got pants on, so you boys won't get dick envy. No need to say thank you. Oh, and there's like twenty freaky ass shifters heading this way."

Coti jumped out, landing next to the large red-skinned son of Satan. "Thanks, Creed."

Creed nodded. "No problem. We need to finish this quickly, my female wants me home, so we can watch chick flicks."

Xan coughed, the sound of pussy made Coti wince. "Don't kill him, he's a good fighter."

Kellen and the others jumped out of the train car, lining up to face the contingent of shifters coming toward them. "Damn, son, you sure do know how to piss off a man."

Coti raised his head, sniffing. "Let's show 'em what fucking with the Iron Wolves will get them."

He stood shoulder to shoulder with Damien on one side, Kellen on the other, knowing when the bodies settled, he'd have a lot of explaining to do. But first, his claws itched. "Should we offer them the chance to back off and live another day?"

Creed sighed. "Damn, there's always one of you who has to be the fun ruiner. Hold please."

The big man in his partial shift walked forward, eating up the space in long strides, his voice booming. "Stop, you vile beasts. If you want to live so you can go and hump your females another day, turn around, tuck your tails and run screaming to your mamas. Continue on your path now, and I'll render you from gut to throat and feed your entrails to my pets."

Xan put his hands up under his chin and sighed. "Goddess, I love him. He has such a way with words. If I were female, and not mated to a male as magnificent as myself, I'd totally look down and want him."

Creed looked over his shoulder. "I knew it, you dirty bastard. You all looked down. There's no shame in admitting it. First step in all programs is admittance. Damn, I feel them breathing. They're continuing on the forward journey, which means they went with option B. Why do the idiots always go with option B? Do they think I have no beasts to feed their insides to?" He turned back around, swatting a couple of wolves away.

"Let's do this," Kellen roared.

Chapter Nine

Each man held his human skin as the ones coming toward them didn't shift. The stink of shifters came at them, but they weren't all wolves. After seeing what NeNe had become, Coti figured there had to be bears and wolves mixed into the group. He'd never come across a mixed pack, yet his musings had to be put on hold. The crazy bastard, that was Creed, was making good on his promise of gutting men left and right, making several turn around and run back the way they'd come. Coti narrowed his eyes, searching for the supposed alpha of the pack, Mac. His enhanced sense of smell was filled with too many other scents. Although he'd catalogued Mac's unique blood trail in his brain, the open field was filling with death and blood, too many others to get a bead on the one he wanted.

He dodged a meaty fist, hitting one of the brawlers he'd seen fighting the night before in the throat, crushing his windpipe in one blow. Before, he'd always pulled his punches to keep from damaging his opponents to where they wouldn't heal properly. The ones coming at him and his friends were given a chance to turn back or fight. They chose wrong.

He took a hit from the side, grunting at the small injury. The shifter who hit him with the tire iron smirked, showing pointy canines. "Is that all you got?" Coti asked.

His swords would end the fight before it had a chance to begin, but Coti allowed the man to swing his weapon again, jumping backward before it could connect with his head. He felt another shifter sneaking up behind him, along with one on his right. The man in front was the distraction while his friends were the ambush. Poor bastards, they thought they could get the drop on him. Coti pretended to not notice the others coming at him, allowed the man in front to think he was engaged in a fight for his life. At the last minute, he pulled both katanas out of their scabbard, spinning in a smooth half circle and swung right and left, neatly removing the approaching men's heads. When he spun to face the first man again, he'd blanched, dropped his weapon and shifted, his clothing ripping, hindering his shift.

"Well shit, boy, don't go losing your balls now," Coti growled. He contemplated shifting, changing his mind when he saw most of the others hadn't. He wasn't sure what his shift would look like and didn't want to find out in front of Kellen his friends.

The big wolf snarled, bits of torn fabric clung to him, making Coti laugh. "Dude, you look like a fool. Didn't you learn to take your clothes off before shifting?"

His snarl warned Coti he was going to attack seconds before he launched forward, his hind legs lending him strength. If he'd been of the mind, he could've played with the wolf, but he wasn't. Instead, he ended the shifter's life in midflight, his yelp of pain cut off. Coti didn't watch him fall to the ground, knowing the Goddess would take those who were worthy home with her, the others would fall into Creed's father's realm. A roar shook the ground, making him flinch. Kellen tossed a man away from him, into Creed while two more jumped onto his alpha's back. His roar wasn't one of pain, but frustration. Coti saw one of the men had tried to jam a knife into Kellen's back, a sure-fire way to get dead.

Two more men, much larger than any of the others he'd faced broke from the fighting. Bears. He scented them, their smells reminding him of Mac and NeNe. He sheathed his katanas, wanting to rip these men apart with his bare hands. "What up, boys? Looks like you two went to the same store to buy your clothes. Was it lumberjacks are us, or what?" He sneered, eyeing their ripped flannel shirts that had seen much better days. Not that Coti didn't like flannel, hell his closet was filled with them. However, when your shirts had more holes than a barrel on a shooting course, you should get rid of it.

"You think you're funny? You won't be laughing when we make your bitch ours."

Coti looked at the man who spoke, his words ran around his skull on replay, making everything appear black and white. He didn't see anyone else on the field, couldn't hear anything but a ringing in his ears. His skin split, claws ripping out from beneath the tips of his fingers. "You will never touch what is mine," he promised, his words came out deeper, almost incoherent.

He took a step toward the men. The ground shook, the earth sinking in with each step he took. How he was still on two legs, instead of all four, he wasn't sure, he'd never done a partial shift like Kellen, but he couldn't stop his beasts from their mission. Kill. Their fear fueled him, making him hunger for more. In several strides, he had the man, who'd dared to speak, in one hand. "Where's your alpha?"

The bear shook his head, making Coti roar. He kept his eyes on the shifter, taking in each motion down to the way his hair blew back from his face.

Coti knew there was something majorly wrong with him, but his own beasts were in control, only he too was on board with them. Kill. Yes, they were going to kill each and every shifter around them. The sound of bones snapping while the stupid shifter tried to take on his bear form made Coti laugh. "Don't you think it's a little late for that?" He dropped the fool, looking around for his partner. The other man was backing away, trying to escape. Coti pointed his finger, his claw longer than ever. "Shift," he ordered. As if his word was law, the man bent, groaning in pain while his bear was forced out of him.

"Holy fucking shit, Coti, what the hell you doing man?"

Coti turned, pinning Turo with a stare. "Stay out of this."

Turo raised both hands. "I'm on your side, brother."

He nodded, turned back to the bears and waited. He'd not felt blood on his claws for what they'd done to his mate. Taking a look around the field, he saw the others had eliminated the threat. In his head, he counted how many he'd taken out, but none of them were the one he wanted. These two, the bears in front of him, were part of Mac. His beasts wanted their blood.

In a forward lunge, he picked up one, tossing him several feet away. A sickening crunch echoed around them.

"Yo, maybe we should ask them some questions before we off them?" Xan spoke up.

Coti turned, pointing at Xan, then at the bear who reared back, roaring. "He's pack to the one who turned my NeNe. They all need to die."

Creed moved between him and his kill. "I get that, really I do. I'd want them all dead, and I'd even delight in their deaths. However, do you know where this Mac is? You might want to slow your roll on the crazy beast mode a bit and see if we can't get some info out of him. Afterwards, you can totally rip his head off and play pickleball with it if you want."

"This one's dead," Bodhi yelled.

Kellen sighed. "Thanks for the update."

"I could've told you that before he went all the way over there," Xan said, nodding toward Bodhi who was jogging back to them.

"Who's gonna clean this mess up, is what I want to know?" Slater asked, his hands on his hips, a look of disgust on his face. "Seriously, I'm all for a good rumble, but I'm not about to dispose of bodies."

Damien and Lucas both sighed. Their loud gusts of air made everyone turn toward them. "First of all, he can do it if he knew what the hell he was," Lucas said pointing at Coti. "Since it looks like he's as clueless as the rest of you, we'll get it taken care of. You, cousin from way down the line, need to get right in the head. That's not right." He waved his hand up and down Coti.

Coti growled, his fangs snapping together. "Why don't you come over here and say that?"

Damien laughed. "Because, we both happen to like being in our Hearts Love's good graces. If we hurt one of hers, even if you are on both sides of the fence, she'd be angry. I'm not sure how, or who can even you out, but right now, you're all kinds of fucked up. For real, I think even Lula would freak."

Xan opened his mouth, but Kellen slapping him on the back of the head silenced him. Coti took a deep breath, then another. He searched for a calmness inside himself where he'd only been feeling rage. Slowly, color appeared around him, the grass became green again. His body cracked, the joints popping while everything became larger, back to normal. Bending at the waist, he took in a gulp of air, followed by another and another, resting his hands on his knees for support. "Fuck, what the hell happened?"

"Well, I'd say you went Beastly on us. Kinda like Hellboy, only way uglier." Turo squeezed his shoulder.

"Yo, why you gotta have my name in your mouth like that?"

Coti stood, looking up at Creed. "Did I at least have pants on?"

Creed tossed his hands in the air, walking away mumbling.

NeNe eyed the pink dragon, her body too heavy for her to make stand. God, what had she taken that was making her hallucinate? Memory came rushing back to her, swift and brutal. She'd done what all stupid women did in horror movies. "I'm so stupid. Mark my name next to the ones that are too stupid to live and put a check mark next to my name," she groaned.

"Oh, but you're so pretty and soft. I don't want you to die. Me thinks you should just get your furry butt up and learn to accept your new self. Come on, up you go. You can do it. It's like riding a bike. Can you ride a bike? I can't but that's because I don't have one. If I did, I'm sure I'd be able to. Nevertheless, the sentiment is the same. So, you getting up, or do I need to rig a harness?"

Wait, she heard the other woman, but the dragon didn't open its mouth. Now that she had a moment to orient herself, she realized she'd not been speaking either. *"Are you in my head? Am I dead, and you're like, God?"*

Laughter filled her, then the dragon moved closer, nuzzling over her. *"You are most certainly not dead, and while I like to pretend I'm a higher power, I'm assured daily, I am not. And, since you sort of asked, I will answer. We're speaking telepathically. I believe that is the human term for this way of communicating. Although, you're not technically completely human any longer. My name is Lula, by the way."*

NeNe looked down at what she rested on, seeing huge brown furry arms. She gasped, jerking backward. Her arms flailed, only they were the furry ones. She stopped moving. Her breath froze in her throat as she raised and lowered first one arm, then the other. *"What am I?"*

"You're a magnificent bear shifter. I believe grizzly is the species. Yes, that is correct, grizzly. I just double checked, and since you're not black you are a grizzly. Do you know anything about bears?"

Lula sat next to her, picking up her paw, examining the long black claws.

She shook her head. *"I...no, I only know they're big and to be avoided if encountered in the wild."*

Lula released her paw, then nodded. *"Well, you are a predator, so that is a good rule for most to follow. There is much for you to know about your new existence, and a short time to learn it. Are you ready, Danielson?"*

NeNe looked over to see a petite pink-haired girl sitting where the dragon had been. *"I was slipped some sort of hallucinogen, wasn't I?"*

"One would think that, yes, but I fear that isn't the case. This is your new normal. Welcome to Fey, sweet NeNe. Here, you'll learn how to be the grizzly female you are now and merge her with the human you. Right now, your mind is fractured. I had to put the bear to sleep. Your bear's a fighter. Do you think you can handle all of that?"

NeNe glanced down at the body that wasn't hers, wondering what Coti would think of her if he saw her. A sob welled up. *"What do you mean, put*

the bear to sleep? I'm still a bear. I can't. I don't
want this. Can't you take it out of me?"

Sadness crossed the other woman's face. "I couldn't reach you, the human so I made the other sleep. You've been given a great gift by the Goddess, NeNe. To turn it away would be a great disservice. Besides, there is no take backs on this matter. You either merge with the bear, or the bear takes over."

"That's not fair. I didn't ask for this."

"Life isn't always fair, young one. So, what's it to be?" Lula asked, standing and holding out her hand.

What was she to do, place a paw in her hand or her head? She'd never navigated a world with such uncertainty, not even when she'd lived with her dad and brother knowing their drunken tirades could lead to violence. She imagined what a bear did to stand, feeling all four limbs like they were her own, which she guessed they were, and stood on them. Her entire body shook like a newborn colt who'd just been born. *"Dear lord, what am I supposed to do now?"*

Lula's hand rested on her head. "Now, you let me teach you."

NeNe shifted again, her body flowing from bear to human with ease. She wasn't sure how long she'd been with Lula. Days, weeks, heck for all she knew, years had passed. Her heart ached for Coti and what could've been, should've been. Yet she knew there was no way she could go back to him as a bear. She wasn't even sure she was ready to go back to Earth, not knowing there were shifters like her. An image of Mac appeared in her mind, her bear rumbled beneath the skin, itching to seek the man out and make him pay.

"Hi, Miss. NeNe. Whatcha doing out here?"

NeNe smiled at the young girl named Asia. "I'm just enjoying the afternoon. How are you doing? Did you get your schoolwork done?" It still amazed her to find the women from Earth inhabiting the home. Once she'd shifted and shown Lula she was safe, she'd been brought to the castle-like home, shocked to find the mother and daughter duo living happily amongst the Fey.

Asia grinned. "Of course I did, silly. You think my mama would've let me out if I hadn't. I'm so happy here," she whispered.

"It's beautiful," NeNe agreed. She knew a little of the girl's and her mother's pasts and understood why they preferred to stay in Fey, but for NeNe, each day made her miss home. More specifically a tattooed bad boy.

"You know when Laikyn and the others were here, we had a party to celebrate Team Styles. That was before she had all them babies. Maybe they'll come up to visit while you're here. Do you know them?" Asia asked.

NeNe felt the world stop at Asia's words. Why would her old friends have come to Fey? Her mind spun with reasons. She got up off the swing, backing away. "I...are you sure they were here and not on Earth when you met them, Asia?"

The little girl stopped swinging, her eyes widening. "Absolutely. Jenna's the Queen, and she's besties with Kellen. Although, I don't think he likes it when she calls him wolfie, but maybe he does." She lifted one shoulder.

Her eyes narrowed. If Laikyn and Kellen had been here, then they could very well be part of the group who'd hurt her. A growl rumbled out of her, her fingers clacked together, making her aware her bear was pressing forward. "Asia, go inside and lock the door." She hadn't lost control of the beast in forever, yet the betrayal from her friends made her want to rip anything and everything to shreds. In between one breath and the next, she shifted, letting out a roar. Pain, betrayal, anguish mixed inside her.

Little Asia made it inside the house, the lock clicking into place before NeNe fell onto all fours. She swiveled her head toward the huge castle like home but didn't want to rampage there. No, she wanted to go to Earth, wanted answers from the people who'd lied to her.

"NeNe, stop it, right this instant," Lula roared.

NeNe skidded to a stop, looking up the rise to see the pink dragon standing next to an even larger dragon. Belle, Lula's mother flexed her wings but didn't say a word.

"Why didn't you tell me my so-called friends were like me? Did they have a part in making me like this?" Her words were a growled accusation.

"You say 'like this' as if it were an abomination. Being a shifter is a gift many would do anything to be. Many have done much to attain such a gift, child. Why are you so angry?" Belle asked.

"Because the man I love, have loved forever, will never want me now." She sobbed, a little piece of her dying at the thought of Coti's disgust when he saw her.

Belle looked at Lula, then they both laughed, making NeNe want to tear their wings off. Of course, they were both three times her size, so she controlled the urge. *"You two are not helping."*

NeNe shifted, hating the talking in her head. She understood it was natural for Lula and Belle, but to her it was intrusive. She put up a wall like Lula had taught her. "I just want things to go back to the way they were." NeNe rubbed her brow.

A burst of sunlight made her wince, and then a heavily pregnant woman was there. Her curly blonde hair was pulled back in a haphazard pony tail. She looked tired, but NeNe thought she'd never seen a woman more radiant. Words failed her as the woman waddled toward her.

"It's not nice to refer to my gait as a waddle, NeNe, dear." She placed a hand on top her rounded stomach. "You in there, stop it this instant, I have things to do before you make your grand entrance."

NeNe held her hand out when she thought the petite blonde was going to fall over. "Are you alright? Do you need to sit down?" She looked over toward the hill, searching for the dragons.

"I sent them away so I could have a little chit chat with you. Let's sit, shall we? I'm Jenna by the way, nice to meet you." She waved her hand, making chairs appear.

At the comfortable looking furniture, NeNe wasn't sure whether she should be awed, freaked, or go with the flow. Her choice was made when Jenna pointed and uttered the word sit in an authoritative voice. Hell, if the other woman would've told her to hop on one foot, NeNe had the distinct impression she'd have done that without question as well. "NeNe," she replied taking a seat.

Jenna nodded. "Yes, I know. Ah, that feels lovely." She put her feet up on a stool, leaning back and closing her eyes. "Now, you want to undo the shifter in you, yes?"

To hear it said in such plain speaking, NeNe felt a sliver of unease. No, she hadn't wanted her bear. Now, the being inside her felt like she was…her. Although NeNe didn't always feel in complete control when she was in her shifted form, the grizzly wasn't some evil entity trying to take over, just the opposite. She'd learned a lot when she'd shifted, allowing the animal part of her to show her what she missed when she was human. "Yes, no, I don't know. Why did this happen to me?" If Mac hadn't attacked her, she'd not be faced with these problems. It all came back to that bastard, the one she wanted to wrap her paws around and rip into two. Something a human couldn't do.

Jenna opened one eye, pinning her with a purple heated look. "You can't have it both ways, child. If I were to take your bear out of you and send you back none the wiser, would you be happy?"

NeNe wrapped her arms around her stomach. On one hand, she could go back to being just normal NeNe, but on the other, if she did that, she'd not have the ability and knowledge to fight against what happened, if it happened again. Plus, she kinda loved her bear. She allowed her mind to imagine Coti and all his sexy glory to appear in her minds eye. Fuck, the man was too damn handsome for her anyway. At over six feet five, dark hair, green eyes and more tattoos than she could count, he had bad boy on lock. His smile could melt the panties off of any woman from sixteen to sixty, plus his muscles. Damn, his biceps were bigger than her thighs when he flexed. She couldn't imagine him going to the gym, but he clearly worked out regularly. Their time together hadn't given her the option to trace his eight pack with her tongue the way she'd fantasized, and if she moved forward, she probably never would. The alternative though, she couldn't live with. "Damn rock and bear place," she joked. "To be a bear, or not to be, that is really not fair. Can you magically make Coti okay with it?"

"Of course I could, but he's already on board with the entire shifter gig," Jenna announced. "Now that's all cleared up, I think my nuggets are getting restless. They're kinda like their fathers, wanting to decide when they arrive and when they don't. I told them," she paused, looking down at her stomach, a hand on each side. "You two need to stay in there and cook a little longer." Jenna sighed, rolling her head back on the seat, meeting NeNe's stare. "What? Doesn't every expectant mother tell their young to cook a wee longer?"

"I'm pretty sure babies are the bosses when it comes to delivery." She stared in awe at Jenna's belly, amazed to see the rippling that was visible through her shirt. "Holy shit. Does that hurt?"

Before Jenna could answer, there was a slight stir of air, something she'd never have noticed had she been human. Instantly, her bear was rising, bringing her to her feet and next to Jenna. Her claws came out, ready to defend the female.

"At ease, we are here to collect our Hearts Love and young."

"Do I know you?" One of the men asked.

"Damien, Lucas, this is NeNe. NeNe, these are my mates, fathers to my nuggets." Jenna's voice sounded strained.

NeNe shook her head. "I'm not even gonna say what's on the tip of my tongue. As for knowing me, I'm pretty sure I'd remember if I'd met you." One didn't forget meeting gorgeous men, especially twins. Holy crap on a cracker, the two men were almost as good looking as Coti.

Jenna laughed, then groaned. "I'm glad you think my guys are handsome. They can be a handful."

"How are you in my head? I've got a wall up." She shook her hand trying to get her claws to retract, sighing as they disappeared.

One of the men moved closer while the other circled around, picking up Jenna. NeNe didn't back away, waiting to see what he was up to. Her bear didn't rake at her, which was odd.

Once he was within in a foot of her, he snapped his fingers. "Bear, you're the bear," he yelled, making Jenna jump.

"Dang it Damien, inside voice. Of course, she's a bear, did you not see her claws?" Jenna asked.

Damien shook his head. "I was calming our little ones."

Jenna sighed. "Is that why they've stopped trying to rip their way out of me?"

Lucas stood with her in his arms. "Let's go home. I think they've cooked long enough, love. Now it's time we let nature take its course and allow our wee ones out."

NeNe stared at the trio, wondering how she was going to get home. While she appreciated Lula and everyone she'd met while she'd been in Fey, she needed to see where her life back home was. If she even had a life still.

Jenna held her hand out. "NeNe, come here."

Looking at the two dominating men, she eased between them, taking the other woman's hand. "What is it?"

"There's many things you're going to encounter, but one thing you need to remember. Pack is the most important thing in a shifter's life. Kellen is one of the best alphas, along with Niall the alpha of the Mystic Pack. If you don't think you want to stick around the Iron Wolves, I can send you to another pack. But this is non-negotiable, you need to be a part of a pack. You'll be the only bear amongst wolves for now. I see that is all about to change, though."

She gasped, hearing Jenna's words. "Are you saying the Iron Wolves MC are made up of actual wolves?"

Chapter Ten

Unable to pull her hand away from Jenna's strong grip, she had no way to fight the knowledge flowing into her mind. Good god, the woman, no the Fey Queen, pushed information into her mind, flooding her with details. NeNe held onto the small hand like a lifeline, jolting with each new revelation. Her friends, Lyric, Laikyn, Syn, and even Joz were shifters. They couldn't tell her because she hadn't been one. Through Jenna, she could see how hard it had been for her friends not to tell her, but they'd accepted their fate, leaving NeNe to go on without them, the little beotches.

"Alright, mia cara, I think the little female has enough to fill her mind for now."

NeNe wanted to agree, for crying out loud her brain felt like a scrambled egg that'd been beaten a little too much if that were possible. "I feel fairly positive I won't go on a rampage when you take me back home." Dear god, was that croaky voice hers?

Yeah, the only one she planned to maim, kill, and all around dismember was Mac, but nobody would miss that fucker. One of the GD men patted her head.

"What does GD mean. I've heard of GQ, which hello, I get." The one holding Jenna asked.

She growled. "Why can all of you get into my head? For fucksake, is nothing sacred here?" Seeing she wasn't going to get out of telling them, she looked at the smiling pregnant woman, and then at the sweating man holding her. "Why are you sweating?" she asked instead of answering.

Her words made Jenna glance up at her mate. "Lucas Cordell, are you taking my pain?"

"I bet if she were on the ground she'd have stomped her foot when she asked that," Damien joked. "Now, back to GD." He stared at NeNe.

"God Damn. It means God Damn Man." She looked at the stomach of the tiny woman, a frown pulled at her brows. "Are you okay?"

Jenna nodded. "We need to get back to Earth. Pronto! All aboard the Fey Train. We outta here.

You wanna come with, you need to grab one of my goddamn men and hold on."

NeNe was going to correct her on the pronunciation of GD, then decided to hold her tongue when Damien grabbed her arm, his touch firm just before a swirling vortex of death took her. Holy mother of gawd, what the ever-loving bit of horseshit did she step into this time?

"Girl, you really need to have a conversation with someone. I'm not sure what all is going on in that head of yours, but I'm pretty sure you ain't right," Damien said, releasing her quickly before she could punch him.

She growled, not her bear, but a girlie one. "Warn a woman before you decide to take her down a tunnel of darkness and throw in a swirly for shits and giggles. Oh god, I'm gonna be sick," she gasped, bending over seconds before she yacked up the contents of her breakfast over his shiny black shoes.

"Are you kidding me?" he roared.

"What the hell?" Kellen asked.

"Can someone please open the ground again?" NeNe mumbled, keeping her head down even though the view she had was of an unappetizing one of pancakes that looked better going in.

"Ah, you didn't get the happy juice I see. Where's Jennaveve?" Kellen patted her back, seeming to not notice he was extra close to vomit.

"Our Hearts Love wasn't in the best of moods. Our young are not being very nice to their mama." Damien glanced down at his shoes, took a step back, and made a motion with his hands.

NeNe glared at him when she saw his shoes were clean, looking as if he'd just bought the damn things. Fucker. "I think you should go see to your, whatever the hell you call Jenna before I let my bear out and eat you."

She was pretty sure the alpha of wolves sucked in a startled breath, but she ignored him, focusing on gathering her dignity from somewhere around her ankles. Damien lifted his hand to his forehead, gave her a jaunty salute, and ghosted. Damn, why couldn't she be gifted with those nifty abilities.

Instead, she had a beastly bitch inside her who clearly couldn't hold her cookies. She wasn't going to split hairs.

"You going to stand there and pretend I'm not here?" Kellen asked.

"Are you going to disappear if I do?" she questioned, turning to see his expression. He may be a big bad wolf, but her bear wasn't a cuddly little thing. No longer was she going to cower from anyone.

Kellen nodded. "I see we got us another alpha bitch. Just what I need around here. Your man will be glad to find out you've come back in one piece. Come on inside, I'll get you something to rinse your mouth out. And, in case you were wondering, that wasn't a request."

She eyed the big guy. Now that she was where she wanted to be, NeNe wasn't sure what she was going to do with her life. The plan to trek it across the country as far from her family seemed like a lifetime ago. Jenna had said she needed a pack.

"You're a wolf?" she blurted. Gah, she wasn't usually a blurter, dammit.

"Yep, so is just about everyone you know around here. You're a bear, a grizzly to be exact, from what we've been told. How do you feel about that?" Kellen crossed his arms over his chest, the muscles bulging, making her think his wolf was itching under his skin.

"Is your wolf trying to get out and fight my bear?" NeNe was surprised her beast was actually quiet for the moment. Maybe the travel and sickness had sent the big girl into hiding.

Kellen eyed her up and down. "No, he's not raking to get out and fight you. Yes, I can feel the apex predator in you, but my wolf doesn't see you as a threat. Don't take that as a put down. It just is."

Coti picked up his phone, looked at the caller ID and groaned. Someone from the club had been calling him every couple hours for the past few days, checking to make sure he wasn't going crazy.

Or crazier. The fact he knew where his unclaimed mate was, yet she was unattainable to him had him on edge. He'd known he couldn't be around the others of his pack, fear of hurting them kept him locked in his home. "What?" he barked into the phone after swiping his finger across the screen.

"I love you too, man." Bodhi's voice was loud, the music in the background making Coti wince.

"Dude, go make out with your mate and leave me alone." Everyone had mates they could touch, while he'd had one night with his. Why hadn't he claimed her then and there instead of thinking he needed to do the gentlemanly thing? "'Cause I'm a damn idiot, that's why."

"In that we all agree, but I thought I'd let you know your girl is here. Well, she's outside with Kellen and one of the Cordells. She actually tossed her guts all over the shoes of that slick motherfucker. Funniest shit you ever did see. Whoa, why you yelling?"

Coti looked at the phone and then at himself in the hall mirror as he passed. "I need you to rewind and explain why NeNe is with the Cordells."

"Not sure on the whys, only know Kellen stormed out of here like his ass was on fire and told me to stay inside and keep my eyes and ears open. I saw and heard your girl, figured you should know." Bodhi's voice became slightly muffled. Coti heard him yelling for someone to get off the bar. "Gotta go, Syn and some of the girls decided to get on the bar and dance. Which would be fine, except Turo is being Turo. See you in a few."

He could picture the ladies on Turo's bar. Although it wasn't technically his, since he was the head bartender and the one who usually kept the peace when a fight broke out, the man took his job very seriously. Plus, if he was there, then his mate Joz was probably with the other ladies, on top the bar. He'd let them have their drama, at least their mates were safely with them, while his was...shit she was back and he was fucking off. He ran his hand over his beard, looked down at his black T and worn jeans with a shrug. He snatched his wallet up off the side table next to his bed. After slipping it into his back pocket, he attached the chain to his jeans, stomped his feet into a pair of shitkickers, then walked into his garage. His first thought was to ghost to the club, his inner peace still amazed him since he'd allowed his beings to merge. "Fuck it," he said, changing his mind and dematerializing. The need to get to NeNe too great. He'd worry about explaining to her about himself afterward.

Outside the club, he coasted on the wind, searching the area before he allowed his body to reform. The sweet scent of woman hit him along with a noxious odor. He walked over, seeing what the nastiness was, shaking his head at the pile. "That's not a good sign." With a thought, he cleared the mess away, not wanting to leave a trail for anyone to find. If he could scent her, then others might be able to as well. He'd not been able to find Mac, the soon-to-be dead bastard. Although the overlying scent didn't remind him of the shithole where NeNe worked, he wouldn't relax his guard when it came to her safety.

The door swung open, Bodhi's big body stood in the entryway, his mohawk a little disheveled. "Where's she at?" he asked the other man.

Bodhi tilted his head toward the inside. "They went into his office, but then, the girls decided they wanted to talk, and well, shit sort of went south at that point."

He heard some chants, and female growls, but surely, they weren't allowing the women to fight. "What the fuck's going on?"

"Sometimes, women need to slap the shit outta each other in order to get their heads on straight, ya know?"

No, he didn't know. His female wasn't one to hit anybody.

A deep rumble shook the room, making the fine hairs on his arm stand up. "Fuck me, is that my little warrior?" He and Bodhi moved away from the door, heading toward the back of the bar. In through the back entrance, there was another door that led to a shifter only area, one where they held fights. The cage sat in the center, lights overhead illuminated the area, showing him NeNe surrounded by his female pack members. "Fucking bullshit. They all going to take her on?"

Bodhi grabbed his arm. "You know our females aren't like that. If they're all in there, then there's a reason, Coti. Don't do something stupid, brother."

He shrugged Bodhi's hand off of him, picking up his pace till he was outside the cage. "NeNe, what the hell is going on?" he yelled.

NeNe turned to face him, black eyes stared out at him. "Don't," she snarled.

"Fuck, her bear's in control." He walked to the door, knowing the big beast would tear the females apart.

Kellen stepped in his way. "No, let them be. They got a beef they need to settle, or the pack will never be level, feel me?"

Coti pointed behind Kellen. "She's going to go killer bear on those females, and then all you are going to be mateless," he warned.

"NeNe's in there, and I'm banking on the fact she still loves her friends. Loves them enough to not kill them. Smack them down a little for being beotches, her words not mine, yes. Kill, not gonna happen. Come on, let's get on with it then," Kellen yelled.

Unable to believe the alpha of his pack was taunting NeNe, he waited, knowing he'd step in before she did something they'd all regret. He met Rowan's intent blue gaze across from him, knowing the man had to be worried seeing his mate in the cage, but the ex-SEAL nodded, then looked back at the women. Bodhi, Turo, and Kellen surrounded him, the three men clearly thinking to hold him back. He mocked Kellen's stance, folding his arms over his chest. "NeNe, do what you gotta do, armina. I need to talk to you." Her head swung around, pinning him with an angry glare.

"Dude, she looks ready to bite your head off. I'd shut the fuck up if I were you," Xan said. "I'm glad my girl never pissed in your female's pool."

"Please excuse him, sometimes I forget to walk in first with a warning sign," Breezy announced.

Xan grinned, wrapping his arms around his mate. "And what exactly would that sign say? Warning, sexy man walking?"

Breezy snorted but a sigh escaped as Xan's hands slid under her top. Coti turned away from the couple, jerking as the cage rattled. A feminine cry of outrage erupted from the center. The tiny woman mated to Turo, named Joz, jumped back up, but he'd missed why she'd landed against the far side. "Can you shut up, so I can focus?" he growled the angry words directed at Xan.

"FYI, your girl just tossed little Joz across the cage like she was a doll she was tired of playing with," Bodhi explained.

Joz stood up, her hands flexing at her sides. "Ah, you wanna play like that?" She ran at NeNe, jumping up and kicking out toward NeNe's head.

The sound of the other woman's foot connecting with NeNe, along with the way his mate's head twisted to the side as if in slow motion, made Coti's stomach drop. His mate lifted her hand, wiped her lip, then turned to face the women who stood in a group. "Nice kick," she said, cracking her neck. Her nails clacked together, black claws had sprung out after Joz's attack. "Next time, don't stop when you got the momentum. All you did was piss me off."

"Aw, sheot, I think we might've bit off more than we can chew," Lyric whisper yelled.

Syn clapped her hands. "Ain't nothing we ain't done before, girlfriend. Remember that one time," she laughed as Lyric said, 'At band camp', finishing Syn's sentence. Both girls laughed and gave each other a high-five, then like two crazy women, they attacked.

If Coti hadn't seen them in action before, he'd have wished for a recorder, so he could hit rewind and see exactly what they'd done. Instead, he focused on NeNe, and her reactions. She spun, trying to figure out where they would attack. Only problem was each female moved fast, and in opposite directions, punching, kicking, and then moving out of NeNe's range. The scent of his mate's blood filled his senses, sending his beast a rocking.

"Settle, Coti. She's got this," Kellen pointed at the cage.

NeNe fell to one knee while Joz leapt over her from behind. She reached up and grabbed one of Joz's feet pulling hard and fast. Joz hit the mat, the wind knocked out of her. NeNe put her face close to Joz's, her hand now holding her throat. "Submit," she roared.

Lyric jumped on her back, some sort of war cry that hurt his ears coming from her mouth, her fist beating at NeNe's head. Fuck, his woman's dome was taking a beating, but she didn't even rock from the hits. Instead, she reached up with her free hand and tossed Lyric up and out of the cage, yelling, "incoming". Her aim was true, giving Rowan a chance to move a step back and catch Lyric.

Syn stood in front of NeNe where she held Joz, her face bruised and battered. "If I were to say, run and aim a kick at your head, what would you do?" he heard the female ask.

In a very bear like way, NeNe tilted her head. "I'd catch you like I did Lyric, then I'd probably knock you and this stubborn one's head together. Both of you submit and we call it done," she rumbled.

The sound of an angry growl had him looking over at the door to the bar. Turo stood with one of his babies, an AR-15, in his hand. "Joz, don't make me unload this fucker. Submit."

"Fine, but I'm not showing her my throat," Joz growled.

NeNe released her. "I don't want your throat. I don't want anything from any of you. You all thought I was nothing but trash, while you were too good to hang out with me anymore, well now, I'm trash that just whooped your asses."

"Baby, I'm gonna need you to hold that gun for a bit," Joz called out, then the crazy little female wrapped her legs around NeNe's head, flipped her over while Syn hopped on her chest. That same damn war cry came from outside the cage, then from inside as Lyric joined the fray. He made to stop them, coming up short as his alpha, along with the mates of the other women, blocked his path.

"You all realize I can dematerialize and ghost right through you, right?" he asked them.

Each man nodded but didn't move.

"Just for clarification, if I scent she's hurting, physically, nothing will stop me. I won't hurt your females, but I will get mine. Feel me?" He looked Kellen in the eye, not blinking.

"I would expect no less," Kellen agreed. "When they finish, and you settle shit with her, we got shit to sort out. I gave you a reprieve, because you weren't level. I can tell you're as level as you'll ever be. I'll give you twenty-four hours." Kellen stepped aside, turning his back to Coti.

He knew his alpha wasn't disrespecting him, just letting him know he trusted him not to do anything stupid. If Kellen only knew, stupid was his middle name. However, he kept his feet planted while the women held NeNe down, screaming back and forth.

"Can any of you understand what the fuck they're saying?" Xan asked.

Breezy elbowed him in the stomach. "Sssh, they're talking it out."

Xan looked around, whisper yelling to Coti. "Is this like one of those telenovela things where you have to understand their language to get it?"

"That's what I just said," Slater agreed.

LeeLee rolled her eyes. "Be quiet so we can hear."

NeNe pushed her beast back, listening to her friends yell as they explained why they'd kept their distance. Yeah, she got they had to keep the whole shifter business a secret, but they still could've called her.

"Beotches, if you don't get your skanky asses off me, I'll bite whatever part of you is closest to my mouth. Syn, that's your left tit. You like that tit, don't you?" She warned the other woman.

Syn moved back, shoving NeNe's arm back toward the floor. "Now do you understand? Lyric and I have always been this way, so it was easy for us to blend into the human world. We didn't have uncontrollable shifts. Joz here, she's not as controlled as us, or wasn't. She's got super wolf over there for a mate. He's been working with her, plus a dragon or something in her line."

"Plus, we had all this shit hitting us, accidents that nearly killed us, yet here we are a couple days later looking fine. How do we explain that to one of our besties? If we told you, then Jenna would have to come and mindfuck you. Trust me, you do not want that." Lyric shivered.

She huffed out a breath, her arms falling beside her, making Syn and Lyric collapse as well. Their oof made her smile. "Newsflash, I got the mindfuck from Jenna, it was a doozy."

Joz touched NeNe's teeth. "My what big teeth you have."

She narrowed her eyes. "Wrong fairytale, that's for the wolf. I'm a damn grizzly bear." She shivered, thinking again how different she was from her friends.

"Well, I for one think that's fucking awesome. I mean, hello. When someone claims they're being a bear in the morning, you can actually mean it. Am I right?" Lyric asked, her smile bright.

NeNe lifted her head up off the mat, staring at her friend. "Did I hit you too hard? You got a few screws loose or what?"

Syn lay down beside her, staring up at the ceiling. "Yeah, she's a little looney, but we love her. But seriously. Imagine when you have kids, we can say, don't mess with mama bear." She held up her hand, waiting for someone to high-five her.

She closed her eyes, hearing a loud clap followed by another, knowing her ex-friends, maybe still friends, were slapping palms. "I'll totally bitch slap you all back into yesterday if you don't quit it."

"Alright, ladies, I'm gonna have to ask you to break it up," Kellen called from the side. "I have a mate and four little ones at home I'd like to go see, but until I know the shenanigans around here are over, I can't."

"Did he just say shenanigans?" NeNe asked in a tone loud enough everyone heard.

Chapter Eleven

Coti waited until the women exited the cage, then he entered. NeNe sat with her legs drawn up to her chest, looking a little lost. "Hey, how you feeling?" he asked.

He was glad to see her eyes were no longer the black orbs of her bear. Her bruised and battered face from before she'd been taken to Fey had healed. Even from her brawl with the females from his pack, she didn't seem to be showing the amount of damage as the other females when they'd limped out. Seconds ticked by without her answering. Coti got down on the mat next to her, then decided he needed to wrap himself around her even if she didn't feel the need like he did.

"What're you doing?" she asked.

Her scent was the same, the sweet combinations of nutmeg and peaches would forever be etched in his mind, reminding him of NeNe. His mouth watered, thinking of what she'd taste like, wondering if she'd have a different flavor since her turning. "I'm holding you," he answered.

She twisted her head to the side, looking up at him with narrowed eyes. "You realize I'm not like you, like any of you, right?"

He inhaled, rubbed his jaw over her hair. Hell, in the wild, they'd say he was marking her. Shit, in the club, he was totally marking her. He'd stop just short of pissing on her, because golden showers weren't his thing.

"Did you hear me?" NeNe nudged his abs with her elbow.

"Of course I heard you, and yes, I know you're not like me. Nobody here is like me." He buried his nose in the thick mass of her hair, relishing in the fact she was there, alive.

"Coti, you're kinda freaking me out," she said, but she relaxed against him.

He nudged her head to the side with his, nuzzling along her shoulder to her neck. His teeth ached to sink into her flesh and taste her, claim her, mark her for all to see. Goddess, he needed her like he needed air. Scratch that, he probably didn't need air to live. "I missed you, my little warrior."

Her hands came up, covering his where they held her around the waist. If she tried to get away from him he'd let her go, but his beasts wouldn't be happy, neither would be the man. Shit, he tensed, waiting for her to pull his hands apart.

"I missed you too," she whispered, running her fingers over his.

His heart thudded against his ribs while his wolf did somersaults inside his head. Shit, he imagined his two beings were rolling around and hugging each other as NeNe relaxed against him, letting him take her slight weight. "What do you say we blow this place and go back to my house?"

He heard her heartrate increase, the sweet smell of anticipation wafted off of her. "I'd like that. Um, I should apologize to the others," she mumbled, looking around the room. "Where'd everyone go?"

Coti took advantage of her distraction, floating them to their feet. "Kellen said the party was over, so everyone left."

NeNe turned in his embrace, blinking up at him. "Except you and me."

"Except you and me," he agreed.

"You still want me even though I'm—I'm a bear. Fuck, I can't believe I'm even saying that, and it's not like a joke. Not that I'm not a bear in the morning before coffee, but I'm a freaking grizzly bear, Coti."

Her voice broke at the end, making his heart stutter. "NeNe, we're all a little different, but that doesn't mean we aren't the same inside where it matters. Now that you know I'm not just a man, do you not still want me?" His mother's people called their one and only a Hearts Love, while his father's people called them their mate. Waiting for NeNe's reply had his heart thudding hard. He was sure if she looked down she'd see his shirt moving from the pounding, but she didn't break eye contact with him. Goddess, he wasn't sure if he was still breathing while he waited what seemed hours for her answer.

"I've wanted you even when I thought you were a criminal. The fact you're a wolf isn't even a blip on my radar." She stood up on her toes and kissed his chin.

He opened his mouth to tell her everything there was about him, giving her the entire truth of what he was before she tied herself to him. The jangle of keys had him stopping to see one of the pack members walking through. He paused, raised his hand in greeting, then he inhaled, his eyes widening. "Oh shit, what the hell?" He backed into the wall, fear shadowed his face.

Coti decided he'd had enough. His pack was either going to accept his mate and him, or they wouldn't, but they wouldn't be afraid of them. With ease, he jumped with NeNe in his arms from the center of the cage, landing in front of the young shifter. Not asking for permission, he pulled his name from his mind, making sure he didn't hurt the kid. "Erik, you have nothing to fear from my mate or me. Reach out to Kellen. Do it now," he ordered. The alpha in him he kept leashed rose.

Erik's eyes were as large as saucers, but he did as Coti instructed. His head bobbing up and down while he spoke with Kellen through the pack link. Slowly, his scent went from fear, to one of embarrassment. He looked at the floor, the walls, anywhere but Coti.

Taking pity on the kid, Coti placed his hand on his shoulder. "Be at ease, kid. Things are changing around here, but it just means there's more protection for all of us. Go on, I assume your staying in one of the apartments." He jerked his head toward the doors that led to the housing area behind them.

"Yeah, my parents are the new managers. They took over after the, um, other couple left." Erik nudged his tennis shoe on the floor, clearly ready to go.

The other couple didn't leave but betrayed the pack, which led to their ultimate deaths. No, Coti wouldn't be correcting the kid, but he'd be keeping an eye out. If he or his parents had a prejudice against other shifters, Kellen would need to know.

"Go on home, Erik." Coti moved to the side, feeling NeNe's hand grip his tightly. She didn't say anything. He was proud of her for not gasping or screaming when he'd launched them into the air like he'd done. Brave mate, his wolf growled.

Erik stepped around them, his steps hurrying toward escape.

"Hey Erik. Where were you tonight?" NeNe asked.

His mate turned around, meeting the younger man's gaze before he could disappear through the door. "I was with friends." Came a petulant reply.

NeNe stalked him, her face up close and personal to his. "Your friends, huh? Do they happen to be from the other side of town?"

Erik pushed NeNe away, his wolf rippled beneath him. "What's it to you? You're not pack. Kellen said I had to be nice and treat you with respect. I will do as my alpha says but keep your nose out of my business."

Coti let the young wolf skitter out the door, waiting for NeNe to explain what the hell just happened. She held her hand up, her finger against her lips. He gave a nod, waiting for her to join him by the door. There was a lot they needed to discuss once they got to his place, their place if he had his way.

NeNe allowed Coti to take the lead, followed him like a docile little woman when her bear was roaring at her to go back and beat the little shit named Erik senseless. She could smell her brother and his friends on him. How she could, she didn't know, but her bear filled her with rage and knowledge as the kid passed her. "How we getting home?" she asked.

Coti looked at her and then the seatbelt, waiting like he had all the patience in the world. "My truck was here getting an oil change." He waited with a brow raised.

"You realize I'm a damn grizzly. A little accident ain't gonna kill me," she snarled but snapped the harness into place out of habit and to get the big man moving.

"You keep throwing the fact you're a bear up in my face like it's a curse. Being a shifter is a gift, baby. Stop growling, cursing, and hating the fact you have a beautiful being inside you."

Her bear rumbled. If she'd been a cat she was sure the bitch would have purred, rolled over, and shown her belly. "I'm not, not really. I've come to accept her. Rather, we've come to accept each other, but it's a steep learning curve. I never did watch the discovery channel or nature shit. I don't know dick about bears or wolves, for that matter." She felt her beast roll big brown eyes, the image almost comical.

"Well, I would imagine what you saw on television, and what you have inside you are polar opposites. For us wolves, we're pack animals like natural wolves. We have a lot of characteristics that they have as well, but that's where the similarity ends. Well, I assume they do. We can link telepathically, we obviously have two forms, and our sense of humanity doesn't leave us when we shift. If you embrace your bear, melding the two of you together, you'll understand her a lot better."

His words made sense, if only she'd been turned by someone she loved. Mac put a beast in her. The female was a brawler who thirsted for a fight. It took a lot for NeNe to get the grizzly behind the cage in her mind. If Lula hadn't helped her in the beginning, she knew she'd never have found her way out. Her beast growled, her need to be free making her skin itch. "You don't—you can't imagine what it's like."

Coti's hand landed on hers where she was inadvertently rubbing over the bite Mac had given her. God, or Goddess, that was another revelation she was becoming accustomed to, she wanted to sink her claws into the bastard who made her, ripping him from top to bottom. Only when his life bled from the earth would she feel free.

"You're right, I don't know what it's like to be turned like you. All I can do, all I can promise is to be here with you every step of the way. Let me be

here for you?" He squeezed her fingers, the softly
voiced question completely out of the norm for the
huge alpha male she knew Coti to be.

"You still have some things to tell me, like how
you flew us out of that cage," she said. There were a
lot of things about the gorgeous man who owned
her heart that she didn't know. He said he'd tell her
once they were at his house. She prayed she was
strong enough to handle whatever blows he planned
to hand her. No, they may not be physical ones, but
in the past however many days, she'd been through
the ringer. For just a minute she'd like to breathe
and pretend everything was rainbows and fluffy
clouds with sunshine on the horizon. Oh, and for
shits and giggles, since it was her fantasy, she
wanted to be rich as fuck and Coti to love her.

They pulled into Coti's yard, her eyes seeing
clearly even though there weren't any lights on. "I
love your place," she remarked. The log cabins
many of her friends lived in were gorgeous, but the
concrete and glass house suited the man.

He grunted, tapping a rhythm on the steering wheel while he waited for one of the garage doors to open. "It's a better defensible place for my kind." He held his finger up. "I'll explain when we're inside."

His truck filled the section closest to the door. They both waited until the bay closed before Coti got out and came around to help her down. Why she allowed the gesture she didn't know, only knew he enjoyed being the gentleman. "Thank you," she murmured once her feet touched the ground.

"You're welcome. Come here, let me program your palm into the sensor so you can get in or out." He explained how the doors were all set to automatically lock behind him when he exited the house. She pressed her right palm to the faceplate, electricity tingled beneath her as the machine took her scans. The entire operation took less than a minute. When a green light popped on, he smiled. "Alright, lets see if it works. Place your hand on the center. It's relatively simple, if your palm touches the plate, the door will unlock and open."

Again, there was a small electrical sensation, then the door locks disengaged before the door slid into the wall. "You take safety very seriously, Mr. Sharp. How thick are these walls?"

He tapped her on the ass. "Thick enough. In you go," he ordered.

Ah, at his rumbled words, her mind conjured up all kinds of dirty things. He was thick, everywhere. Her body went soft thinking of their one night together.

"Armina, don't. We need to talk," he growled.

Shit, shifter sense of smell meant he could smell her arousal. Embarrassment had her moving away from him.

He stopped her exit, his hand soft yet firm on her arm. "Don't be embarrassed about a natural reaction, NeNe. Look at me." He pointed down at his pants. "I had a boner since I smelled you. It's only gotten harder as I watched you kicking the other ladies' asses, and now, smelling your fucking sweet scent." He inhaled. "If I didn't think you needed to hear everything before I take you again,

I'd have your pants shredded and your legs around my neck while I alternated between licking you 'til you had nothing left to give and fucking you until my balls were empty."

She shifted her legs back and forth. "Why does that sound like a really good plan?"

"'Cause I'm really brilliant and come up with the greatest ideas. Now, stop teasing me with your sweet pussy elixir and sit down. You want a drink?" He turned away, the bulge in his jeans clearly visible.

"Did you just say sweet punani elixir? Is that even a thing? I'm so going to file that in my bank of shit to pull out for later," she laughed.

Coti lifted his hand, raising his middle finger. "It's now a thing because I said so. Drink?" He held up a bottle of beer in each hand.

Suddenly, she was extremely thirsty. Nodding, she accepted the cold bottle, tipped her head back at the same time as Coti, and drank almost half the bottle in one long swallow. They both sighed. "Alright, spill." She pointed her bottle at him.

He tipped the bottle back to his lips, downing the rest of the beer, then tossed the empty into the trash. "While you were in Fey, I'm sure you saw a lot of other beings. Dragons, obviously fairies. You remember Damien and Lucas, Jenna's mates?"

She nodded. "Yes, they were drop dead gorgeous but looked as though they'd happily kill you and then go home and braid Jenna's hair like nothing happened."

Coti laughed. "If you mean they seemed like homicidal men, you might be on to something. What I mean is, did you scent what they were?"

NeNe shook her head. "I didn't even think about it at the time. Are they Fey like Jenna?" She pictured the two men in tights with wings, snorting at the image.

"No, they're nothing like Jenna. As a matter of fact, I'm related to them, loosely." He turned his back to her, then spun back to face her. "Their father is Damikan, the Vampire King. Their mother is Luna, a wolf shifter. Both men are over three thousand years old."

The bottle slipped from her fingers, crashing on the polished floor. What the hell else was he going to tell her? Demons from hell come out at night and steal babies or virgins from their bedrooms? Coti's hands held her face between his palms, his words penetrating her brain. He'd said he was related to the men. No, the vampires.

She jumped backward, putting space between them. "So, you're a what exactly?" Her eyes strayed to the broken bottle, then to his face. He looked like she'd gutted him. Dammit, it wasn't her fault. Was he going to want to drink her blood? Did he sleep in a coffin? No, she remembered they slept in a bed together. Wait, he walked out in the day. So did the other men. "You lying to me? Trying to see if I'll freak out or something? 'Cause I'll tell you right now, that's not the best way to get laid."

Coti shook his head, coming toward her. "No, and just so you know, we're not like the movie or book vampires. The Cordells are hybrids. I guess I am too, but my mother was the vampire. She was also a gypsy wolf, but my father didn't know about the vampire part until after they bonded. When they mated, he knew she was his, but somehow, he'd convinced himself she'd enthralled him. Her people were gypsyies who came from Romania. There are stories that they could do things that other hybrids couldn't, but the first-born son was gifted special powers. A strength, a being of three in one.

"You're the first born?" she asked, already knowing the truth.

He nodded. "For over a hundred and fifty years, I've fought the others, keeping the vampire side of me hidden, embracing only my wolf. When I was twelve, I was already a head taller than my father. He feared me, feared I'd take his place as head of our family. At twelve winters, I only wanted to please the man," he sighed, raking his hair back from his face. "Hell, at five I shifted into a white wolf that killed grown men, solidifying fear in my own father and clan."

Chapter Twelve

Retelling his story was harder than he'd envisioned. If NeNe turned away from him, the need to continue on would disappear. Endless days and nights had been spent thinking what life would be like with his mate. Having her within his grasp, only to lose her, he wouldn't survive.

He told her of the first year after his father made him leave, then the long years he'd spent searching for the woman his family said would fix him. "If I had this elusive female, I could go home, you see." He looked at her, watching how she took his words.

"So, you did what, fuck your way across the world?" she snarled.

Coti laughed, her jealousy welcome. "NeNe, I can smell my mate. I can feel my mate. My others, inside," he took a deep breath, tapping his head. "Know our mate. She was nowhere to be found. I went to the Cordells' grandfather once out of desperation. I wanted him to end me. I'd tried everything, but nothing worked. The old bastard sneered at me, and said I wasn't worthy of his sword."

The familiar ache of being cast out by another member of his family made him look away, not wanting to see her do the same.

"Do you think he did that so that you wouldn't expect him to actually kill you? Or I don't know, maybe it was his way of being noble. What did you do after he did that?" She pressed up against his back.

Coti didn't dare turn around, her soft breast against him gave him hope. "I decided I'd learn how to use a sword and go back and challenge the fucker. I mastered Kenjutsu, Jaijutsu, Jaido, and Ninjutsu. They were my preferred choices after seeing the katanas. Of course, I forged my own blades, and when I was confident I could take the old bastard—I decided he wasn't worth it."

She wrapped her arms around him, her head resting between his shoulder blades. "I'm assuming those are all some totally kickass fighting things?"

He laughed. "You could say that, yes."

"Back to the vampire thing. You want to suck my blood," she said in a weird accent.

Coti shook his head, then nodded. "I don't need blood to survive. I think the Cordells and I differ in that way as well. If I'm severely injured, I go out and hunt on four legs, the blood of an animal, like a deer, works to heal me. However, since we were together, I've changed. My other beings have settled, come to an agreement of sorts. Hell, I don't know, but now, my body aches for yours. My teeth ache to sink into your flesh and mark you, mate you, claim you for ours. I want to replace every bad thing that's happened with good, make you so damn happy you never want to leave me."

"Coti, look at me," she whispered.

He stood from his slouched position over the counter, seeing his nails had grown during his speech. Go big or go home was a saying he figured he'd embrace. Or in this case, run his mate off. NeNe didn't move back, making it hard for him to turn around without bumping into her.

"I'm not going anywhere, even though you got some freaky eyes going on right now." She pointed toward his face.

He had a feeling he knew what she was referring to. When a vampire was in extreme situations, their eyes turned red. Since his beast was no longer locked down, it was making itself known, fucker. Coti blinked, willing control to surface. His wolf seemed to laugh at him. "Better?" he asked.

She nodded. "Will I become a vampire if you do take my blood?"

"Not if I do, but when I do. Armina, you understand you're it for me. You stay with me, I'm going to do all the things I said I was. This calm façade you see before you? Its not going to last. I've worried about you, feared for your safety for too long. If you don't think you can accept all of me, you have access to get out. Take one of my rigs and go. Do it now," he gritted.

"You didn't answer my question. I'm thinking a vampire bear will not be a very sexy beasty." She ran her hand up his chest. "Does it hurt?"

He gripped her by the hips and spun them, settling her onto the counter. "I'd never hurt you. Ever. You want to know how it works?" He licked his lips, then let his incisors drop, showing them to her. "I'll lick along your neck, finding the vein that calls to me. I'll make sure you were aroused, then lick that sweet pulse, suck your skin into my mouth so you'd have a little bruise to remind you I was there. When my teeth finally sink into you, you'll feel nothing but pleasure wash over you while my incisors act as needles sort of. Only instead of injecting, they'll allow me to take your essence into me. Unlike movies, there's no pain, no blood filling my mouth to drip down your shoulder when I finish. I do have anticoagulants in my saliva, so the wound will heal up almost instantly once I removed them and licked over the area."

Her hand lifted, one finger aiming toward his mouth. "That doesn't sound too bad. How about this mate, mine thing? What exactly does that entail?"

Coti growled. "Armina, you ask too many damn questions."

She grinned. "Hey, you've known about all this for...holy shit, you said over a hundred years, grandpa. Give me a break."

He grabbed her finger, sucking it into his mouth. "I'll show you grandpa."

The sweet smell of her arousal filled the air. He knew he needed to explain the truth about mates and the fact they didn't divorce. There was no such thing in their world. He didn't understand why her bear wasn't raking at her the way his two beings were.

"How about your wolf? Does it feel like he's always trying to take control? Like it's competing with your human counterpart?" She looked down, then up, her nose scrunching.

His chest hurt as he imagined how overwhelming it all had to be on her. "Sometimes it can be a little much, but for me, I've been the way I am since birth. For those who are turned, especially those who were changed against their wishes, I think there's a major adjustment to their entire lives. I imagine there's even a constant battle for supremacy, but you're strong. Not everyone could survive what you did." He didn't want to mention the survival rate was less than fifty percent for those who'd been forced into their world. She already looked on the verge of tears.

"Lula said as much. She's different, in a good way. I think she's the reason I survived." she swallowed, looking away from him.

He shook his head. "You're the reason you survived. Every shifter needs to learn to accept their other being, finding a balance within themselves. Most need a strong alpha to guide them through their first shift, which doesn't usually happen right away. You're an anomaly in that respect as well. Already, I can see you're controlling your bear, not the other way around."

Coti could see she was letting his answers process, thinking what else she should and shouldn't ask. He didn't want to invade her private thoughts, knowing they were forging a bond built on trust. Usually, he didn't like answering questions. If he was being honest, he loved knowing she trusted him to give her what she needed. His dick jerked when he thought of what else he could give her.

"When I first changed I…I don't have much recollection. Once Lula brought me out…does that sound right?" She bit her lip. "Lula was all of the sudden inside my mind, and I could feel the bear. She was so angry, wanting to rip everyone and everything to pieces. When I realized that the bear was me, I tried to hide, but Lula wouldn't let me. She forced me to take control, which was really weird being as I was taking back my own body." A laugh escaped her, but her hands trembled.

"How many times did Lula make you shift before it became easier?" he asked, finding it fascinating to hear about her journey. His only regret was not being there to help her.

A grin lifted one corner of her lips. "If you were to ask Lula, she'd say elevendybillion. I told her that wasn't even a number, which of course she claimed that was because nobody had tried and failed at shifting as much as me," NeNe laughed before she continued. "Honestly, it was her tough tutelage that made me want to prove I could do it. Like she said, this is my body, I just share it with the bear. Once I owned that, it was easier."

The next time he saw the pink haired dragon, he was going to give her a hug. "Any more questions?"

She licked her lips. "One more. I, of course, reserve the right to ask more in the future."

He brushed his thumb over her lower lip, wiping away the dampness. "I would expect no less. Alright, what's your last question, right now."

NeNe reached for his hands, bringing them up to her mouth. Her hands were so much smaller than his. She loved the differences between them. His dark, tattooed fingers with the battle scars looked like they could take on the world and come out the winner. She kissed each knuckle, glancing up at him through her lashes. "I don't want to be your almost mate. I want to be your true mate, or whatever it is you call it. My bear wants it too, although she's sort of growled at your wolf."

Coti moved forward, his free arm pulling NeNe's body into his, her legs wrapped around his waist. "Mate, I prefer mate," he growled.

She opened her mouth to respond, but he tugged her head backward, then his lips were pressing against hers with near desperation. Her bear grunted in her head, the sound almost comical as she imagined the big girl rolling on her back for the wolfman. The heat from his body warmed her, and she felt him tugging at her mind, asking instead of taking. She let him in, felt his relief in her acquiescence. She traced his bottom lip with her tongue, then grinned as he took over, humming low when he deepened the kiss.

"Forever mine, NeNe, you're mine, my mate forever," he growled, nipping at her lip before covering her mouth once again. His hard body against hers didn't give NeNe a chance to respond while he kissed and held her, claiming her mind and heart.

"Are you going to claim me on your kitchen counter then?" She gasped when he finally let her up for air.

"First, I'll claim you anywhere and anytime I want. Second, you'll fucking love it. Third…where was I going with that?" He pulled her off the counter and began walking toward his bedroom.

NeNe wrapped her arms around his neck. "I've no clue, but I do like the way you think." She bit his earlobe, loving the shiver that wracked his frame. Coti didn't try to hide how he felt from her like some men would've tried.

"Let's see if you like what else I do." They entered his room, lights coming on automatically set on a dim setting.

He tossed her onto the bed, making her yelp, but then his eyes were such a bright green she had another question. "When you're in your shift, do your eyes change?"

Coti blinked taking a deep breath. "Some do, but mine stay green Kellen and many other alphas will have blue. They call them alpha eyes. My

254

family are Gypsy Wolves, a different breed of shifters, although we are wolves, they don't seem to follow the same rules. My other, the vampire side, I'm told will have my eyes turning red, but only when my control slips."

She leaned up on her elbows. "How about me, are mine different?"

Their gazes held, and she wasn't sure if he was going to answer her. "I believe once you have more control, they might not, but right now, when you're in your bear form, your eyes are that of the bear."

NeNe wiggled until she was leaning against the mound of pillows. "Okay, that's all I got for now. Information overload. Now, I need you filling me," she said, not expecting the blast of lust that hit her from their connection. Good lord, the man had an imagination that set her pulse pounding.

"If you like those clothes, I suggest you strip," he ordered.

She didn't waste time arguing as she wanted everything he had to give and more. Coti tossed the last of his clothing to the side, watching her while she stripped her final piece of clothing off. For some reason, being the one to bare herself for him made the act even more sensual.

Coti put one knee on the bed, his hands reaching for her, pulling her down until she lay flat. She leaned up, kissing his neck, a low throaty growl vibrated beneath her lips. The sound sent an answering growl within her. Need had her burrowing her hand between them, seeking out what she knew would ease the ache he'd created. Her hips thrust upward, searching for contact with his naked body. God, she'd never experienced such out of control hunger as this.

His hands smoothed over her, grabbing hers from between them, locking them inside one of his. "Damn, need to slow," he muttered.

"Fuck slow. We can do that next time." She arched her pelvis up, then like a beacon, his neck called to her. "Mate," she growled, lunging forward erasing the scant inches to where she could suck the skin on his neck into her mouth. Salty, male, all Coti filled her.

"Ah shit," he rumbled, the sound reverberating through him and into her as his hips collided with hers, sliding the tip of his cock into her.

NeNe felt the impact of his entrance with her entire being. His growl combined with his pulse beating beneath her teeth, she felt her bear rising up, wanting to claim Coti. She wasn't sure how the mating happened, only knew the bear part of her was taking over, slightly, her teeth sinking into his flesh. Memories flooded her, his time as a young man in a time she couldn't imagine. Her heart ached for the young boy he'd been. She and her bear took in the knowledge he had, filtering through things that angered the female as she saw him mating with others. NeNe pushed the animal back, releasing Coti with a swipe of her tongue over the wound. "God, I'm sorry," she whispered.

Coti met NeNe's eyes, hoping his weren't red like his beasts. Fuck, it took all his willpower not to slam into her like a madman until he came. His body twitched, his balls were so tight he feared they'd explode with one move. "My turn," he said.

He tried not to lunge for her creamy throat, wanting his claiming to be completely different from her change. He licked over the injury, his beast and wolf growling in unison, then his canines sank into her, making her cry out in pleasure. NeNe's climax hit with the first suck, her tiny body spasming under his, her nails digging into his ass. He didn't think the steady clench and release of her pussy would end up drawing him farther into her. Licking the wound, thrusting slowly, wanting to add to her pleasure, he kept up the pace of his thrusts.

"Holy shit, holy shit," she muttered over and over.

He felt their link lock into place, the mating bond complete. His past was now hers. He vowed to protect and love NeNe for the rest of his days and nights, ensuring she never worried whether she was worthy ever again. To him, she was more than worthy, she was everything.

His lips drifted upward, kissing that mouth she used as a weapon. "Damn, you're my perfect match in every way. Gonna love you forever, and even then, I'll love you longer."

A sweet smile crossed her face, her eyes glowing green. She bared her throat to him again. "Claim me again, Coti. I know your wolf did, but the other needs to as well."

Coti froze, unsure what she was talking about, then his beast rose, his fangs dropped, taking what she offered. He sucked deep, his hips pounding out a furious rhythm while she moaned. He only took enough to satisfy the beast within him, then sealed the wound, shocked to see the old scar healing, his bites the only visible injuries. "Goddess, you're beautiful, smart, perfect in every way, NeNe. How'd I get so damn lucky?"

He asked the question, but he really wanted to tell her she was insane. Beautifully insane for courting all that he was. However, she'd accepted all that he was. There were no take backs, and damned if his body wasn't happy.

His cock shuttled in and out, balls so tight he feared he'd blow before she did. Arching back, he licked one tight nipple, sucking the hardened tip into his mouth before moving to the other side and doing the same with it.

No other woman could hold a candle to his sexy mate.

"Oh yes, Coti. Why am I so horny?"

He chuckled against her breasts. Opening their link, he gave her more, letting her feel what she did to him, the feel of her tight wet heat as he shuttled in and out of her.

"Oh fuck, that's so, shit," she screamed, her pussy constricting around him.

Coti closed his eyes, rearing back as he finally let go. The sweetest agony he'd ever felt was as he pumped his seed inside NeNe, watching her eyes close and her chest rise and fall while she screamed his name in pleasure. Another spasm had her clenching down on him, making his eyes cross. "Fuck. Oh fucking hell, NeNe, you're the sweetest, most perfect female born."

When they were both finally spent, he eased to the side, still locked inside her while holding her tightly to him. The thought of releasing his hold on her didn't seem right just yet.

"That was—was so much more. I don't have words, Coti. I felt you in ever fiber of my being. Like, every single inch of me is filled with you."

He felt her words all the way to his very soul. "That's the way it's supposed to be with Hearts Loves and mates. I'm so glad I found you, armina."

Chapter Thirteen

NeNe ran her leg up Coti's bare thigh. Her multiple orgasms took her by surprise. She'd actually never had one before being with Coti, at least not with another person. The steady beat of his heart seemed to thump inside her where his cock was still deeply imbedded. "I think I could get used to this," she murmured.

Coti chuckled. "Good, I plan to give you multiple Os, often. By the way, I'm glad I was your first."

She groaned and buried her face against his chest. "That connection thing is going to be something I need to get used to. Upside? Bear seems more settled. I don't feel her rattling around as much. Does that make sense?"

He lifted her chin with his finger, placing a sweet kiss on her lips before answering. "Yeah, it does. I was inside your memories. I saw what you went through when she was forced in you. Bear was pissed like you were. Now, she's content, even though a wolf wasn't her ideal mate, she likes us."

"So, we can talk to each other through our minds no matter where we are?" She settled more comfortably on him, soaking in his peacefulness.

"Yes. I know Kellen can connect with anyone in the pack no matter the distance. From what I've heard, mates can as well. For us, it'll be a learning curve. I could probably ask Jenna or the Cordells, but I really hate to bother them, right now." He smoothed his hand down her back, stopping at the curve of her ass, squeezing gently.

"So, they're really thousands of years old?" She shut her eyes when his fingers trailed between the cheeks of her ass. Goodness, they'd just made love, and she was already feeling her body heat up, wanting him again. A thought hit her. "Holy shit! What about you and I? I know you're like old, but I'm human, or was. Will I become old and wrinkly while you stay hot as fuck?"

He boomed out a laugh, his dick jerking against her leg over his hardness. "Ah, armina, you're so damn precious. To answer your question, now that you've turned, you'll live a lot longer. I'm not sure on the length. With you taking my blood, you're not only a shifter, but I can sense my vampire blood flowing in you as well. Since joining the Iron Wolves, I've kept that part of myself hidden from them, which if you were paying attention, Kellen is none too happy about. I'm going to have a come to alpha meeting with him soon."

She looked into his sparkling green eyes, worry furrowing her brow. "Is that like a come to Jesus moment? Will he kick you out of the pack? Damn, am I part of his pack? Are there like some wacky rituals I have to go through to become one?" She tried to sit up, questions tumbling out as she imagined everything they'd have to do.

Coti pulled her on top of him, holding her down with both arms banded across her back. "NeNe, let me erase a few of your worries, and then no more questions. Look into my mind, search for any questions you might have. Love, you have all the knowledge you should ever want at your disposal within our link. Now, Kellen as the alpha, has a right to be pissed that a member of his pack, someone who'd pledged to him, has basically lied, albeit by omission, for years. So, yes, I may have to face his wrath. However, I'm not worried about getting you or I kicked out of the pack. If it came to that, then so be it. As for you being an Iron Wolf, you became one when I claimed you. There's no crazy hoops you need to jump through in order to become one. Of course, Kellen still has to welcome you and create a bond that links you to him and the pack, but that's only a formality."

She opened the link between them, searching for the truth. Kellen was an alpha who didn't fuck around. If he thought Coti, or she, posed a threat to the pack, he wouldn't accept NeNe, nor would he hesitate to boot Coti out. "You hid what you were out of fear they'd shun you," she said, knowing it was the truth. His own father had done just that.

His deep exhale lifted his chest, and her, up and down. "I'd never hurt anyone in my pack, even if they kicked me out."

"Of course you wouldn't. Heck, your own father is probably still living, which is a testament to that fact. My bear wants to rip my dad and brother to shreds and hunt yours down," she snarled, instantly regretting her outburst when she saw Coti's eyes flash red.

"I'll take great pleasure in teaching both men in your family the error of their ways, my little warrior," he promised.

NeNe maneuvered her legs over his sides, done with the talking about what could be, should be. "Let's forget about our screwed-up families. There's a much more pressing issue we need to deal with right now."

"Hmm, and what would that be?"

Slowly, keeping her eyes locked on his, she kissed her way down his body, flicking her tongue over his flat male nipples. Coti didn't hide his reactions from her, the link allowing her to feel his emotions. When she reached her destination, her mate gave full access, opening his legs, giving her room between them to kneel. Staring upward, she pressed a closed-mouth kiss to the tip of his cock, then licked over the head.

Coti moaned, gripping the sheets in both hands. "Damn, I love your mouth."

Before he'd finished speaking, she took his cock deep, holding his balls in one hand while she pumped him with the other. Their eyes locked, her tongue rolled around the heavy vein underneath, and she felt him swell even further. The sexy moan he expelled made her groan, her lips tightening.

"Gonna come," he warned.

Her hand moved faster, wanting to taste him.

Without warning, he pulled her off him, startling a gasp from her. "What's wrong?"

"Want in you," he growled.

One big hand fisted in her hair, bringing their lips crashing together. She reached between them, wrapped her hand around the base of his dick and guided it into her, sighing at the tight fit.

Their simultaneous moans filled the room. She'd never felt so full, so complete until Coti. Her pussy tightened around him, her body primed for a release from sucking him.

Coti gripped NeNe's hips, pushing her up and down on his dick while she squeezed him like a vice. The undulations tugging at him made his balls draw up with every clench and release of her inner muscles. Never had he thought to find a woman made just for him. Goddess, her pussy was so tight, so wet and hot he was ready to blow.

He growled, the sound coming from deep within his chest, making her eyes brighten. Oh yes, his sexy mate was with him every step of the way. Her hands on his chest raked him with claws, drawing blood as she leveraged herself up, sitting straight so she could take him deeper, rolling her hips. "Growl for me again," she ordered.

Fucking-A. Coti growled again, then growled even deeper, letting it draw out. The wicked smile on her face turned to pleasure. Using his hands, he helped slam her up and down on him. "God yes, don't stop. Don't stop, Coti."

A damn horde of demons could rush in and he didn't think he could stop. His wolf, vampire, and Coti himself had surrendered completely to their sexy little mate. Pushing her down harder, faster, he fucked her like an animal.

"Fuck, yes," NeNe screamed.

He forgot everything except he and his mate, sweat trickling between them. The sound of their bodies slapping together, her breasts bouncing up and down, had him racing toward orgasm. "Come for me, NeNe." The sexy symphony they made with their bodies coming together was the most erotic thing he'd ever heard. Her moans and gasps had his cock throbbing, his blood pulsing, his fangs dropping, making him harder than ever before.

He worked a finger between them, finding her clit, rubbing back and forth over the swollen nub. Her pussy contracted around him, holding him like a vise. Her throaty moan came from deep within, and he felt an answering one swell in him all the way to his balls.

Shoving upward faster, while pushing her down harder, had a pained sob of pleasure wrenching from NeNe. She swiveled her hips above him while he added a second finger to his ministrations to her clit.

The clenching around his dick, the clamp and release signaling her orgasm was his undoing. He lifted her higher, shoved her down harder, relentlessly taking her over and over. She rode him, beautiful in her wild abandon. Coti needed to seal their joining, his entire being wanted to taste her again.

Her eyes glowed, the bright green called to the primal part of him. In that moment, he knew he loved her. Not because of his wolf or his beast, but because he loved her, NeNe, the woman. His arms wrapped around her, hips still shuttling up and down, he brought her to him for a deep, soul-searing kiss. His mind opened, letting her see what she meant to him.

NeNe broke away from their kiss, flipping her hair to the side and offered her neck, the side he'd marked earlier. "I love you, Coti. Take what you want, what I want."

As his teeth entered her flesh, the pussy surrounding him clenched, drawing him in deeper, locking him inside while he came. The clasp of her wet heat milked him, taking all that he was even as he drew her essence into him. His muscles clenched, holding onto NeNe's body while he arched his body into hers, the welcoming heat too much, their come mixed, running between their bodies as he continued to release.

He licked his mark. Using his hand on her head, he guided her to his neck, wanting to feel her teeth in his. Remarkably, his dick jerked as he came some more. "Fuck, I've died and gone to the Goddess," he swore.

Her dainty little tongue licked over him. Exhaustion pulled at her when he finally rolled her over, using his powers to cleanse them. The thought of leaving the evidence of their lovemaking inside her lasted about a minute, until common sense kicked in. She'd sleep better without being sticky, but damn if he hadn't thought about it.

NeNe fell asleep with her head on his shoulder, her hand over his chest. The beating of their hearts was in sync. Tomorrow, they'd tackle the pack.

Coti came awake instantly, his mind opened while he searched for what had disturbed him. He reached for the security around his home, seeing nothing out of the ordinary. NeNe's back was to him, goosebumps rose on her flesh from where he'd kicked off the blankets. He pulled the sheet over her, then kissed her shoulder before rolling out of bed quietly. After all she'd been through in the past weeks, she needed rest.

He tugged on a pair of jeans, then padded into his kitchen to grab some coffee. It took a few minutes to fill his cup. While he waited, he mentally knocked on Kellen's mind, figuring he'd be polite this morning. His alpha didn't make him wait long before responding.

"You're up early, sunshine. I'm assuming you sealed the deal with your mate, finally?" Kellen sounded chipper.

Coti took a sip of his coffee, grinning at the word chipper coming from Kellen. *"Yep. Never thought I'd have the pleasure,"* he answered honestly.

"Denying who your wolf knows is your mate is hard as fuck. I let Laikyn go unclaimed almost too long."

He could hear the anger in the other man's tone even through the distance. *"Yeah, I was a dumbass, too."*

Kellen growled like Coti knew he would. Calling your alpha a dumbass could be considered foolish, or even a wish for a beatdown. Coti wasn't either, usually. *"Boy, I'll let you get by with that, this time. Now, when you coming in so we can have a meeting?"*

"You realize I'm older than you by over a hundred years, yes?" As soon as he asked, he wished he could call the words back. Shit!

Kellen's growl echoed through his head. *"Pretty sure that's gonna get covered in the sit down. Be here within an hour and bring your mate."*

It wasn't a request. *"We'll see you then. Is the entire pack going to be there?"*

"You and your mate are safe and will be under my roof," Kellen promised.

"See you soon." Coti cut the connection instead of waiting for Kellen to respond. He knew if Kellen said they'd be safe, they would be. Whether they'd continue to be part of the Iron Wolves was still to be seen. He rolled his shoulders and finished his coffee, running his hand through his hair as he thought of where he and NeNe would go. He had enough money they could literally travel for however long they chose, find a place and settle amongst humans if they wanted. But, her bear was going to need other shifters to keep her level. He wanted to be all she needed and would do everything in his powers to be that. However, he wasn't a foolish pup. Some things a female needed,

a newly turned shifter, he alone couldn't provide. "Fuck," he swore.

"That doesn't sound too good," NeNe said.

His head turned toward the hallway where she stood wearing one of his shirts. His mouth dried at the picture she made. He could see her tattoo peeking out from the bottom. "Come here." He held his hand out, waiting. She came to him, her arms going around him like they'd done it hundreds of times. "No matter what happens, we'll be fine. You know the history behind the phoenix?" At her nod, he continued. "Like the phoenix, you and I'll rise, just as we've always done. Look at you, you're the original phoenix to me. You rose from the ashes more beautiful than ever. You're exactly the hope that can lift anyone. If someone would've asked me a year ago if beauty can come from a tragedy, I'd have said no. I'm not saying what happened to you is a tragedy, but it wasn't how I wanted to bring you into my world. Fuck, I'm probably screwing this all up." He took a deep breath, wondering how to explain.

She pressed her hand over his lips. "I get what you're saying. Granted, I hated the how, but I love where I am now. So, you just spoke with Kellen, and he's ready for this big powwow, right?"

He chuckled. "Pretty much. We don't call it a powwow, at least not to his face," he told her.

NeNe shrugged, the action made his shirt fall off one shoulder. If they had more time he'd strip her bare, right then, and there. "We need to get dressed and head there now."

His little mate took a step back, her grin positively wicked as she reached down and lifted the top off. "I seem to have nothing to wear. Whatever shall I do?"

Coti growled. "You're going to make us late, armina."

"Have you heard of a quickie?"

He lifted her up by the waist, slamming his mouth down on hers while he willed his jeans away. In a swift move, he was buried balls deep inside, hoping they wouldn't be too late to the meeting with Kellen.

Kellen sat in his large recliner, his fingers steepled while he waited for Coti and NeNe. Laikyn sat on the arm, her fingers sifting through his hair, petting him in a soothing motion. Goddess, he loved his mate. "They're late," he growled.

Laikyn laughed. "They're a newly mated pair. How many times do you think we were late to things? Oh wait, I think we can safely say we lost count to the point we no longer gave a time."

Several people laughed, while Kellen glared.

A knock on the door had everyone in the room quieting. "Enter," Kellen said.

Coti walked in first, pulling NeNe in behind him. Kellen was unsure if he'd bring the bear with him or not. He tilted his head, his nostrils flaring. The fact he could only scent wolf and bear angering him all over again.

"How the fuck do you do it?" he asked.

His enforcers stood around the room, ready to take action should the need arise. If only they knew.

The man was more of a threat than they realized. Coti shrugged but didn't come further into the room. "You want to send some of these guys outside to wait?" Coti pinned Kellen with a hard stare.

Oh yeah, he was an alpha. Kellen tapped his fingers together. He'd never bring Laikyn into a room full of dominate shifters either. "Out, everyone but Xan and Lake." He didn't need backup to talk with Coti and his mate.

The wolves were exiting, but then NeNe grabbed one of the younger wolves by the back of the neck, shoving him up against the wall. Kellen got up, a snarl escaping. "What the fuck is going on?"

Coti held his hand up, freezing the other wolves except Xan and Lake. "Erik you better explain before my mate rips your throat out in front of Kellen. Trust me, I'll have her back no matter what."

Erik's eyes widened as he looked at the other wolves who weren't moving. "Alpha, kill them. Don't let them get away with this."

Kellen quirked a brow. Erik was new to the enforcers, a young pup he wasn't sure would last in the role. "Why don't one of you start explaining what the fuck is going on before I get fucking pissed."

Laikyn touched his hand, their bond opening. *"I heard a whisper of something, but I wasn't focused on him at the time."*

"Me either," he admitted. He could easily tap into the young pup's mind but wanted to see what Coti and NeNe did next. Their actions moving forward would show him if they'd fit in with the pack, or not.

NeNe drug the kid toward Kellen, shoving him to the ground in front of him. "This kid has some crazy idea that you're going to kill me. He also stinks of my brother, which tells me he has terrible taste in friends. You want to kill me, Kellen?"

Kellen stared down at NeNe, her green eyes flashed to brown, then red before settling back to green. His mate gripped his arm. The scent of her worry had him reaching out through their link to soothe her. *"Easy, I've no wish to harm either of them."*

"She's a whore, alpha," Erik snarled, his wolf eyes tinged yellow.

He reached out a hand, touching Erik's forehead, soothing the wolf. Instantly, he wanted to wretch at the filth filling him. As the alpha he felt his pack, yet Erik had deadened his link to Kellen with drugs, taking up with humans and other shifters who weren't part of their pack. "Why?" he snarled.

Erik's glassy eyes glared up at Kellen. "Being low man on the totem pole isn't where I want to be. I'll never be anything here except a bitch. I'm too good to be your bitch," he spat, the liquid barely missing Kellen as Coti jerked the kid backward.

"How did you know?" he asked NeNe, ignoring Erik for the time being.

He listened to her and Coti explain about the evening before, narrowing his eyes as he thought of others in his pack feeling the same as Erik. He barreled through the kid's mind, searching for answers. What he saw made his wolf rake at him. Erik had been the only one in their group who'd been sneaking off, giving the other pack information. "You little bastard. You told them about my young?" he said in a low tone.

Laikyn gasped, her hand going to her throat. "Oh Goddess, no."

Finally, the kid began to understand the trouble he was in, the stench of his fear hitting Kellen. "Rowan and the others are watching them. All is well," he promised her.

"Let me handle the punk," Xan said coming to stand next to Kellen.

Kellen shook his head. "It is my duty, my right as alpha. Take him to one of the holding cells." The fact they now had several pissed him the fuck off. Their world was changing, yet it didn't seem like it was for the better.

Laikyn tugged at his shirt. "It's for the better," she murmured.

Looking into his mate's eyes, seeing the love and acceptance there, he had to agree. "Coti, we need to talk still. You and NeNe have a seat. Release the others. Please," he tacked on.

Xan laughed. "Can I record that last bit? I don't think I've ever heard him say please before."

When Laikyn opened her mouth to respond, Kellen pulled her in front of him. "Mon chaton, I suggest you keep that sassy mouth shut unless you want to find yourself over my lap counting."

The sweet scent of his mate's arousal filled his nostrils, making him groan. "Fucking hell. Why are we here again?"

Xan raised his hand to answer, but Kellen pointed one finger at him, silencing his best friend. Smart second, Kellen swore he wouldn't be held responsible for what he did if Xan cracked a joke. Breezy was too young to be a widow. Xan chuckled as if he knew what Kellen was thinking, raising his

middle finger to scratch the side of his nose, the
fucker.

Chapter Fourteen

NeNe and Coti sat down on the couch across from Kellen, the alpha scared the bejesus out of her. Both Kellen and Xan took the huge recliners, each of them were big and took up a lot of space. Her mate, which she was getting used to calling him, was every bit as big if not a little bigger.

"Can I get either of you a drink?" Laikyn asked.

Kellen groaned. "Baby, do you think this is a social gathering?"

Laikyn slapped Kellen on the arm. "Don't be rude. Drink?" she asked again.

NeNe licked her lips. "I'll take a water, please."

Coti shook his head. "Nothing for me, thank you."

"Did you drink from the vein already, vamp boy?" Xan asked with no outward anger.

She felt her bear still inside her. Something else stirred, making her pause as she looked at the other man. "You'll watch your tone and not speak to him as if he's beneath you, feel me?" Her voice didn't sound like her own, yet she didn't regret her words.

Xan, the sexy as fuck man blinked, focusing his blue stare on her. "Well I'll be a goddamned motherfucker, look at that." He pointed his finger at NeNe.

A growl swelled up from her chest. "I said, do you hear me?"

"No, you said feel me, which I am not risking any of my body parts to do. However, I understand and will adhere to your wishes," he said with a laugh. "Why are we always getting more alphas than betas?" He turned to look at Kellen.

Kellen tipped his head back, looking up at the ceiling. "I don't fucking know, brother, I honestly think I pissed off a Goddess or something." He sat up, pinning NeNe with what she knew was his alpha stare. "You got control of all your shit?"

She didn't take offense at his wordage. "I have control for the most part. Obviously, I could've killed that asshole earlier, but I didn't. Now, I haven't been tested in extreme situations like someone trying to harm me or mine. Ps. Coti's mine," she warned.

Kellen tossed his head back and laughed, then his hand went out, stopping Laikyn as she walked past him. "Of that we are on the same page. She's me and mine. Feel me?" he echoed her words.

NeNe looked at where his thumb rubbed up and down his mate's wrist, saw little goosebumps pop up on her flesh and could smell Laikyn's arousal in the air. "Oh god, can everyone smell me when I want him?" she asked, turning to look at Coti.

Her mate covered his mouth with one hand trying to hide his smile. "Armina, it's nothing to be ashamed of. Hell, we males can't hide our obvious need for you females either." He pointed out.

She so was not going to look to see if Kellen had a VDL.

"What the hell is a VDL?" Coti asked.

Heat crept over her, making her hyperaware everyone in the room was looking at her. "I'll tell you later," she whispered.

Coti picked her up, placing her in his lap. "Now," he said.

She put her forehead against his. "Visible dick line."

Xan's laugh had her groaning while Kellen sputtered. She was sure he said he was going to remember her words, which didn't comfort her.

"I can't wait to tell the other ladies about this. Here's your drink," Laikyn said, passing a bottle of water to NeNe.

"Just for the record, I didn't look to see." She took the cold bottle, rubbing it against her hot cheeks.

Laikyn patted her arm. "Rest assured, he totally has VDL all the time."

"Laikyn, get your ass over here and cover my visible dick, now." The big alpha roared, making his mate hurry over to him. Her husky laugh dispelled any thought she was scared.

"Watch it brother, you'll be getting led around by your cock in no time." Kellen shifted Laikyn to his thigh. "Now, I want to know the truth. Why don't you start from the beginning," he ordered.

She sucked in a breath, feeling as if something was pressing in on her.

"Stop it," Coti pushed out between clenched teeth, his hand ran up and down her back soothing her.

NeNe found it harder to breath while Kellen stared at Coti. Her hand went to her chest, gasping. "What's going on?"

"Take a deep breath and look at me," Coti instructed.

She looked away from Kellen, the suffocating presence receded, replaced by waves of love and reassurance. "You only need to do this when you feel another trying to force his will upon you. She's trying to show you," he murmured aloud.

Inside herself, she followed where he led, seeing the strength within that was reinforced by not only her bear but something else. "Oh my god, I'm," she stopped and stared at Coti, watching him nod.

"Yes, you are. I'll explain to Kellen and see where we go from here." He kissed her quickly, taking away any objection.

Taking a deep breath, he placed NeNe next to him. "My mother's family were hybrids, but different from the Cordells in the fact they were Gypsy wolves. Most wolves turn the same color as the hair on their heads, except a gypsy wolf. I, along with the rest of my clan, are all white when we shift. Had you never wondered about that?"

Kellen shrugged. "Honestly? It never crossed my mind. In our wolven form, you were a tough fighter, trustworthy, or at least I thought you were, member of the pack, and someone I relied on to protect others. You were part of the enforcers before I took over from my father but weren't part of the old way of thinking, which was why I asked you to become one of my enforcers."

Coti could hear the thread of anger in his alpha's tone. He couldn't erase what was, yet he wanted to explain. Staring the other man in the eye, he told him of his childhood, explained about his being kicked out. "You see, my mother hadn't fully mated with him, so he didn't receive her vampire strength like many mates. Back then, he claimed her because he said she was his mate. She knew he lied, but he was her one and only. Being a Gypsy wolf and a vampire, my mother and her clan, that's what they were called, settled in with the pack. She'd hoped that him being her Hearts Love, he'd eventually feel the same. She had me, who only made things worse as I got older and bigger than the man of the house. I was a threat he had to get rid of." Coti shrugged. Those years had been hell except he'd had his mother and her clan.

"What about her clan? Why did they allow you to be kicked out?" Kellen's wolf was on the surface, his nails lengthening.

He took a deep breath. "The clan was diminished to only my mother, her mother, and my aunt. My father's pack was a lot larger. My aunt had mated fully with a young shifter, but my father threatened them. Plus, my mother had my sister and brother, both were more wolf, not other like me. I knew if I left they'd all be happier, safer. I thought it would be no time before I'd find my mate and be able to come back. That's what my family told me anyway."

Kellen snorted. "Yeah, that's a crock of shit. Where are they now?"

"I've no clue," Coti answered. He truly hadn't cared after the first hundred years.

"Now, this is the question I need answered honestly." Kellen sat forward, his hands dangling between his knees. "Why did you hide your other side from us all these years?"

"After being kicked out of my family for being different, I roamed for years, decades, until I finally went to the Cordells for answers. The elder Cordell turned me away as well. Not Damikan, but his father. Being different has gotten me nothing but shunned. Finding a clan isn't something I ever searched for, but this pack called to me. I hadn't been searching so much as called here. When I landed outside of town all those years ago, your father was the first person I ran into. He looked me up and down, said 'wolf' in his deep baritone, then said 'well, come on then.' I followed him like a lost puppy and never left."

Kellen chuckled. "Sounds just like the old bastard. Man of few words is my dad. I'd say if you were a danger, you'd have already fucked some shit up. Although, now that you've mated, you'll be a little more on edge. You still want to be a part of the pack?"

Coti nodded. "Absolutely, but only if NeNe is."

Kellen stood, motioning Xan to stand. "NeNe, you ready to pledge to the Iron Wolves?"

NeNe licked her lips, nodding. "You're not gonna piss on me or ask me to like take a blood oath, are you?"

He groaned. "Armina, where do you get these ideas?"

She elbowed him. "It's in all the books."

"Hey, at least she's not asking about fucking Bambi then killing it like some people." Xan looked at Kellen who shook his head.

"I don't think I want to know what you're talking about." NeNe bit her lip.

Kellen growled, pinning Xan with a stare before turning to NeNe. "I don't know what books you read, but if there's pissing on one another, you need different reading material. Not that I'm judging if you're into golden showers or any other kinky shit." He grunted from Laikyn's punch to his arm. "Come here, you two."

"Err, no golden showers for me." NeNe shook her head as she spoke, looking at Coti who nodded in agreement.

Coti stood, tugging her to stand with him. He hated the way her legs shook. His fierce little warrior mate was scared at what she didn't know. They walked toward Kellen, their hands clasped together.

"Coti, you've been an Iron Wolf for years. I plan to have you around for a lot longer. More than likely you'll be here long after I'm gone. Do you vouch for your mate NeNe?" Kellen's deep voice rumbled, his alpha powers melding with the man.

"I do, alpha," Coti answered.

"NeNe, you're a shifter amongst shifters. Most here are wolves, but to us it doesn't matter what form you take or if you don't shift at all. Do you agree to protect pack no matter if they be human or other?" She squeezed Coti's hand, then nodded.

"I need you to speak, female." Kellen's tone was deafening as it boomed out.

"Yes, alpha." She blinked, feeling the heaviness trying to push her down.

"If you agree to become part of the pack, we connect mentally. Open up to me, NeNe. Giving me access proves you trust that I won't take advantage of that power."

Coti gave her fingers a reassuring squeeze, wanting to give her comfort, knowing she had to do this on her own.

His mate blinked, then he felt a wall come down between them, keeping him from her. Xan held up his hand, giving a slight shake of his head that kept Coti where he was.

NeNe allowed Kellen into her mind. His presence wasn't like Coti's, yet she didn't feel as if he was invading so much as just there.

"Thank you for your trust. I'll leave you now, but this is the link to me should you have need. I know this is all new to you, but all pack members can reach out to me at anytime here. You might want to mentally knock first in case I'm busy." His laughter made her smile.

"Will you be politely knocking as well if you need to speak to us?"

"Hell yes. Trust me, after accidentally interrupting that sick bastard Xan, I'll knock before interrupting anyone's mind."

NeNe blinked then nodded. "So, do I bow, kneel, and kiss your ring, or what?"

Kellen patted her on the head. "You'll fit right in here, NeNe girl. Alright, let's have a round of drinks, shall we?"

"If you mean be another disrespectful female who will forever be a pain in our collective asses, then bottoms up, brother." Xan agreed, holding his glass up with a smile.

"His mate must really like him," NeNe muttered.

"Nah, I give good head." Xan winked.

Kellen groaned. "What did I tell you about TMI, fucker?"

Coti wrapped one arm around her, grounding them both. Through her link with him and now Kellen, she felt like she was one of them. Even Xan and his dirty mouth, she knew he'd die to protect those he cared about. Her mate accepted a bottle of beer from Laikyn, then he lifted his bottle, holding it in the air. "Iron Wolves," he said.

In those two words, she felt accepted. Kellen swallowed his drink whole, sighing like he needed the hard bite of the liquor.

Xan sat his glass down, the empty glass clinking on the hard table. "Damn fine liquor, alpha."

Laikyn shook her head. "It's not even noon yet."

NeNe looked at Coti and his half empty bottle. "It's five o'clock somewhere, right?"

Coti grinned and leaned down to kiss her. "Damn straight it is. Besides, we're wolves. Takes a lot more than a drink or two to get us drunk."

She was pretty sure Laikyn mumbled something about a truckload, but Kellen had covered her mouth with his. Seeing how Kellen and the rest of the pack didn't shy away from touching their mates, whenever and however they pleased, made her feel a little better knowing they'd been aware of her response to Coti. She still had a slight bit of embarrassment knowing everyone would've smelled how much she'd lusted after him, but that couldn't be changed.

"I need to find my Breezy, too much sex going on in here," Xan announced.

Coti coughed, settling NeNe in front of him.

"You trying to hide your VDL?" Xan asked, quirking his right brow.

"Why don't all of you go out to the club and leave me and Laikyn alone so I can take care of my lady's needs." Kellen looked up from where he held his mate, his blue eyes brighter than she'd ever seen.

"NeNe and I have some things to take care of," Coti began only to stop when the door to the club burst open without warning.

"I just got a call from one of my feline friends. We've got trouble." Turo stood in the doorway, his eyes landing on Coti and NeNe. "Shit's about to go down, boys and girls. Let's get the females to safety and meet it away from here."

Kellen nodded, already moving toward the door with Laikyn next to him. "I'm getting my mate and kids together. Rowan and Lyric are with them now. Have you…" he stopped at Turo's grunt. "Of course you have. Alright, let's go."

NeNe pulled on Coti's hand. "They're coming for me," she stated.

"What do you mean?" Kellen asked, turning back to pin her with a hard glare.

She took a deep breath, linking with him and their alpha. His pride swelled at her show of trust and lack of fear. "Look at my memories. When he turned me, he wanted me. Not one of the other women, but me. I don't know why, but he was fixated on me when I started there."

Through her memories, Coti could see the other man's constant attempts to engage NeNe in any sort of interaction. What his mate didn't see, when she looked at him, was the way his eyes hardened, the entire thing flickering to the solid black of his grizzly.

Kellen flicked his gaze to him, nodded and turned. "NeNe stays with us. If he comes, it'll be her he's searching for."

"Meaning anyone within range of me is in danger. Maybe I should run?"

Coti growled, his wolf and beast denying the thought of their mate leaving their side. "You'll stay with me."

"I'm going to the lower level to meet Lyric and the kids. You go do alpha shit," Laikyn said.

"Wyck, you and Lou go with her, make sure she's safe," he ordered.

The bar was filled with a dozen Iron Wolves, all ready to do whatever Kellen ordered them. Coti felt the need to warn them exactly what they were up against. "We aren't facing a pack of just wolves. I know Mac's a bear, and I fought a lion. I scented wolves, so fuck if I know what else might be in that menagerie of a pack out there. They don't follow the same rules we do where pack is sacred. I fought a shifter who was beaten down, yet he was a beast I would hate to tangle with if he'd been free. If they have others like him, not on a leash, we could potentially be in for a bloody battle."

Arynn and his mate moved forward. The man had recently found his true mate and was the father to two preteen girls. "We ain't just a bunch of wolves either, Coti. My Sheila's a fierce dragon. Hell, little Joz is too, damned if that's not still freaking Turo out," Arynn laughed.

Turo flipped Arynn the bird while the tiny Asian woman named Joz stepped around his hulking frame. "Hi, NeNe, we need to have a girls' night and catch up. So much to talk about, starting with you being a bear, me being a dragon. Do you know the possibilities of that happening are less than…" Turo covered her mouth with his hand, then grunted before picking her up and kissing her silent.

"Seriously, she knows the numbers and will give us the rundown, later. For now, we need to head out. Ace said the fuckers were moving around, gathering up their strongest to take back their queen. I'm thinking that's you." Turo nodded at NeNe

His wolf rumbled while his beast pushed forward. "Over my dead body."

Stillness filled the air.

"Aw sheot, he's a vamp and a wolf. That's fucking awesome," Bodhi whooped. "Let's go kick some ass and call it done so I can get home. I was in the middle…" he stopped at Kellen's warning growl.

"Motherfucker, do not finish that sentence or so help me my baby sister will be packing ice between your legs." Kellen pointed his finger toward Bodhi.

Coti laughed at the big blond man who mimed zipping his lips while his eyes shined with mirth. "You realize we all sound like a bunch of damn idiots joking before we go out to cause bloodshed, right?"

Turo swung a gun over each shoulder before passing another to his mate. "Your point?" he asked.

"Just wanted to make sure we were on the same page."

"Same page, same book. Let's go. No misting for you and your vampiness. We go in as pack. What you do when we get there, or how you get it done, is up to you, but nobody's going rogue." Kellen slapped him on the shoulder, leading the way toward the door.

"I love this pack," Joz whispered.

"That's because you're my crazy little female. You best not get hurt, you hear me?"

Coti didn't turn to see what Turo and his mate were doing. If he had a choice, he'd wrap NeNe up in bubble wrap and stow her away from what was to come. One look at her stubborn face and any thoughts of shielding her left him.

"Such a fast learner." She pecked his cheek, then hurried forward and out the door.

Fuck, he was pussy whipped. Twenty-four hours properly mated, and he was wrapped around her like a boa constrictor would his prey.

"When we get back to your place, I'll wrap something else around you." NeNe said through their link, showing him an image of her lips wrapped around his dick.

He needed to get her to understand it was their place, and now, he was the one sporting a VDL, thanks to her.

Chapter Fifteen

NeNe tried to calm her racing pulse. The last time she'd been at the campground, she'd been attacked, twice. Gah, she really hated those memories. This time, it would be different. She wasn't your average human up against shifters who were ten times stronger than her. Her bear stretched in a lazy way. "I think my bear is tired."

Coti enfolded her hand in his while they rode in the back of Xan's XV. "Nah, she's shoring up her reserves for the coming battle."

She tilted her head to the side, wondering if the animals talked without them knowing. Coti must've read her mind since his smile was quick in coming. "They don't talk, but I know how my wolf is before a fight. When I need to expend energy, like many of us, we'd hit the cage at the club. Inside there, where you and the girls brawled, we can let go without shifting, yet our animals get to stretch within us.

Like now, my wolf knows he's going to get to come out and play so he's content to chill."

"My wolf is always stretching the restraints I put on him," Bodhi said from the front.

"Do you think it's because we were made, not born?" NeNe knew the other man had been turned when he'd been a child thanks to her connection with Coti.

"Nah, I think he just likes to let me know he's there." Bodhi turned back around, conversation seemingly over. "My niece wants a wolf in her. My sister hasn't decided. Maybe you can talk to them?"

A feeling of hope swelled within her. When she'd been in the Fey realm she'd gotten a glimpse of his sister and child, but Lula hadn't introduced them. At the time, she'd been a snarly bear. "I'd like that," she said.

"My niece said you looked like a cuddly bear who needed a hug." His eyes met hers through the rearview mirror, making her laugh.

"Yeah, I'm pretty sure I resembled a grizzly that needed to be put down."

Coti touched her leg, his touch warm through her jeans. "Even when you were snarling and frothing at the mouth, you were gorgeous."

She buried her face in her hands. "You didn't need to add the frothing part, did you?"

"It's best to have honesty in a relationship, my mate says. It's why she and I are perfect for each other." Xan nodded like he'd just extolled the best advice.

"Does your mate always call you on your shit?" Coti asked.

Xan looked backward, one hand on the wheel while he flipped Coti off. "Absolutely. If she doesn't yell at me at least once a week, telling me she's going to cut my dick off, I know I ain't doing something right."

She opened her mouth, then shut it. What the hell the man could do that would cause Breezy to threaten to castrate him weekly puzzled her. "Alright, I give. Why would she do that, and why do you enjoy it?"

The crazy wolf had one hand hanging over the wheel while he sipped on an energy drink, taking his time before he answered. NeNe was coming to the conclusion the wolf, although one of the most handsome men she'd seen, next to her mate, would make her crazy, too.

"You see, I like to take things slowly. Everything in her life moves at warp speed, but at our home, I set the pace. Sometimes, it drives her to say things that I then like to punish her for. Now before you get all up in arms, know that my mate is very, very satisfied by the time I finish." He winked back at her, his meaning clear.

"Let's pull the rigs over here and go in on foot. See those vehicles?" Coti pointed at a group of cars. "That's Ace and his team."

"We sure they're on our side?" Bodhi asked before opening the door.

Coti nodded. "Yeah, he has strong blocks, but I'm stronger."

"Stay outta my head, or I'll make sure you will wish for eye bleach," Xan warned.

"Trust me, I don't want to see any of your dirty bits, sicko." Coti popped the door open without waiting for Xan to reply, holding his hand out for NeNe to slide across to him.

She allowed him to help her down, taking in a deep breath. "Yuck, what is that smell?"

"That, my sweet newbie, is the stench of bad shifters," Ace drawled.

Coti held his hand out to Ace, pulling him in for a back-slapping-hug. "Thanks for the other night and for this. How many are with him?"

Dalton sighed. "About thirty, but most are green. He and his crew have turned humans. I would say only a dozen are born, not that the made ones are weak, but he's not giving them what they need to survive in the long run. It's like they're toys to them."

Kellen growled. "How did I miss this?" He waved his hand at the compound before them.

Standing upon the hill, they could see the layout, which was large.

Coti squeezed his shoulder. "I didn't even realize there were shifters there until I almost fell upon them. There's something or someone shielding them. Hell, probably both," he snarled. He thought of NeNe and the way she'd turned almost instantly instead of days began to make more sense. "Could there be Fae amongst them?"

A chorus of fuck echoed around them.

"I'm gonna give the Cordells a call. I know they don't want to leave Jenna's side, but we might need them." Kellen looked around, meeting each man's stare. "I'm not going to lose a single one of you because I was too confident."

Seconds ticked by while they waited. NeNe flexed her fingers in and out, moved her head back and forth like she was preparing for a fight. "Calm, armina," he whispered next to her ear. The waiting was getting to him as well.

"Yoohoo. Did someone phone a friend?" Lula asked, her pink hair pulled into an intricate bun on top of her head.

Coti blinked, staring at the tutu around the dragon female's waist. "Um, Lula, did you just come from dance class?"

Lula stood on her toes, twirling in a circle. "No, but I would totally rock at being a ballerina. Wait, do ballerinas rock?" She tapped her lip. "Never mind that. We gonna go slay some baddies who put bears in people who don't ask for them?"

The ground shook behind them as Creed arrived, splitting the concrete from the force of his landing. "Oops, my bad. Lula, can you fix that?" He pointed at the ruined area.

Lula smiled like he just gave her the golden key, then the ground smoothed out. "Bam, who's your dragon?" She held her hand out for Creed.

The man moved through them, tapping Lula's raised palm. "You are. We doing this, or what? Damien and Lucas will be along shortly. Probably right after we do all the hard shit, so they can pretend they helped."

A stir to Coti's right had him shoving NeNe behind him. Damien appeared with Lucas, scowling at Creed. "You're a damn cheater."

Creed blew on his fingers, the black nails growing longer. "There's two of you. How is it cheating if I shove one of you in order to beat you to where we are going?"

Lucas lunged toward his brother-in-law, while Creed hopped backwards laughing. "You shoved me into a damn realm, asshole."

"Did your brother get you out?" Creed blinked innocently back at them.

"That's not the point, you dick. What if I couldn't have traced him, or the realm you sent him was like the soul fuckers one?" Damien roared.

Creed rolled his eyes, looking toward Kellen. "Listen to them, crying like babies. You made the bet you could beat me here. You didn't lay any rules out. I, however, do have enough sense to not want to upset my Raina by offing one of her beloved brothers. You're welcome, by the way." He turned and began walking toward the compound.

"Can I kill him?" Lucas asked.

"Many have tried, all have failed. You're welcome to put forth the effort, though. I would like to inform you I'm recording your threat for future use." Creed didn't turn, his finger tapping his head.

"See, that's why I love that crazy bastard," Kellen said.

"Why, because crazy is as crazy does?" Damien growled.

Kellen nodded. "Pretty much." He began following Creed.

"You realize that wasn't a compliment, right?" Damien asked.

The alpha held up his middle finger on both hands. "Potato, tomato as a great female says."

Lucas groaned. "He's quoting our Hearts Love. We're so screwed."

Coti stared after the two craziest men he'd ever met, then looked at Damien and Lucas. "Thanks for coming."

Lucas nodded. "When this is over, we've gotta talk."

"It's never a good thing to hear those words coming out of anyone's mouth, let alone one of you," NeNe said.

Damien bent until he was eye level with NeNe, making Coti's beast rise. "Easy, cousin. She's more than shifter," he stated.

"We'll talk about it later. For now, let's go before those two get us all killed."

"Nah, they're likely to fit right in, until they don't want to." Bodhi moved around them. "However, it's best if we don't let them try it."

The humans from before, who'd manned the entrance, slept inside their pickups or outside in tents. Coti shook his head when he noticed the mound of liquor along with the stench of drugs. "How is it the law hasn't come out here to at least check on this shit?" He nudged a beer bottle with his boot, keeping NeNe close to his side.

"I saw a few local officers at the races. Maybe they pay them off."

Her nonchalant tone didn't fool Coti. "I'm sure there's more you're not telling me," he growled.

She blinked up at him. "You guys are removed from a lot that's going on that doesn't directly involve you and your people. If you have money, you can do just about anything you want and get away with it."

Coti stopped walking, planting himself in front of his mate. "You're one of us, too."

"Now I am, but only a couple weeks ago, I was on the outside looking in. I was this close to being gone." She held her thumb and finger an inch apart.

His wolf pushed forward, making his voice sound deeper. "I'd have hunted you to the ends of the earth."

"You were still in denial, remember?" Anger and hurt rolled off her.

He wanted to deny her words, but she was right. "I'm sorry." He couldn't say anything else.

She pulled his head down, kissing him with the kind of passion he was coming to expect. "You're forgiven. Let's go kick some baddies asses."

Several of the wolves groaned at her words. Coti bit her lower lip, licking over the wound before setting her back on her feet. "Damn, I'm a lucky motherfucker."

"Don't you forget it," she agreed.

NeNe was having third and fourth thoughts when they tromped through the campground. The others called it a compound, but it appeared more like a huge camp for fuckups. Like a traveling circus, except there weren't any fun rides for kids. Now that she knew it was a shifter encampment, she understood how they'd been able to get everything in place without an issue. The huge track they used for quarter mile races was one of the main event areas with the octagon cage fighting on the other side. Mac, the leader, had his platform seating area directly in the middle of both, raised up high enough he could overlook the entire place without having to get down. She shivered at the thought of him and his enhanced hearing and sight.

"What's wrong?" Coti asked, pulling her closer to him.

"I was just thinking about the times I'd thought I was out of Mac's eyesight or hearing. When in truth, I probably wasn't. More than likely, he heard Gracie and the others tormenting me and heard about my plans to leave after my last night. I'm betting he knew those bitches were going to fuck me up." Her bear flashed images of the women bleeding beneath her claws.

"Makes sense. If you were injured, you'd probably agree to a turning. In his fucked-up head, since he's the alpha here, if he turns you, then you're his by right and might."

She rubbed her hand over the mark Coti had made, glad the gruesome one Mac had inflicted had been repaired by her mate's bite. "I'd like to rip his balls off and shove 'em down his throat."

"Ah, another blood thirsty female. I love it. Alright, children, looks like it's gonna be a rumble." Creed pointed toward the area where races took place.

"Why aren't they rushing us?" NeNe asked.

Creed pointed at his head. "I've cloaked our presence. Figured we could get the lay of the land first, make sure there's no surprises like the last time."

Blinking, she wondered what he was referring to, but none of the men said a word.

"I feel Dark Fae here, but I can't pinpoint where," Lucas stated, putting his hands on his hips with a scowl on his face.

"What's a Dark Fae?" NeNe asked.

Creed walked back to her, shaking his head. "Hold please," he said, then touched her forehead.

She thought she heard Coti yell no, but her mind was immediately swamped with knowledge. Images flowed into her along with years of life she had no way of filtering. Her head felt full, yet her bear and the other that seemed to reside within her soaked up the knowledge, taking it in and settling.

"You're better prepared, yes?" Creed stepped back, his left arm out.

She looked to see Coti pushing against an invisible wall. "Yes, thank you. Can you let him go?"

Creed looked over at Coti. "You gonna play nice?"

Coti flashed his teeth that didn't look wolfish but had fangs. "I'll fucking kill you if you hurt her."

"Blah blah blah, heard that one before. Clearly, I'm still here, and now, your female has the knowledge she needs to be an asset instead of a liability. You're welcome." He released the invisible hold he had on Coti.

NeNe placed herself between the two men. "I'm fine, truly. Strangely, I actually feel better. Remember all those questions I had?" She waited for him to nod. "I don't think I have anymore. At least not about what I am or how to be the new me. Thank you, Creed."

"See, she's smart. I already said you're welcome." Creed turned and walked away as if he hadn't a care in the world.

"He's not a shifter, is he?" she asked Coti.

Her mate looked up at the sky. "Goddess no. He's most definitely not a shifter. Come on, that's a discussion for another day."

"How do we want to do this? Surround them and then have Creed do his thing so they know we're here?" Xan asked.

"That seems like a bitch move. I say we do like in the old days. We're pack, we go in as one and slaughter them all," Turo growled.

Joz sighed.

NeNe blinked at the iridescent black scales flickering over her friend's skin. Damn, here she thought she was a badass apex predator. Joz had her beat if she was a kickass dragon.

"I'm going to keep the humans asleep even if they're on the enemies' side. We don't need to bring that type of attention down on us." Creed pointed to the right where tents were set up. "There's a couple dozen in there. We'll take care of them afterwards. I don't feel anything below us, so looks like it's go time, kids." He clapped his hands twice; the boom sent a blast of wind toward the area, making dirt and debris fly at the shifters who were gathered.

Chapter Sixteen

Coti allowed his powers to rise, forming his katanas. "Did you soak up how to use these?" he asked NeNe just before the barrier went down. At her nod, he handed her a set, then created another. "Stay by me. If you have to shift, do it." Looking into her mind, he double checked to make sure the knowledge was there, satisfied that she was prepared.

"If you're focused on me, you'll get hurt or worse. Trust me, I'm not stupid," she said with conviction.

Through their link, he could see she was ready for battle thanks to Creed and him. The blast echoed around them, followed by a silence that was almost deafening. As if in slow motion, the shifters in the center of the track turned as one, facing the threat. Coti pointed one of his katanas at Mac. "You're dead," he growled.

Mac's eyes widened for only a moment. "Kill them all."

The shifters who came at them were slow to change from man to beast, their animals misshapen. Several what the fucks were growled out from his fellow brothers, but none hesitated to take the animals out.

Coti took a hit from the side, bumping into NeNe who was busy slicing the arm off a bear. The huge beast roared, his face coming too close to his mate's twisting body. Before Coti could intervene, NeNe flipped backward, slashing upward as she went, coming back to make a clean slice, taking his head. The huge animal lay with his innards out, his head feet from him, while NeNe prepared for the next attack. Goddess, she was amazing.

"You might want to take that one out, he looks to be getting up." NeNe pointed at the one who'd bumped into him.

"Shit!" Coti shoved his sword into the animal's chest. The thing had clearly been damaged by one of his brothers.

He and NeNe continued forward, keeping in their human forms. He lost count as to how many animals had fallen. A sadness welled within him at the senseless loss of life. The bastard that was Mac had turned the humans into something they shouldn't have been. A growl split the air, but he and NeNe were busy with a group of men who were born not made.

"Hello, bitch. You really should've chose our side. We'd have treated you like a queen." A huge mountain of a man said, spitting on the ground.

NeNe rolled her eyes. "Oh, and as the queen would I have been passed around to all of you to fuck?"

The three men laughed, elbowing each other. "You'd have liked it." one of the men said, grabbing his dick.

"See, there's not even a VDL, which means I most assuredly wouldn't have," NeNe laughed.

At the narrowed eyed stares, Coti knew things were going to go south, fast. "That would be visible dick line, which none of you have," Coti informed them, pointing his sword in the general direction of their crotches. "I have a proposition for you, boys. You can walk away and promise to be good little bear cubs, and we'll let you live another day. Or, you die."

He made sure his tone suggested the latter. These men would've gladly taken NeNe against her will, brutally. For that alone, they deserved to suffer.

As one, they attacked, their focus on his mate. Big mistake. NeNe ducked, her elbow slamming into the side of one of the men. The force of her blow sent him into Coti. Using his feet, he kicked him backward, the sound of ribs cracking made him smile. He stalked the man, intent on killing him quickly.

"Gotcha."

Coti turned to see Mac dragging NeNe by the hair.

He twisted the man's neck, killing him quickly then was up and chasing Mac. The other two men moved to intercept him, shifting into their bear

forms. Coti tossed one of his katanas at the one
who'd spoken first, embedding the sword deep into
his chest, the tip coming out the other side. The
other sword went flying, taking out the bear's right
eye and continuing through the back of his head.
Coti didn't stop to see if they fell or not. Mac was
fast, even though he was dragging a struggling
NeNe. The scent of Dark Fae hit him.

"Creed," he yelled. The other man was halfway
across the football sized area, but Coti knew he'd
hear, or at least, he hoped like hell he did. If Mac
had the help of the evil ones, he'd need more than
himself to defeat the bastard.

His beast rose, roaring out in denial. Coti shifted
to mist, moving faster than he could as man or wolf.
The scent of NeNe's fear hit him but mixed in with
it was also determination. What was she doing? He
had a feeling his mate was allowing herself to be
taken. "*When this is over, I'm going to tan her
damn hide*," he promised.

"*Good luck with that*," Creed said, invading his
thoughts.

Instead of debating with the man, Coti grunted. "Can you smell the evil?"

A moment passed, then Creed was the one to grunt. *"Yep, stinks worse than that one time my father had a horde of Krumkin Demons fighting over dinner."*

Coti had no clue what a Krumkin Demon was and was sure he didn't want to know. As the son of Satan, Creed had seen and experienced things none of them would want to. *"I'm assuming that's pretty bad."*

"Yep. Come on, looks like he's hiding in one of those rail cars. They must've figured you boys were allergic to silver or some shit since that thing is coated with it."

Coti saw NeNe and Mac heading for the last car, her little body struggling behind his, the scent of her blood hitting him like a bomb going off. He lost the ability to stay in his current form, dropping to the ground behind them, startling Mac into releasing NeNe.

"Hey, asshole, why don't you pick on someone your own size?" Coti cracked his knuckles. He moved forward intent on taking Mac's head off.

"Coti, he's got my mom," NeNe whispered scrambling to her feet.

He pulled her next to him, eyeing the bastard up and down. "So, I'll kill him and get your mother out of here."

In her memories, when they'd bonded, he'd only seen glimpses of a woman NeNe referred to as momma. Other memories showed NeNe as a young girl, wishing her mother was there, and deep sadness, but he'd assumed she'd died. Not once had he imagined she'd been taken by this bastard.

"He says she's a shifter now, but he won't help her unless I go with him." Her voice quavered.

Through their link she felt a tug. *"Do you feel your mother, armina?"*

"I felt drawn here from the very beginning. Something called me here, but I didn't know what. There was always a tug that kept me here even when I knew I shouldn't," she answered.

"You can scent a lie. When he spoke, did you smell truth?"

"Yes," she said.

The conviction made him nod, knowing he would do anything to help her save her mother.

"You two done with the chit chat. You want to save your bitch of a mother, you come with me alone. If not, she dies." Mac shrugged, his bear form rippled beneath his skin.

The last thing he could do was allow his mate to go off with the other male. "You know I can't let her go without me."

Mac inhaled, no doubt searching for his mating mark. "I'll erase you from her the same as you did me. Besides, it'll be a family reunion." He whistled, like one would do to call a pet.

Two men Coti recognized ambled out from behind Mac. Their black eyes belying their humanity had been replaced with bears. "It's time you came home, girl," NeNe's father growled.

NeNe's spine stiffened when her dad and brother lumbered out. They smelled like bear and drugs, just like the other shifters they'd encountered. Behind them, she could hear roars and screams as her pack battled. She wasn't sure where Creed had disappeared to, but she'd felt him before Coti had dropped to the ground. She was glad Mac hadn't realized Coti was anything other than a wolf. "Oh, is this home now, daddy? Last I checked it was a trailer on the other side of town. Of course, this tin can might be a step above that piece of shit."

Her father lunged forward, hatred burning in his dark eyes. Mac held out his arm, clotheslining him. A roar broke from her dad. The fierce sound of an angry grizzly in a rage coming from a human male was all kinds of weird. "Yikes, you should get that checked out." She motioned to her dad on the ground twitching.

Mac held up a device, laughing when her father stopped moving. Her brother moved forward, glaring at her. "You're nothing but a whore, you know that?" He lifted the older man off the ground.

"Your opinion of me doesn't mean dick. How does a son let his mother suffer?" Her bear growled, thick black claws burst from her fingers.

"Enough, you come with me, now, or I give the signal for Gracie to kill your mother. You remember Gracie, don't you?" He smirked.

Rage burned through her at the mention of the other woman's name. "She touches my mother, I'll kill her. No, scratch that. I'm going to kill her regardless of what happens."

Mac laughed. "I knew you'd be a great bitch for me. Let's go." He held out his hand.

She looked at the big palm held out, then at a silent Coti. Their connection was oddly quiet. "I trust you to get me out of there," she whispered.

When he didn't respond, she touched his face, shocked at the strange coldness. Turning toward Mac, she walked around him. "Touch me, and I'll cut whatever appendage you're using to do so, off."

He grabbed her arm, unaffected by her threat. "Did you see how your supposed mate just stood there? If you were mine, I'd have battled to the bloody end before I allowed my female to walk away with another. That's the difference between a mangy wolf and a bear."

The cold man who stood so still was a shell. She didn't know what Creed and Coti were up to, but she knew he wouldn't allow her to walk into danger alone. A soothing presence spread throughout her mind. The words 'Mate' reverberated in Coti's voice, giving her the strength to allow Mac to lead her through the maze of rail cars.

Her mother had left when she'd been a toddler. NeNe had very little memories of her except she cried a lot, which had made NeNe sad. Then one day, she'd left and not come back.

"Here we are." Mac lifted the flap of a large tent.

She smelled Gracie and the other two females along with her mother and a male.

Gracie stared at her, a smile playing at her lips. "Oh, you come back for another round?"

NeNe let her bear push forward, the long thick claws extending. "You want to play, puppy?" Three wolf bitches against one bear didn't seem like a fair fight, but NeNe felt sure she could take them all.

"Why did you make her a bear instead of let one of us turn her?" Gracie snarled at Mac.

Mac was across the space and lifting the woman into the air by her throat. "You don't question me, ever. Get your skanky asses out of my sight until I call for you," he roared.

She would've laughed had her attention not have locked onto the couple in the corner. The big man crouched in front of her mother, his eyes wary. "What's going on?" His deep voice rumbled through the room. "You said you'd let her go, if I did what you asked."

"I need her for one more thing, then you both can go."

NeNe heard the lie and wondered if the other shifter could as well. "You need my mother to lure me here, then what? You going to kill her?"

Her words had the shifter protecting her mother growling louder. "Over my dead body. We've given you what you wanted."

A moan came from the cot on the floor. "Alaric, what's happening?"

"You both have served your purpose." Mac motioned to someone behind him.

The acrid scent hit her. A Dark Fae was helping him. The thin man moved forward, reminding her of the guy from the Poltergeist movies. With blurring speed, she placed herself between him and her mother. The animal within her allowed her to use the other being's powers, knocking the man backward.

"Well, isn't this interesting?" he said, tilting his head to the side, his words came out a hiss.

She felt the shifter behind her moving but didn't take her gaze off the man or Fae. Where the hell was Coti? Her eyes caught Mac moving, his hulking size eerily quiet as he tried to sneak behind them.

"Others are coming." The man her mom called Alaric shouted, his warning came before she smelled them. Mac had clearly called the bitches back along with a few others. Fucking great. He needed the cavalry for little ole her and the shifter protecting her mom.

"If you call me kicking your ass interesting, then yep, interesting it is," she agreed, drawing his attention away from the couple. A shift to the left showed her Mac was moving in.

"Alaric, is anything keeping you from fighting?" she asked.

"Not anymore."

She wanted to look back and see what her mother looked like. The urge to do just that almost had her missing the hand moving back and forth, weaving a spell she was sure. "Yo, Creed, a little help here," she yelled.

"Got him," Creed called, snatching the little man out of the air.

NeNe covered her mouth at the sight of Creed's hand entering the tent through a hole, his huge red face smiling like a kid on Christmas Day. "Um, thank you."

"Aw, would you look at that. I didn't even have to say you're welcome first. Be back shortly. Don't do anything I wouldn't do." He stood up from his crouched position, making her spin around on a gasp. "Oops, forgot to tell you not to look down. I guess I should've said not to look up. My bad."

She laughed, then the sound froze in her throat at the sight that met her eyes. Mac and Alaric were facing off. Although Alaric was big, Mac held a woman in front of him. NeNe knew without a doubt the woman was her mother. She also could tell she was a shifter, and she was pregnant. By whom was the question she didn't have an answer to. If Mac felt it was his right to claim any female in his clan, then he would no matter if they were mated to another. Of that, she had no doubt.

"Mac, you really don't want to do that?" Coti said, coming up beside her.

The sound of her mate's voice gave her strength.

"Why is that? You wipe out my clan so now you going to offer me a way out?"

NeNe's mother opened her eyes, dark brown orbs of fury stared at her. She gasped, wondering why there was so much hate and rage directed toward her. "I'm going to take my breeders and leave. That's right, little girl. Your mama's a breeder, just like you were meant to be."

Alaric growled, his wolf rippling over him, white fur coating both arms. "My mate is not your breeder, you sick son of a bitch. You kept her drugged, forcing her bear out so the human side of her had no respite."

She stared at Alaric, then at her mother. "How long?" she whispered.

The man didn't pretend to not understand. "He grabbed her over twenty years ago. Your father took the money he offered and walked away. I assume he thought he'd never see either again."

Mac laughed. "Your father was a dumb ass then, and is an even bigger one, now. He offered you up on a platter. It was fun to watch you, a little human in the middle of predators, while your mama was so close to you."

Her mind worked furiously, wondering why he was standing there talking. His Dark Fae was taken, yet he acted as if he had an ace in the hole. *"He's got a plan or another weapon,"* she warned Coti.

The ground shook beneath her feet. "Is that an earthquake?"

Mac tossed his head back, bellowing out a laugh. "You threw in with the wrong side."

As soon as he finished speaking she heard Kellen yell. The battle that seemed to have ended began again outside the tent. Only this time it sounded as if they were surrounded.

"You didn't think I was that dumb, did you?"

Coti grinned. "Pretty much." He nodded toward her mother.

The crazy look disappeared, her mom blinked then she smiled showing huge bear teeth. Her nails were long black claws. NeNe blinked, shocked that Mac didn't seem to notice the woman he held was partially shifting in his hold.

"Jules," Alaric whispered.

Mac heard the whispered name, but it came too late, her mother reached behind her with one clawed hand. The roar Mac elicited as she ripped at his groin had the men in the space covering their own anatomy.

Jules didn't stumble away as Mac released her and fell. Her hand fell to her side covered in blood. She locked eyes with NeNe, a tear fell from one eye then the other. "Renee?" she asked.

Nobody called her by her full name. She'd been NeNe since she started school. However, she heard the longing in her mother's voice. "Mama," she whispered.

Uncaring they were both a little battered and bloody, NeNe wrapped her arms around the woman she'd thought left her all those years ago. "Oh god, you're so thin." NeNe held her mother tighter.

Alaric came to stand behind her mother, his hand resting on her back. "She'll get stronger," he assured them.

The sound of battle stopped outside as a sonic boom rent the air.

"Creed," Coti said.

Kellen and Xan walked inside with several others following, their faces hard. "Tell me he's dead." Kellen asked.

Coti pointed to the side and a still breathing Mac. "Not yet, but I think he wishes he were."

Alaric moved in front of Kellen, stopping him from reaching Mac. "It is my right to end his life for touching my mate."

"And you would be?" Kellen asked, pinning Alaric in place with his stare.

Alaric looked around the tent, his eyes falling on Coti. "I'm Alaric Chlodwig."

"What the fuck?" Coti growled.

Chapter Seventeen

Coti looked at the man he'd fought that they'd called Champ. "Explain?" he ordered.

"You're not my alpha, brother." Alaric stood to his full height.

"Brother? How is that possible?" He inhaled, taking in the familiar smell of his mother and father. "Fuck!" he roared. "You can have this." He ripped the ring off his finger. "I'm not taking over anything. I don't want nothing to do with that bastard or his shit."

Alaric looked at the ring Coti had thrust into his hand. "I don't want this," he said, a loneliness echoed in his words.

For the first time, Coti looked inside his brother's mind. He saw his mother laughing with a young Alaric. As he searched, he could see his parent's happiness had indeed been true with Alaric, unlike with him. When he'd left, Alaric had been an infant. "What do you want?"

His brother looked at Jules, then at Coti. "I want my family. I came here looking for you but found her. She's mine, even if you don't want to accept me in your life."

"Well, shit, I think this is a discussion best held somewhere other than the middle of a blood bath." Kellen's tone brooked no argument.

Alaric stared at Kellen. "You're his alpha then?"

Kellen nodded. "Yep. You got a problem with authority, son?"

His brother laughed. "You do realize I'm much older than you?"

"Age don't mean shit to me. Grab your woman and let's go. We'll figure this out back on our turf. I have a feeling this place is about to get a cleansing. Ace, you and your crew joining, or what?" Kellen turned to face the felines.

Ace shook his head. "Nah, we'll just stick around and make sure there's no stragglers lurking about."

NeNe's head went up, a growl emitted from her before she launched herself out the back of the tent. He tried to discern what she'd smelled that had her bear going off, while chasing after her. He came to a skidding stop as he, Xan, Bodhi and Kellen glared at the three females corralled around Gracie and her girls.

Lyric waved at Xan. "Creed said all was clear and that our girl might need some help. Voila, the bitches are here."

Coti scratched the side of his nose. "Aren't they the bitches?" he asked pointing at the snarling trio.

Syn shrugged and blew a kiss at Bodhi. "Hi, honey. Be a dear and hold my earrings." She tossed a set of huge gold hoops toward her mate.

"Karsyn, you get hurt, and I'll beat that pretty little ass," he warned.

"Fucker, I'm right here." Kellen pointed at his chest.

NeNe moved next to Lyric and Syn. "Wow, you girls sure do know how to show up late to a brawl."

Coti contained his snort as the three females shoved each other around, then turned to the women they planned to beat down. Next to them, Gracie, Kris, and Paula were like Amazons, yet none of the Iron Wolves females showed an ounce of fear.

"Since you three like to gang up three to one, we thought we'd even shit out." Lyric waved at herself and Syn, then NeNe.

Gracie huffed. "How's that evening things out?"

Lyric smiled a wolfish grin. "'Cause we're a lot badder than you three. We don't need to gang up on anyone, let alone a little human to prove we're tough." Lyric reached up, not missing a beat and brought Gracie's head down to her knee. The movement was smooth, fast, and vicious.

Coti almost missed it.

"I taught her that," Xan said from beside him.

"That one's mine," NeNe yelled at Lyric.

Lyric released a bleeding Gracie. "My bad. Here you go." She tossed Gracie to the side, ducked a swinging blow aimed at her head from Paula, and tackled Kris.

Coti and the others stood with their arms crossed while their females commenced to beating the shit out of the shifter women who'd hurt NeNe. His mate landed on top of the one he knew had caused the most damage to her, raining down blow after blow on the other woman. NeNe was so focused on hitting and cursing while she pummeled Gracie, he feared she wouldn't see the woman's hand shifting into that of her wolf. He opened his mouth to warn his mate but froze as Kellen shook his head. "Let her be." He tipped his head toward the fight.

NeNe grabbed Gracie's arm, snapping it backward. The crack loud to his shifter ears. Gracie's howl of pain was even louder. Minutes later, the Iron Wolves' females all stood back from their opponents, a little battered, a whole lot bloody, but they smiled.

Lyric held up her fist, knuckle bumped Syn, then NeNe. "We the baddest bitches," she announced, then howled.

The rest of the pack howled along with her.

"Time to go home." Kellen clapped him on the shoulder.

Coti waited for NeNe to come back to him. She stopped by where his brother stood with her mother, her hand shook as she ran it over her mom's head. They had a lot to talk about, but now that Mac and his merry bunch of fuckups were taken out, they had time. He met Alaric's gaze. The empty black orbs were replaced with green, the same as his. Fucking family. His kept growing.

"You ready?" NeNe asked, staring up at him.

"Yep." He'd face anything as long as he had her with him.

Coti and the others cleaned up before gathering in the office at the Iron Wolves. His brother sat holding Jules who appeared to be getting stronger with every passing minute.

"So, how is it that you're his brother?" Xan asked. Breezy slapped him on the arm, but he just stared at Alaric, demanding an answer.

Alaric shrugged. "I guess I take after my older brother. My soul was very determined long before I came into this world. Even when I was just a little sperm surrounded by all those other little sperms that were stronger than me, had a longer tail than mine, swam faster than me, I fought my way through. I even got knocked into other sperms, it was a battle all the way, but look at me now, I made it to the end."

"Holy fuck, another one?" Kellen gazed up at the ceiling.

Laikyn climbed into his lap. "I think you're getting paid back for all your bad deeds."

Coti closed his mouth with the help of NeNe's hand. "Did you just refer to yourself as a sperm fighting other sperm?"

Wyck handed him a beer. "Yeah, he did. Freaking weird. I like him."

Alaric nodded. "Thanks. It was a tough time to be a sperm." He winked.

Jules sighed. "Please stop speaking of sperm and you in the same sentence, honey."

Coti laughed as his mate used his hands to cover her eyes. "Where's Creed when I need a distraction?" she asked.

"Damn, did you get an eyeful as well?" Syn asked.

Several men growled around the room. NeNe turned and kissed Coti. Ah, his little mate was most definitely in for a reminder of whom she belonged to. She may have been unclaimed, but from now on, he'd make sure everyone knew she was his.

They stayed at the club for a lot longer than he wanted, yet he gave NeNe a chance to be with the pack. Jules yawned, making Alaric stand with her in his arms.

"Do you have somewhere to go?" he asked his brother.

"I have many homes. My instinct called me here, though. I thought it was to find you and maybe it was, but I think it was also for her." He kissed Jules on the forehead.

"Renee, you're a wonderful young woman. Exactly who I wish I could've helped shape you into being. As parents it's our job to teach our children," she whispered. "Children give us the ability to appreciate with grace the lessons they teach us as well. I was robbed of that with you." Jules wiped a tear

NeNe hugged her mother. "We'll have time to get to know one another. Life didn't go as you planned, but we can swerve with it. I love you." She put her hand over her mom's slightly rounded stomach. "I really hope you're having a girl; my last brother was a dick."

Her mother blushed. "Alaric says she is. Our children are the mirrors that reflect back to us the shadows of ourselves. They show us the shame and our own insecurities. I would've loved and nurtured you as a child, ensuring you grew as an adult to be the brave woman you are today. I'm going to do everything in my power to make sure I am for this one."

"You will be," Alaric assured her.

Coti's brother grunted. If they wanted to know for a fact, he could find out, but until he was asked; he wouldn't intrude. No matter what gender, he noticed his mate wasn't asking if his brother was the father or not. Again, Coti could tell them that answer but didn't since nobody asked.

He couldn't wait to get her home and show her how much she meant to him. If and when they had children, he'd do everything in his power to be a great example to them. Nothing like his own father. He'd seen through Alaric's memories happiness and love, given and received from both his mother and father. For a brief moment, he'd felt bitter jealousy at the life his brother had compared to what he'd grown up with.

Holding the door to his truck open, he winced at the bruises on NeNe. "I swear, I'm going to wrap you in bubble wrap. You seem to be a walking bruise." He ran the back of his hand down her cheek.

NeNe held his hand to her face. "These don't even hurt. Actually, I feel pretty fucking awesome after handing Gracie her ass."

He chuckled. "There is that."

"Hey, you got a minute?" Alaric called out.

Coti settled NeNe into his truck, wondering what his brother wanted. Kellen had already offered him the use of one of his vehicles, so he could get back to where he'd been staying before Mac had captured him. He'd seen how the Dark Fae had been used to enthrall him in order to keep his animal at bay while he fought, holding Jules over his head. What else was there to say?

"I'll be right back." He kissed NeNe on the lips, tasting beer and her unique flavor combined.

She sat back and sighed. "I'll be right here." Her eyes closed as he shut the door.

In three strides he met Alaric in the center of the parking lot. "What's up?"

Alaric tilted his head to the side. "You didn't ask about our parents or sister?"

"I heard you say you were the last of our family. I'm assuming they're no longer alive?" He ignored the ache in his chest.

His brother nodded. "That's right. When father passed away, it was his time as happens with shifters due to age. I think he still thought our mother would bond with him fully and extend his life. She asked him throughout the years if he would ask you for forgiveness, but he was a stubborn male until the very end. With mother on one side and me the other, he did."

Coti waited but Alaric didn't continue. "He did what?"

"He said he was sorry for what he'd done. Said it was his pride that kept him from reaching out to you, up until several years prior. However, he said he did try to link with you, but there was no bond. He said his heart nearly felled him when he'd thought you'd died. I realized in that moment he'd sent men out to find out what happened. Those men returned weeks later with a tale of a man who could do amazing things but wouldn't tell us where you were." Alaric paused. "I never heard our father speak with so much pride as when he talked about you, his first born Ulric. Your name means Wolf Ruler, did you know that?"

Coti laughed. "Some ruler I am. I never wanted that damn title, not like he did."

Alaric sighed, then looked Coti in the eyes. "I was never able to measure up to you. When we fought, even though my wolf was locked down, I really wanted to defeat you."

A grin split Coti's cheeks. "I kinda got that, what with the way you tried to take my head off. Look, it's been long enough to hold grudges. I wish I could've met the man you called father and felt love for, but that's not what I had. For you and me, we have today, tomorrow, and whatever else we're given, moving forward. Sure, we could hash over the past, but what's that going to get us but angry.

You pissed because I don't give a shit about an old man, and me pissed because you had a happy childhood." Coti put both hands on Alaric's shoulders. "Your mate in there, along with your cub, needs you to focus on them and your future. You need a pack to keep you level. I know Kellen will welcome you, and NeNe wants to get to know her mama. All that other shit is just that, shit. You think your sperm was strong, clearly mine was too. Now, let's hug it out so I can go fuck my mate."

His brother mimicked his pose, gripping his shoulders. "You realize I'm now your father-in-law, right?"

"Ah, fuck me. Don't even start with that bullshit." He tugged Alaric in for a hug. "Get outta my face, brother," he laughed. For maybe the first time, he actually felt a familial connection blossoming. He'd severed the one he'd had when he'd been turned away from the Cordells. Damn, thinking of the wolpires made him realize he still had another conversation that needed to happen. "I know you didn't get any of the vamp blood from

our mother, but you're still cousin to the Cordells.
When I have a chitchat with them, you're coming
with."

Alaric nodded. The poor bastard had no clue,
which Coti planned to keep it that way until it was
too late. Maybe having his baby brother as a shield,
he wouldn't have to deal with them, much. One
could hope.

"*Keep thinking that,*" Creed murmured in his
head.

"Fuck. Get out of my mind," he roared out loud.

Alaric and NeNe stared at him. He pointed at his
head. "Creed." The one word was all he had to say.

They drove home in silence, each lost in their
own thoughts. He wanted to find out where she was
mentally after all the revelations of the day. Her dad
and brother hadn't made it out of the campground
alive, which in his opinion was a good thing. Most
of the shifters who were made had to be put down.
The ones who were salvageable were now in the
care of Ace and his crew. Kellen had seemed

relieved to not have to deal with a menagerie of shifters. If he was being honest, he was too. Their pack had a lot of changes recently and could deal with less stress for the foreseeable future. Half-crazed made shifters that ranged from lions, bears, to wolves needed a smaller pack, something Ace was willing to handle.

"You're thinking awfully hard over there." NeNe rolled her head on the leather seat to stare at him.

He'd never get tired of looking at her even when she was sporting bruises. "How do you know I'm thinking?"

She reached across the space and rubbed between his brows. "You get this crinkle right here," she explained.

Coti grabbed her hand, kissing her fingers. "I'll try to think quieter."

"Hmm, I like your thoughts." She turned toward the front as they pulled into his drive.

Neither said another word while he parked inside the garage or while he came around to open her door. As she went to slide out, he reached in and took her into his arms, exhaling when she snuggled into him. Her warm breath fanned across his neck, making his dick instantly hard.

At the security panel, NeNe placed her palm over the sensor, a beautiful smile brightened her face when the door slid open. "I love that," he told her.

"What?" she asked.

He strode through the house, stopping at the fridge for two bottles of water. He placed the cold beverages in her hands, then continued. "I love the way you smile. I love that you're here with me, that I get to wake up with you beside me."

They entered the master suite, and he paused. "Is there anything you want to change here?"

She looked around the room. "Not right now. Well, I want us naked, but I'm pretty sure that's not what your eeep…" she squealed when he made both of their clothes disappear.

"Your wish is my command, armina." He took the water from her, setting them on the side table next to the bed. "Anything else you wish for?"

NeNe's eyes went down his body, stopping at his erection. "There's something I really do want to know." She began, then scooted onto the bed, turning until she was on her hands and knees. Looking over her shoulder, she licked her lips. "Does this bed make my ass look big?"

Coti tossed his head back laughing. His mate had a wicked mind, but goddess he loved her. "Hmm, I think I need to get a closer look." He moved closer, the smell of her sweet arousal teasing him. Seeing her creamy white ass in the air, begging to be touched, Coti reached forward and gave her a swat on first one cheek then the other, making her yelp. Before she could scramble away, he bent down and kissed the red flesh. "Beautiful ass."

He pushed her forward, closer to the headboard, then eased down on his back, wedging himself between her thighs. Hands locked around her hips, he moved her back and forth, licking and sucking her pussy until she came with a keening cry. Just as he was preparing to start all over, his mate growled and launched herself down, taking him inside her in one swift move.

"Goddess, yes," he groaned.

She moved up and down, setting the pace, her head tossed back. Coti needed more. Flipping their positions, he caged her below him with his body resting on his forearms next to her head. Staring down at the woman who held his soul, he slowed his thrusts. Her lips were moist from where she'd licked them. He bent, licking over her top lip, which was plump and made the perfect bow when puckered. Next, he traced her bottom lip, then delved inside, tangling with her tongue. Their bodies moving together and apart slowly, until the need for more overcame them.

NeNe's eyes darkened, not to that of her bear, but of need. He lifted her legs up higher on his hips, hissing as her nails dug into his shoulders. With one hand, he grabbed first her right, then her left hand, pulling them above her head. The move made her chest lift, her hardened nipples rubbed against him with each thrust. "So damn gorgeous. My balls ache," he growled.

"Fuck me harder," she demanded.

Coti let go of her hands, leaning back on his haunches. NeNe lay with her arms above her head, her legs wrapped around him, completely on display. "You want it hard?" he asked.

She nodded.

"On your hands and knees." He didn't allow her to maneuver. Using his strength, he had her flipped and in the position he wanted, pressing her face to the bed. "Hold on, baby." Coti slammed back inside her, his cock bottoming out over and over as he did as she ordered. He was so close to coming tingles were racing up his spine. While he still had an ounce of sanity left, he released her right hip, smoothing over her stomach and down to the hardened nub. Within a few swipes of his finger, her inner walls began to clench, contracting around him.

"Yes, faster, Coti." She slammed her ass back into him, her hand pressing against his between her legs.

"Show me what you need, how you need it." He covered her hand, moving both their fingers over her clit while he fucked her harder, faster, pistoning in and out like an animal.

Her inner walls clamped down on him so tightly he was sure he saw stars. The constant milking drew his orgasm from him with a roar. "Love you, NeNe. Always will, my heart forever."

"Oh god, I think you killed me," she muttered, shoving hair off her face sometime later.

Coti still had his semi-erect dick inside her and had no plans to leave his favorite place for the foreseeable future.

NeNe snorted. "What if I need to go to the bathroom?"

"Do you?" he questioned lazily.

"Not the point," she said around a yawn.

He jerked a sheet over them. "Get some rest, then I'll see about letting you out of bed, after."

His mate laughed, but she pulled his arm tighter around her, then slipped his hand between her thighs. "Fine, keep your hand where I can feel it," she giggled.

Coti didn't see how he was going to get any rest, but hearing his world, the only female for him make a little snore, he realized he'd do anything for her. Besides, holding onto something as precious as her pie corner of succulence wasn't a chore.

"I'll hold your fornicating tool for you next time," she mumbled.

Yep, he was definitely a lucky bastard.

Want to read about Jenna, her Wolpires, & the birth of their twins?

Keep Reading!

Epilogue

Jenna glared at her mates. "Why are you back here? I told you to help my wolves. Go, I'm not having the nuggets until I know everything is okay with them." She breathed out steadily, feeling one of her precious babies moving down.

Lucas sat next to her on the right. "All is well with them. We left after seeing all safely back to the club."

"Woman, our babies want out, and your body wants them out. Stop being stubborn and let's do this," Damien ordered.

She looked behind one of her mates, blinking at Lula. "Are you wearing a catcher's mitt?" A pain seized her, making it impossible to speak. Son of a monkey's butt. Poor Laikyn giving birth to four. "You two did this." She pointed at her stomach, then grit her teeth on another wave of pain.

"We can take away your pain," Lucas offered.

"I told you I was doing this like humans, and I'm gonna do it." Why she was doing it was stupid, but she had said she would, and she would.

"Alright, its time for you to let me see where you're at, Jennaveve." Belle moved around Lula, shaking her head. "I've finished the courses and could be a baby doctor if I so chose, which I am not, I just wanted to reassure you."

"Hello, two doctor hubbies here." Lucas waved a hand at he and Damien.

Jenna clamped down on his hand, making him turn a weird shade of blue. "You are my mate, not the doctor, today. You and you," she pointed at Damien. "are to be up here, not watching my vagina stretch out to the size of…holy shitake," she yelled.

"Looks like we're ready to start pushing. On the next contraction, I want you to bear down like your going to the bathroom." Belle sat in front of the bed wearing a set of light purple scrubs, a darker pair of latex gloves on and even a mask hung around her neck completing the outfit.

Jenna focused on the crazy that were her people until the pain hit, then did as instructed, even though she feared she really would accidentally drop the kids off at the pool like she'd heard Breezy talk about. Who the heck wanted to shit in front of their mates while giving birth, and who decided to call it dropping kids off at the pool?

Lula was breathing in and out, counting to ten, the hehe hoo gave her another thing to think about.

"Good job, I can see a head. Just relax and on the next one, do it again." Belle sat, the ever-resilient mother dragon, waiting.

Two more pushes, and out came her first baby. She watched as Damien and Lucas both touched her, each man working together to cut her cord and open her airway. Her lusty cry made Jenna's eyes fill with tears, but another pain hit her. "Oh," she whimpered. She hadn't cried out since the beginning. Her mates, she was sure, had a hand in controlling the pain, but at the moment she didn't care.

Lula's hehe hoo started again, then she gasped.
"Give me the baby and help mama."

Jenna didn't know what was going on,
everything seemed to be fading. She tried to blink to
get Damien and Lucas into focus, knowing she
needed to be the one to push their baby out.
However, the last thing she saw or heard was a tiny
cry from her daughter in Lula's arms, then darkness
came.

"Where am I?" she looked around at the empty
space. A glance showed her flat stomach, and her
hand went down, pressing against where she'd held
her precious babies.

"Welcome home, Jennaveve."

She spun, facing the Goddess. "No, I don't want
to be here. Send me back, please." She reached out
for the female who'd given her so much, falling to
her knees on a sob. "I can't leave them. I didn't
have enough time, Goddess." Her body rocked back
and forth, tears falling from her eyes unimpeded.

The Goddess ran her hand over Jenna's head.
"Sssh, I know. It's not your time, child. I took you
away because you're a stubborn fool. You're not
human. You can't do things the human way. Yes,
you, like human females, can give birth in a similar
way, but you are Fey. Your physiology isn't the
same inside. You can move through realms. Can
humans? You can shift time. Can humans? So many
things I can name that you can do, that the human
counterpart, and even our shifter females can't. For
you to be on Earth and go through a birth like a
human, almost killed you. I need you to remember
that although you love all your people, you're not
like them. For your children, and your own sake,
you must never forget that ever again. Do not raise
your precious children to think they are either, for
this lesson you have learned needs to be one they
don't have to suffer through."

Jenna nodded, embracing the soothing love the
Goddess gave her like a mother's arms wrapping
around her. "I promise, I'll never make the same
mistake again."

The Goddess helped her stand. "I'm sending you back now. Your mates and friends are understandably distraught. I'll send you back a few seconds earlier. You were dying, Jennaveve. Remember that. When you look into Damien's and Lucas's eyes, you will see the torment they suffered at the thought of losing you. I will not erase that for it is a lesson you all need to learn."

She wiped her tears away, nodding. "I understand. Thank you."

"No, thank you, Jenna. I could not fathom losing you."

A gust of air sent her back. "Is she okay?" Jenna asked, startling everyone in the room.

Damien and Lucas both fell on their knees next to the bed while Belle held one little bundle and Lula held another. Jenna ran her hands over her mates' heads. "I was foolish," she whispered. Opening her mind, sharing her memories with them.

"Never again," both men vowed.

What they were swearing to, she had no clue, but if it was her never delivering babies on Earth again, she agreed. Never having more babies? That was yet to be decided. She flipped the blanket back, intending to get up.

"Female, are you crazy?" Lucas put his hand on her chest, halting her.

Jenna placed her own hand over his. "The Goddess healed me." She waved her hand down her body.

All evidence of the birth was gone, not an ounce of pain echoed in her being. Oh, she remembered what it had felt like, and vowed to do what she could for her friends like she'd done with Laikyn when their time came to give birth, but she felt as good as new.

"Do you realize you literally took a good hundred years off my life?" Lucas placed his forehead on hers, a tear slid onto her face from him.

She wiped away the moisture with her thumb. "I'm sorry," she choked.

He kissed her gently on the mouth, then made room for Damien. "You're our world. My light dimmed when I thought we'd lost you." His big body shook as he wrapped his arms around her.

The sound of twin cries brought all their heads around to see Belle and Lula bouncing back and forth. "I think they're hungry."

Jenna looked down at her breasts which seemed to be filled. "Bring them to me, please." She settled back onto the bed with Damien on one side and Lucas on the other. Each man helped her latch their child onto her nipple, then stared as she fed their babies for the first time. With her twin girls nestled in the crook of her arms, her men beside her, Jenna swore she would be the best mother, best Hearts Love, and best Fey Queen.

"There's a crazy wolf banging at my head, love." Lucas helped her lift one of the girls up and began to pat her back.

Damien snorted. "He's been doing that for the last couple hours."

She'd been too focused on her babies. Her mind had shut everyone out as she'd given control to her mates and Lula with strict orders to be there for her friends, no matter what. "I'll take over," she announced.

Her mates' unhappy growls made the girls fuss, so they stopped. Jenna patted both babies on their tiny rumps. *"Hello, Kellen,"* she said through their link.

"What the hell happened? My heart nearly stopped when I felt our bond snap, then come back. My boys are going crazy, and I am about to charter a damn jet to find your ass," he growled.

"Do you have low jack on me?" she laughed, excited to hear his voice. It had been hard not being able to help him and the wolves the last few months.

"Jenna," he warned.

She looked at Damien and Lucas. "Brace yourselves, we're going to have company."

Having all her strength back, she told Kellen to gather his children, and whoever else wanted to come for a visit, and that she'd blink them there. "I want to check their fingers and toes."

Damien chuckled. "I think all mothers do." He carefully unbundled the child he held while Lucas did the same to his. She touched each girl's face as they lay on the big bed in front of her, then placed a finger into one of their hands. "They've got good grips already."

Lucas kissed her cheek. "Strong like you."

She gasped when she spotted the tiny heart shaped white birthmark on each girls' hip. Her finger traced each one, checking for any sign of injury. "Is this normal?"

"Yes, love, they're both perfect. That's an angel's kiss." He kissed the tip of one finger, and then, touched the mark on each girl.

Lula and Belle smiled from across the room. "You did good, Jennaveve," Belle said.

"You scared the devil out of me," Lula said.

Jenna laughed as Belle said it was a good thing since Lula didn't need the devil in her.

She swaddled the babies back up just as Kellen and the pack were ready. "I think we need a bigger space." She waved her hand, increasing the room by three times the size, adding couches, chairs, and rugs for the babies.

Kellen strode over with two chunky boys in his arms, their bright blue eyes staring down at her girls.

Lucas put his hand out. "No claiming babies, boys." He shook his finger at Jagger and Jaxon.

"What're their names?" Laikyn asked, carrying her twin girls Everleigh and Enzley, both girls rested against their mother, unlike their brothers who looked ready to jump out of Kellen's arms.

Lucas picked up one of the girls and turned to face the room. "I present to you, Miss. Willow."

Damien lifted their other daughter, then stood next to his brother, motioning for Jenna to stand between them. "And our other little princess is Miss. Piper." At the sound of her dad's voice, Piper opened her eyes.

"Oh my, they're purple like Jenna's," Lyric said with awe.

"This one's are too." Lucas nuzzled his nose into Willow's neck, waking the sleeping baby.

As soon as both girls were awake, Jaggar and Jaxon, who Kellen had placed on one of the large furry rugs began crawling toward them.

"Incoming," Rowan called out. He held his daughter in his arms, laughing.

Jenna knew when Creed and Raina arrived as the little boys scrambled up Kellen's legs.

"So sorry we're late. We were with Liv and...oh my god, they're the most beautiful babies in the world. Holy mother of pearl, lock up your daughters now, brothers." Raina kissed each girl on the cheek, cooing inaudibly.

"Too late," Kellen announced, holding his boys who stared at Creed.

Raina rubbed her stomach. "I'm so glad I'm having a boy."

Creed walked over to Jenna and kissed her cheek. "My mother said you're very blessed as are the girls."

She thought of the little hearts on her babies and wondered if Creed would recognize them. In all the times he'd gotten naked, she hadn't taken the opportunity to check out his nude form. The mark of an angel was distinct, and she was sure that's what her girls had.

"I suggest you keep it that way," Lucas said, their connection allowing him to read her thoughts.

Jenna grinned. "Nobody could measure up to you two," she promised.

Creed coughed, words that sounded like bullshit ringing in the room. Jenna looked around at her friends, the people she had sworn to protect, and knew without a shadow of a doubt they were her people now and forever. Each and everyone had been through some sort of trial and made it out the other side the victor, stronger than they'd ever been. She liked to think she played a small role in their lives and knew without them in hers, she'd only be a shell of a Fey. Now, she was brimming with love and joy and owed it to those who surrounded her. They might not all be related by blood, but their ties were forged through hell and were stronger. She sent a prayer up to the Goddess, thanking her for the life she'd been given and promised to never take for granted all that she was.

"Welcome to the family, little ones." Kellen said, kissing first Willow, then Piper, his boys touching each girl gently.

Yes, they were all welcome in each others' homes, and would always be for as long as she was the Fey Queen.

The End

Want to read the Fey Queen's story and see how she found her men?

Dark Embrace - Buy Links

Dark Embrace
Dark Legacy Book 1

Jenna rolled to the side, the taste of copper filling her mouth making it hard to swallow. She squinted, trying to figure out where she was without making too much noise. The room was huge. Like something out of a fairytale. The thought had the breath freezing in her throat. Her hand went to her cheek, feeling for the cut that had burned like acid soaking straight to her bones. When her fingers felt nothing other than smooth skin, she exhaled, hoping it had only been a nightmare. "Then where the fuckity fuck am I?" she whispered into the quiet of the room.

Shoving the blanket off her legs, Jenna scooted to the edge, her first thought was to blink her way back to her realm now that her mind was clearing. With every inhale of breath, she knew her guys were near, but she couldn't get a clear read on where exactly. Damien and Lucas Cordell, the princes of, well, she wasn't exactly sure what as their father was the Vampire King who was mated to a wolf shifter. Being the eldest of their children, and twins, she guessed they were next in line to take over if he should ever step down. The last time she'd seen the powerful king, he was no closer to releasing his title than she was. Being the Fey

Queen for thousands of years was something she was proud of, yet it was also a burden. The memory of the time when the Goddess had revealed herself to Jenna came flooding back to her in a rush, making her feel lightheaded.

The garden of the Goddess was always a place Jennaveve felt she could go to when life, or more aptly, the fighting, became too much. Today, she was bone weary of all the warring between her kind and the others in the Fey Realm. Watching friends become enemies. Lovers become the complete opposite as they, along with families, destroyed each other, all over their thirst for power. The need for more. Always more, whether it was magic or land, it was always bloody and filled with the stench of death, and she was tired of watching, waiting for it to come to her door. "Dear Goddess, I'm ever so tired," she sighed.

"Ah, my sweet Jennaveve, you are far stronger than you give yourself credit for," a lilting voice whispered over the lilac fields.

Jenna jerked into an upright position, searching around her for the source of the voice. Oh, she knew who the speaker was, had heard the Goddess in her head hundreds of times in the three centuries she'd been alive, but not once had she actually thought to hear it out loud. Maybe she was hallucinating?

"You are quite lucid, child," the Goddess laughed. The sound like silver bells, only much more—magical.

She wasn't sure if she should stand, or kneel, or bow. Heck, she wasn't sure which direction to face or if she should face the ground and beg for forgiveness. Her entire body quivered out of fear. What had she done to bring notice from the Goddess?

"You should do none of the above, my sweet. Sit, let's take a moment and enjoy the quiet before the storm." The Goddess's soothing voice was like a caress.

Her mouth went dry as she stood. "I'm sorry for…interrupting your space," Jenna sputtered. Dear Goddess, she was speaking to the Goddess.

Holy crap! A golden glow became almost solid, projecting the most beautiful form Jenna had ever seen, eclipsing everything else and stealing her breath as she stared.

The Goddess waved her hand. "No apologies. Sit with me."

Fear had her doing as she was told without question. The ethereal woman sat next to her, their legs almost touching as she took a blade of grass between her fingers. "What would you wish for if you had just one wish, Jennaveve?"

A lump formed in her throat as she thought of what to say.

"There is no right or wrong answer, only the truth," the Goddess instructed.

Knowing the being next to her would know if she didn't speak from the heart, Jenna licked her lips. Her mind spun. The first thing most would ask for would probably be power, but Jenna didn't crave the same as the rest of her kind. She'd always been different, which made her more of an outsider in many, if not most, circles, even in her home with her family. What she truly wanted, if she could have one wish, was something her Fey family would scoff at, but in her soul, was what she yearned for. Without hesitating, she took a deep breath, taking in the sweet scent of lilacs, and released it. "I want to be able to rest without fear and have my people do the same each night."

A golden hand brushed lightly over the top of her head, making the tension that had invaded her as she'd spoken ease. Instant lightness flowed through Jenna. "All my children should feel this way," the Goddess agreed. "This is why you were born to be queen. You, my sweet Jennaveve, are my greatest creation. You are destined to be the Queen of the Fey Realm. From this moment on, you will be the one to bring peace to all of Fey, and with my powers inside you, you'll be the strongest, most powerful being in all the realms."

"I don't...what do you mean?" Jenna whispered, her throat barely allowed the words to come out as knowledge began to flood her. A strange power pulsed within her veins.

"All of the beings here in Fey are my children, but you my child, you were created with more. You are a part of me, created by me, from me, for this purpose." Her lilting words were filled with power. The Goddess ran her palms around Jenna, speaking words that Jenna couldn't interpret, but as the last words rang out, a surge had Jenna crying out, forks of white hot power sent her falling onto her back.

"What's happening to me? We are all your children," she gasped out. More knowledge and power filled every fiber of her being, shredding her from the inside out. Jenna feared she was going to explode as the pain increased.

"It's okay, Jennaveve. I'm sorry for the suffering you are feeling, but it's almost done. The power has always been inside you. I just needed to unlock it." The Goddess shook her head; a tear rolled down her cheek completely unnoticed by her.

The urge to reach up and wipe the moisture away had Jenna trying to lift her arm, but the movement was too much effort.

"See, that is why you are the Queen. Yes, all here are my children. However, many years ago, too many for me to recall, I had a vision. In it, I saw the need for one such as you. In the way of my kind, I created what I knew would be the savior of this realm and beyond, then waited for the right time. You needed time to…well, for lack of better terms, experience enough of life to mold you into what you needed to become, before bestowing the mantel of what you were destined to be. That time is now, Jennaveve," the Goddess said, her words echoed around them with authority.

Finally, as the pain was subsiding, and she no longer felt as if her body was being shredded, she was able to take a deep breath without feeling like thousands of knives were digging into her. Moving her head didn't take as much effort, so she rolled her neck to the left and looked at the Goddess who was sitting calmly staring off into the distance. "What do you want me to do?" As the last word left her mouth, the Goddess touched her forehead, more knowledge filled her head like a tsunami. Then, just when she was sure her brain was going to explode, the pressure was gone. The bright rays of the dual suns were replaced by the two moons.

"It is time for you to rest now, for tomorrow you will show all what it means to have you as their queen."

Jenna could only blink, or at least she thought she did. However, the last thing she remembered was loving arms lifting her from the ground, wrapping around her and rocking her back and forth, gently, like a mother would a child. Words that sounded like a song floated through the air singing her to sleep. For the first time in hundreds of years, Jenna rested without fear.

~Present Day~

As her feet touched the ground, her legs wobbled then gave out. The feel of the cold tile slapping against her palms had her crying out even as her knees slammed into the unforgiving surface. "Shit," she moaned.

Why nobody had come at her cry was a little alarming, but it gave her a moment to get her bearings and stand up or attempt to stand. Hell, she'd take leaning on the bed while standing on her two feet at the moment as a step in the right direction. "You can do this, Jennaveve," she cheered herself on, but in all reality, it took more effort than she'd thought. "What the hell happened to me?" A fine sheen of sweat covered every inch of her body like she'd been working out for hours.

She remembered allowing herself to be kidnapped by a scumsucking vampire freak who'd mated with a panther shifter. The jackhole had wanted to kill his wife while his daughter watched. In his mind, which she still wanted to gag when she thought about the things she'd seen in his memories, the bastard wanted to teach his daughter a lesson or something. She rubbed at her temples as she thought back to the night in question.

Yes, she'd only been in his clutches for a couple hours. Her Iron Wolves were coming. She remembered sensing them, along with Damien and

Lucas. Everything was going according to plan, until a stranger came out of the darkness.

Fear had her looking around the quiet room, opening her senses in search of the being who'd come out of nowhere that night. His essence reminded her of the Cordell's only darker. Sinister. Goddess, she'd never felt such a being before and didn't want to ever again. A shiver stole up her spine. "Please tell me I'm not his prisoner?"

No, she couldn't allow herself to think that way, or she'd lose whatever sanity she had left. She needed to get to the Fey Realm and recharge. Once she was back to herself, she'd return and speak, or mate, whatever the wolpires did. Jenna nodded, then opened her heart reaching for her home. When nothing happened, and she was still leaning against the large four-poster bed, real anxiety nearly felled her. "I'm just overly tired. Can someone come and help a girl out." Like before, she reached out for one of her friends, only a vast emptiness met her quest.

Never in all her years had she not been able to communicate with whom she wanted, when she wanted. Never had she been unable to move between realms. Until now.

The door opened to the right, it's slight creak like a shotgun in the quiet room. Jenna raised her right hand, preparing to defend herself. With what, she had no clue as she could barely stand on her own two feet, but she'd be damned if she'd go down without a fight. Of course, she'd probably go down in a stiff wind, but the young female who entered paused, her startled gaze appeared friendly.

"Good afternoon, miss. I came to check on you. We weren't sure you'd be awake just yet. Let me go get…"

"Who are you, and where am I?" Jenna demanded hiding the tremble that shook her by forcing rigidity into her body.

Eyes as wide as a baby doe, the girl kept one hand on the door. "I'll just go let the others know you're awake. Is there anything I can bring for you?"

Jenna wanted to run across the room and make the girl stay, but her body was shaking from standing already. "Please, tell me where I am."

"You're in the guest wing, of course. I'll just go tell them you're awake." The maid began walking out the door.

"Wait. Who are you going to tell?"

"Damien and Lucas of course." The girl bowed and backed out as if she thought Jenna was a crazy person.

Hearing the names of those who were destined to be her mates, had her relaxing. If she was in their home, then she was safe. They'd help her figure out why she couldn't access the Fey Realm or reach out to anyone. The way she was feeling, it was as if she was—human.

The air stirred near the large fireplace. What made her look she wasn't sure, only that she knew something seemed familiar. She expected to see Damien or Lucas, heck her heart actually sped up at the thought of seeing them. However, her body froze as the man from the darkness appeared. "What are you doing here?"

She whipped her head toward the door the young girl had gone out. Although Jenna's senses weren't on track, she was sure she'd been a human, especially since it was daylight. The being in front of her came out of the shadows, allowing her to get her first real glimpse of him without the cover of night or a trick of him keeping his identity hidden. Oh, he was gorgeous, there was no doubt of that. But what was most startling was his resemblance to Damien and Lucas.

"Hello again, Fey. You're looking slightly ill. Are my...family not treating you well?" His eyes flashed from obsidian to red. Where her men had gorgeous eyes that she wanted to get lost in, this mans were cold and lifeless.

His words finally registered. "Your family?"

He raked his claws together, making them clack in a way Jenna was sure he did to scare his victims. *Newsflash asshole, I've faced bigger, badder, uglier, and hopefully deadlier foes*, she thought.

"I'd love for us to stay here and chat, but I fear the big guy is waking, and well, I'm not in the mood for a reunion just yet. By the way." He looked toward the doorway. "Sorry, my pet. I don't usually use females as pawns, but in this instance, it's a must." He flew across the room, eliminating the space separating them.

Jenna fell back against the bed, nearly falling to the floor on her ass. His quick reflexes kept her upright. "What the hell are you talking about?" She pressed her hand to his chest, trying to put space between them.

He shook his head. "You'll find out in due time, my pet. Now, we must go before father-what-a-waste awakens."

She knew the telltale signs of magic and could feel it as the man in front of her began to manipulate the fabrics of time and space. "Who are you?"

He flashed her a smile, white teeth with two canines much longer than the others prevalent. "My name is Khan, son of Zahidda. Bastard son of Damikan at your service."

The door flew open, giving her hope she'd be saved. The sight of Damien and Lucas had her shoving harder against the rock hard chest. "Let me go, asshole. I'm not your pawn." It was like trying to move a mountain if you were a mere human. Goddess, she hated being so weak.

"Jenna, flash away," Damien growled.

"Ah, but your female can't. It seems I'm her cure, little brothers," Khan taunted.

Lucas stepped forward. "Who are you, and what do you want?"

Khan tilted his head to the side. "You have nothing I want. Tell your *father* I'll be in touch. Oh, here," he tossed a necklace onto the bed. "He'll know who I am with that. If not, then you're little plaything will become mine, until I tire of her."

Blackness swirled around Jenna as she heard both Lucas and Damien roar her name. A sick feeling hit her square in the gut, one she knew all too well. Goddess, the memory of the first time she'd come into contact with Damien and Lucas brought a shiver to her. Lucas had been injured and she'd been called to heal him. As soon as she touched him an electric shock had gone through the two of them until it had found Damien, connecting them for all time. The knowledge that they were hers, and she theirs was as clear as glass, but she'd held them off thinking she needed to fix what she'd deemed broken. Now, faced with the possibility of never seeing them again, Jenna cursed herself for being foolish.

Khan was playing a game with the Cordells. One only he knew the rules to, and he had zero compassion for anyone getting in his way unless he could use them for his own gain. Jenna just happened to be exactly what he needed in order to hit back at the man he felt deserved it. Shit, she so could use her Fey powers, or even her bestie Kellen right about now. Or even better, if she'd not been so stubborn and mated with Lucas and Damien, instead of waiting, then none of this would have happened.

"Well, what ifs do nothing but make big girls cry over spilled milk," she muttered to herself.

"What?" Khan asked as he opened the portal allowing light to filter in.

She blinked a few times. "Huh?"

"You mumbled something about girls crying and spilled milk." He carried her over to a couch and set her down. His gentle touch and actions at war with his words to Damien and Lucas.

The light airy room reminded Jenna of a lake cabin, one that families would go to on vacation. "Oh, um, nothing. I talk to myself sometimes."

Khan shrugged his shoulders. "Make yourself comfy, you'll be here for a spell or two." He winked.

A growl rumbled in her throat. "Hahaha, very funny."

He was next to her in a blink. "No, I'm not funny at all. What I am is deadly. You'll do best to remember that." He raised his nails, the longer lengths looking ominous now, reminding her of the night he'd cut her cheek.

"You did something to me when you sliced my cheek open." If he was going to kill her, she'd at least know the hows and whys.

"I didn't realize I'd poison you the same as those ghouls. I spelled these." He clacked his nails together before continuing, "to kill with maximum efficiency. I thought I'd scented something different on you and was just going to take a taste. When I smelled my...the Cordell's blood in you, I realized the chance to finally exact justice on their father was now."

Her world righted itself as she realized why he looked and smelled like her men. "You're their brother?"

"Ding ding ding. Give the girl a prize." Khan walked away, his stride not quite as smooth.

"But, how? I mean, are you?" She was at a loss for words. She'd met Damien and Lucas's parents, Damikan and Luna, and couldn't imagine either of them giving up one of their beloved children. He'd called himself the bastard son, yet it didn't equate with the man who was known as the Vampire King, the one she'd met.

Khan turned around, his eyes glowing red. "Damikan seduced my mother then left her for his queen, the shifter bitch. My mother was ruined in the eyes of her clan, tossed out like trash since the Vampire King wouldn't acknowledge her or me, her bastard son. We had to fend for ourselves, fight for everything we could get, including the ability to sleep without fear we'd be staked at sunrise. All the while, his greatness lived in his grand home with his Hearts Love and created a new family, while me, his eldest son was a beggar in the streets. The things my mother had to do, in order to keep us safe until I was old enough to help, would turn your hair grey. Would you like me to tell you some of them, Fey?"

Jenna swallowed, knowing what he was implying. The thought of anyone, man, woman, or child being forced to do anything made her want to rip the nuts off of the ones who did the making. "No, I don't need the details. However, I don't believe for a second that Damikan knew. He's an honorable man."

No sooner had the words left her mouth before she found herself against the stone floor, an angry Khan looming above her. "You don't know anything. What have you ever had to suffer?"

She wanted to reach out with her powers and soothe his pain away, but had nothing except her arms, yet she didn't want to touch him. "I'm sorry, Khan."

He flashed across the room. "They'll come for you, and when they do, I'll kill them and then, Damikan will know what suffering is."

Jenna gasped, a spark of her powers flared to life at the thought of Damien and Lucas being hurt. "Over my dead body."

Khan raked his gaze over her prone form. "That can be arranged as well."

In a blink, he was gone, leaving her on the cold floor with nothing but a small bit of her former powers. "Goddess, wherever you are, help me please." The last thing she wanted was for her guys to try and save her, only to be hurt, or worse, killed in the process. Khan had powers that rivaled that of Damikan, only darker. No, she'd find her Fey spark and save herself, then somehow, she'd figure out what the fuckity fuck happened all those years ago. How the heck could Damikan have fathered a child, a son, and left him with his mother without giving both of them his protection? By her calculations, he was thousands of years old at the least since Damien and Lucas were over three millennia. Luna was going to rip his dick off. Jenna smiled in spite of her situation. It was either that or curl up in a ball and cry. It had been way too many years since she'd indulged in a pity party for one and didn't think this situation merited another one, yet.

Damien looked at the empty space where Jennaveve had been only moments before then at the shocked face of his twin, knowing his own reflected the same expression. "That couldn't be who it appeared to be." He paced away, his wolf scratched beneath the surface of his skin with the need to find their mate.

The bedroom looked as if an F5 tornado had been through it in the short amount of time since they'd entered and watched the bastard disappear with their woman. He knelt next to the bed, scenting Jenna's blood. A small smear of her precious life force coated the tile flooring. He ran his finger over the red stain, bringing it to his nose, inhaling, focusing on what had caused the injury. Instant jarring took him into the exact moment their Hearts Love had fallen onto her knees, her cry of pain was like a blade slicing through his own heart. "Why did one of us not stay with her?" Anguish and regret filled him.

Lucas's roar had the windows rattling, his wolf every bit as angry as Damien's. "I don't understand this, but we were only away from her for short periods of time. Whoever...that being was, he knew when to strike. It was as if he had a connection to her. He looked like us."

Distaste soared through Damien. He glared at Lucas, wanting him to take the words back. Their Jennaveve didn't belong to anyone but them. "We must summon father. This happened in his household. Surely he has a way to track whoever came and went."

His brother's eyes flashed blue. "Whoever he is, he's a dead man."

Damien nodded. "In that, we agree."

The door flung open, wind pushing him and Lucas backward as Damikan entered, their mother Luna rushing in behind him. "What the hell is going on? First, I feel a breach in my wards, and then I'm summoned," he paused, pointing at his chest. "Me, summoned to a guest suite as if I'm not the King. You have thirty seconds to explain before I teach you and your brother why I am the ruler." The air crackled with power.

It took all his control not to cower in the face of his father's fury as the King of Vampires blasted his dominance at them, the very air became heavy, threatening to push him to his knees. He and Lucas both stayed on their feet, fighting the power, holding their bodies straight by sheer will. Blood seeped from his nose, but he wasn't willing to show any weakness, not now, not when Jenna's life was on the line.

"Enough," Luna yelled, stepping between them, holding her arms out. Their mother's head whipped back and forth, tears falling down her cheeks, blood ran from her nose as well.

"Someone took *our* Jennaveve from your home. He was right here, and he looked just like you." Lucas stabbed an accusing finger toward Damikan.

Damikan's deep rumble made the one Lucas had emitted earlier seem tame as he took a step forward. "What are you saying?"

Damien glanced between his mother and father. No matter how pissed he was, the thought of hurting his mom was something he didn't want to do, but

Jenna's life was on the line. "Look into my memories," he said instead of speaking out loud, thinking their father would rather see it first then explain to their mother.

"Oh no you don't," Luna spat, blood on her face from where Damikan's dominance had pulsed through the room.

Their father broke his gaze from them, sucking in a breath. "Luna, what...come here." His gentle tone at odds with the anger still simmering in the air.

Luna shook her head but moved next to him. "I want to know what's going on, and I won't be brushed aside. Speak, Damien."

With a nod, Damikan wrapped his arms around their mother. "Whatever you have to say, you can say in front of your mother. We have no secrets." As he spoke, his right hand went up and down her body, cleaning the evidence of blood from her.

Luna relaxed into his embrace, the strain melting away.

Lucas came to stand next to him, folding his arms across his chest. "This is the most fucked up thing we've ever encountered, and let me tell you, between the two of us, we've seen and done a lot. I know you've been together since you were both basically kids, and in our world, it's unheard of for two to find their Hearts Love so young the way you did, father. What were you, a couple hundred years old when you and mom bonded?"

Damikan nodded, his chin resting next to their mother's ear. Damien wondered how they were going to react to the next words that came out of Lucas's mouth. He looked over at his brother, waiting for him to finish. "Almost into my third century. Your mother was much younger, though. However, what does this have to do with what's going on here?"

Lucas shrugged. "I started, you get to finish, old chap."

"Fuck," he swore.

"Damien, really, was that necessary?" Luna asked.

Damikan growled.

Every moment they stood there and put the conversation off, the longer Jenna was in the other man's hands. "Use your senses, dad, tell me, us, what do you smell? Who did you sense when you entered? You felt the breach to your wards. Track the intruder and tell us who it was, or who you think it was. Then, I'll tell you who was here," Damien said a little less forcefully.

"Enough of these riddles, Damien. Your Hearts Love has been taken and you want to play games? If it were my Luna, I'd rip the very fabric of this world apart to reach her." His father's eyes flashed to obsidian.

Damian nodded. "It seems there was a woman before our mother who you must've felt something for since you gave her a son."

His words fell like stones dropping down the side of a mountain. Again, the pressure built in the room. His mother's gasp and shocked disbelief was clear on her beautiful olive complexion.

"What the hell are you talking about? I have no other sons." Damikan turned Luna to face him.

"He is not mother's child, but yours. Look into my memories. Both of you." Damien wasn't willing to force himself into his parents' minds, but he opened his memories for them, allowing them to see and hear what the stranger had looked like and said.

"How?" Luna asked, her hand covered her mouth, while the other went over her heart.

Damikan released her, moving around the room in a slow methodical way. His head tilting this way and that. When he reached the far corner near the fireplace, he stopped, inhaled deeply then disappeared.

"Shit, where did he go?" Damien tried to trace and follow, calling out for his father's elite soldiers as he did, only to come up against a solid shield, keeping him locked inside the castle. "No," he roared. They'd been able to trace since they were children, tracking their father should've been easy. However, he'd locked them inside the castle while he'd gone off, leaving them with a sense of betrayal.

At the same time his twin disappeared, then reappeared next to him, his fist bloody. "I tried to break out through the back gates, but he has us warded in. Why would he do that?" Lucas shook out his hands.

Pain and betrayal slashed at Damien, echoing through the twin bond he shared with Lucas. Looking over to where their mother stood, she seemed smaller, more fragile than ever before. He took a step toward her. "Mother...I," he stopped.

Luna held her head up. "Do not apologize for something you have no control over. We will get Jennaveve back, and I'll handle your father." Her eyes flashed blue, fur rippled over her and then, their human mother was replaced by that of her wolf. Anytime she needed time or space, she'd always told them she needed her fur. Now, was clearly one of those times.

"Fuuuck," Damien roared, his wolf and vampire halves battled within him. He wanted to shift to his wolven form and rip through the walls of the castle until he found Jenna but knew she wasn't anywhere near. The link that bound them was tenuous at best, and it seemed to be fading.

"What about the Iron Wolf? They have a...special connection," Lucas spat.

Walking over to the shredded bedding, he picked up what was left of the pillow case, pulling it to his nose. "I think I just threw up in my mouth, when you said that, but it has merit. Can you link with the asshole?"

Lucas opened his mind and concentrated on Jenna's best friend, Kellen Styles of the Iron Wolves. He knew the shifter had just become a father to quadruplets and truly, almost, in a slight way, hated to bug the bastard. However, he also knew if Jenna couldn't reach them, she would try to get into contact with the one she called her bestie. Yeah, like Damien, just thinking that way had him gagging. One day, it would be them she'd look at as her besties instead of Kellen.

Fuck, he was becoming a giant pussy thinking he wanted his Hearts Love to be their best friend. Shit, next he'd be scheduling them regular mani and pedi sessions together. Might as well wrap it up with facials with cucumbers over their eyes, too.

When the link didn't immediately connect him with Kellen, his fists clenched at his sides. He felt a pain behind his eyes as he strained harder. "Motherfucker, why would our father do this to us? It's like he's crippled us here while our woman could be..." He swallowed unable to continue speaking.

Damien waved his hand around the room, putting everything back to the way it had been when they walked in. They could erase the damage around them, but not the memory of watching her frightened face or the words that came out of the man's mouth. "He called us his little brothers. That would mean our father had him with another woman. Clearly, he's walking around during the day, so he's not a full vamp. Is he like us?"

Lucas thought back to the very beginning, rewinding it in his mind then allowing the scene to unfold in slow motion. The man looked almost identical to their father, down to his towering height and the obsidian eyes. He and Damien had blue eyes thanks to their mother but not him. Their father only had blue eyes when he became a wolf/hybrid, and that was if he wasn't angry. His memory latched onto the nails the other man had flashed. The sharp points looked as if he purposely made them sharper, longer. "He wants to appear sinister. Everything he did was to scare Jennaveve, yet his hold wasn't bruising. If he wanted to hurt our dad, killing her would hurt him, but it wouldn't truly devastate him. What is his end game?"

"I don't give a flying fuck what his end game is. I'm going to end *his* game," Damien promised.

He met Damien's stare, nodding. "If he's hurt one hair on her head, he's a dead man, brother or not."

"I'm going to bleed him for taking her and scaring her, no matter what blood runs through his veins, that's non-negotiable." Damien crossed his arms over his chest.

Lucas put his hands on his hips. "Stop looking at me like I'm going to argue, because newsflash, brother, I'm with you one hundred percent."

Damien put his hand out, waiting for Lucas to take it. "Jennaveve is ours to protect, ours to love, ours to get back, no matter the cost."

Lucas gripped his brother's palm, each one shifting until a single nail elongated, slicing into the other's palm, sealing the vow. "We will do whatever it takes to bring her back to us safely. Damned to all who stand in our way." Magic crackled between them as they both made the blood oath.

About Elle Boon

Elle Boon lives in Middle-Merica as she likes to say, with her husband, two kids, and a black lab who is more like a small pony. She'd never planned to be a writer, but when life threw her a curve, she swerved with it, since she's athletically challenged. She's known for saying "Bless Your Heart" and dropping lots of F-bombs, but she loves where this new journey has taken her.

She writes what she loves to read, and that is romance, whether it's erotic, Navy SEALs, or paranormal, as long as there is a happily ever after. Her biggest hope is that after readers have read one of her stories, they fall in love with her characters as much as she did. She loves creating new worlds, and has more stories just waiting to be written. Elle believes in happily ever afters, and can guarantee you will always get one with her stories.

Connect with Elle online, she loves to hear from you:

www.elleboon.com

https://www.facebook.com/elle.boon

https://www.facebook.com/Elle-Boon-Author-1429718517289545/

https://twitter.com/ElleBoon1

https://www.facebook.com/groups/RacyReads/

https://www.facebook.com/groups/188924878146358/

https://www.facebook.com/groups/1405756769719931/

https://www.facebook.com/groups/wewroteyourbookboyfriends/

https://www.goodreads.com/author/show/8120085.Elle_Boon

https://www.bookbub.com/authors/elle-boon

https://www.instagram.com/elleboon/

http://www.elleboon.com/newsletter/

Other Books by Elle Boon

Erotic Ménage
Ravens of War
Selena's Men
Two For Tamara
Jaklyn's Saviors
Kira's Warriors

Shifters Romance
Mystic Wolves
Accidentally Wolf & His Perfect Wolf (1 Volume)
Jett's Wild Wolf
Bronx's Wounded Wolf
A Fey's Wolf

Paranormal Romance
SmokeJumpers
FireStarter
Berserker's Rage
A SmokeJumpers Christmas
Mind Bender, Coming Soon

MC Shifters Erotic
Iron Wolves MC
Lyric's Accidental Mate
Xan's Feisty Mate
Kellen's Tempting Mate
Slater's Enchanted Mate
Dark Lovers
Bodhi's Synful Mate
Turo's Fated Mate
Arynn's Chosen Mate

Coti's Unclaimed Mate

Contemporary Romance
Miami Nights
Miami Inferno
Rescuing Miami

Standalone
Wild and Dirty

SEAL Team Phantom Series
Delta Salvation
Delta Recon
Delta Rogue
Mission Saving Shayna
Protecting Teagan

Delta Redemption

The Dark Legacy Series
Dark Embrace

Made in the USA
Columbia, SC
24 July 2018